The Secrets *of the* Huon Wren

Claire van Ryn is an awarded writer who began her career as a newspaper journalist, but has also filled roles as magazine editor, communications specialist, writing teacher, blueberry picker and shoe fitter. She lives in Tasmania and recently spent a year travelling Australia with her husband and two children in a caravan. Creating is Claire's favourite thing: whether with words, watercolours or whatever else is close at hand.

clairevanryn.com
@clairevanryn
@clairevanryn.writer

CLAIRE VAN RYN

The Secrets *of the* Huon Wren

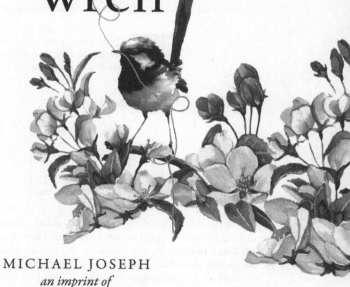

MICHAEL JOSEPH
an imprint of
PENGUIN BOOKS

MICHAEL JOSEPH

UK | USA | Canada | Ireland | Australia
India | New Zealand | South Africa | China

Michael Joseph is part of the Penguin Random House group of companies
whose addresses can be found at global.penguinrandomhouse.com.

Penguin
Random House
Australia

First published by Michael Joseph, 2023

Bible verse on page 101 from The Holy Bible, New International Version®,
NIV® Copyright © 1973, 1978, 1984, 2011 by Biblica, Inc.® Used by permission.
All rights reserved worldwide.
Cover illustrations: wren by Maria Stezhko/Shutterstock;
apple tree by Florabela/Shutterstock; thread by Olga Khorkova/Alamy;
blue texture by MM Photos/Alamy; pattern by Irtsya/Shutterstock
Author photograph by Jac Parsons
Cover design by Nikki Townsend Design
Typeset in Sabon by Midland Typesetters, Australia

Printed and bound in Australia by Griffin Press, an accredited
ISO AS/NZS 14001 Environmental Management Systems printer

A catalogue record for this
book is available from the
National Library of Australia

ISBN 978 1 76104 927 9

penguin.com.au

*We at Penguin Random House Australia acknowledge that Aboriginal and
Torres Strait Islander peoples are the Traditional Custodians and the first storytellers
of the lands on which we live and work. We honour Aboriginal and Torres Strait
Islander peoples' continuous connection to Country, waters, skies and communities.
We celebrate Aboriginal and Torres Strait Islander stories, traditions and living
cultures; and we pay our respects to Elders past and present.*

For Phill.
I love you.

For now we see through a glass, darkly; but then face to face:
now I know in part; but then shall I know even as
also I am known.
1 Corinthians 13:12 (KJV)

Chapter 1

Launceston, Summer 2019

It wasn't Nora she'd wanted to meet that day. It should have been a different corridor, a different door, a different story scribbled into her notebook.

When Allira signed in on the visitor clipboard, under the column 'Reason For Visit' she wrote: *G. Tredinnick*. Her eyes stung with bleach fumes and vanilla air freshener that were masking . . . something. She smoothed her t-shirt into the waistband of her jeans. She'd dressed down today to put her subject at ease. When it came to the interview, she would press record on her phone and slip it out of sight, and then casually write trigger words on her notepad. She would massage the conversation, laugh and maintain eye contact until trust was strong enough to pose the questions she really wanted to ask.

A statuesque woman with a name tag dangling from her pocket marched towards Allira, her footsteps thudding on the industrial carpet. 'Can I help you?'

Allira fiddled with the visitor lanyard around her neck. 'Um . . . I'm Allira Ambrose from *Folk* magazine.'

'I'm not familiar with that one.' The woman hugged her suited elbows, unsmiling.

Allira's right index finger traced the constellation of beauty spots below her right eye. She shifted her weight, impatient to get started. 'Ah, I had an interview lined up with Mr George Tredinnick. Could you point me to his room?' A clock ticked obstinately on a nearby wall and a bald man in red flannelette pyjamas moved at a painfully slow pace towards them using a walking frame.

'I'm Sally Cosgrave, Mercy Place Aged Care Manager.' She thrust her hand into the space between them for a perfunctory handshake before continuing. 'And unfortunately Mr Tredinnick won't be doing any interviewing today.'

Heat shot from Allira's stomach to her throat and she lifted her chin. 'This meeting was approved by Mr Tredinnick himself, and his family. I spoke to them this week.'

The bald man had nearly reached them now and for a moment the two women watched his snail-like progress in silence.

'*Folk* magazine is produced to capture real stories of people who have lived extraordinary lives,' Allira continued. 'My editor, Justin Taylor, tells me that Mr Tredinnick was a prolific boat-builder in Tassie's west, and that his Huon Pine constructions were sold across the world.' Allira preferred to source her own leads, but last week Justin had handballed this one to her. He rarely wrote his own stories any more, and inevitably he would take his frustrations out on those who did.

Finally, Sally spoke. 'Mr Tredinnick died last night. We've only just moved him out.' She looked past Allira, eyes scanning from corridor to corridor, room to room.

'Oh, I'm . . .' Allira's eyebrows peaked. 'I had no idea.'

'You weren't to know. He would have been a difficult interview anyway,' Sally said, ignoring Allira's paling face. 'He had severe dementia.' She smiled thinly, a lip-stretching manoeuvre she clearly reserved for the requisite demonstrations of sadness or pity in her job.

'I've actually interviewed quite a few people living with dementia. It just takes time and patience, and often a bit of research to sort fact from fiction,' Allira said.

The bald man stopped at Sally's side. She pointed his walker towards an empty recliner and began guiding him towards it. Allira tagged along.

'Well, I'm glad to hear someone is taking an interest.' Sally's voice warmed ever so slightly, and Allira was suddenly self-conscious of how fresh-faced she looked in her jeans and ponytail, like she had just graduated from uni rather than her full twenty-eight years. An inexperienced blow-in mining these vulnerable residents for a sensational headline. 'We do our best to meet all their physical needs, to ensure they are safe and cared for. In fact, we have an unblemished reputation for our standard of care. But there are some who just need the ear of someone willing to sit and take the time.'

The man was now settled in his chair and Sally patted him on the shoulder before swinging round to squint at Allira, hands on hips, taking the measure of her. She lowered her voice. 'If you're after a story . . .' Allira was surprised to see her eyes sparkling with things she evidently wanted to say but couldn't. 'Spend some time sitting with these people. There are stories here.'

Allira smiled and looked at her watch. 'I wish I could but—'

'I know. Busy busy. We're all too busy for the elderly.' Sally looked away. 'These places wouldn't even exist if only families operated like families.' The words slipped out like the remnant of a conversation she'd been having with herself. She turned back to Allira and smiled apologetically. 'Forgive me, it's been a long morning. But truly, if you're interested in writing real, raw stories, this is where you need to be.'

Allira rubbed the line of spots on her cheekbone again. The manager's challenge was there in front of her, as confronting as her no-nonsense manner and impeccable skirt suit.

Sally continued. 'I'd start with Nora. She has no family.'

'None at all?'

'None we've been able to track down. Just one letter in the three years she's been here, and her baby doll, of course.'

'What do you mean?' Allira was confused.

'You'll see. Go sit with her.'

Not wanting to commit, Allira looked down at her feet.

'Nice to meet you anyway,' Sally said to Allira's ambivalence. She continued along the wide hallway, leaving Allira standing behind a semicircle of recliners where a few residents were seated, facing a flat-screen television running repeats of *A Country Practice*.

Allira sighed, suddenly tired. It had been too hot to sleep deeply last night. Hamish was on night shift and didn't get home until 1am. He was always so considerate on those nights, taking his clothes off in the dark and gingerly slipping under the covers without saying a word. But she'd been waiting for him.

'Hey, babe,' she had said sleepily. 'How was your shift?'

He'd rolled over and circled her torso. 'One heart attack and a broken arm,' he replied, kissing her neck. 'And we nearly delivered a baby right there in the ambo! We only just got her to the hospital in time, bub was born five minutes later.'

Allira turned to face him. 'She's lucky you were there.' Allira kissed his mouth with tenderness, even as her heart clenched painfully.

Now she rubbed the back of her hand across her eyes to push the memories away and focused back on her surroundings. Grey heads in recliners suddenly bobbed in laughter at something on the television. Allira looked past them, beyond the beige walls and fake plants, beyond the shiny windows and grey car park, beyond the smattering of houses skirting the nursing home grounds. Beyond to the endless blue of the sky. The whole view was soft at the edges, like she was peering at it through a wedding veil. Perhaps a bushfire was burning somewhere, or perhaps it was a mirage of her own brain fog. Everything was fine. But not quite. She dragged her eyes away and looked at her watch: 11 am. *I should go.* As she turned to retrace her steps back to the clipboard for sign-out, her eyes lingered on the hallway to her right. Mint green doors displayed name cards and plastic sleeves for medical records. The first door was open a crack: NORA GRAY.

Before she had time to think, Allira's feet were walking her to that door, just a few metres away, and she was peering in. Sally hovered in her thoughts, the way she had described Nora. No family. A baby doll. Allira shook her head. What was she thinking? She should get back to the office and explain to a no-doubt cranky Justin that the Tredinnick story had come to nothing.

*

'How'd it go with the old fella?' Justin called across the room as Allira walked into the tired second-floor office. Lines of light striped the space, straining through half-tilted venetians onto a hodgepodge of desks huddled beneath a lone heat pump. It was a dance studio once, hence the polished floorboards and speakers mounted at the room's perimeter. One corner had become a graveyard for desk chairs and filing cabinets.

Justin would be annoyed she had nothing to show for her time. She was already in his bad books this week – she had been forty-five minutes late to work on Monday. Allira knew that one of Justin's pet peeves was tardiness, but what she didn't know was how to predict the days he'd be sober enough to come into the office, let alone care.

'Not so great,' she said. 'Your fascinating boat-builder from Strahan died in his sleep last night.'

'Dammit.' Justin raked long fingers through salt-and-pepper hair. 'Got anything else, then? Surely there was some other old bird with a yarn to spill at the home.' His callousness irked her, but what could she do? He was her boss. The fact that he had landed himself the *Tasmanian Herald*-owned magazine when it was on the chopping block clearly hadn't diminished his ego. One of the sub-editors said he'd 'paid' a carton of beer for it to the general manager, who was more than happy to see the back of both the magazine and the rogue employee.

Allira opened her mouth to say something about having some common decency when she saw a flash of bright coral and the shimmy of an ample décolletage crammed into a plunging neckline. It was Rae Benedetti, hovering in the background making warning hand motions, her lips pursed and eyebrows raised like exclamation marks. Just thinking of her made Allira smile. The office would be a dreary place without Rae.

'How are sales on the latest edition?' Allira changed the subject. She could have relayed her conversation with Sally Cosgrave about a home full of stories, but something made her hesitate.

'We've had one hundred-odd more subscriptions since release,' Justin replied, not quite hiding his own surprise with how well the magazine was travelling.

'No way!'

'Yep.'

'All those changes are paying off.'

Justin nodded, despite himself. He knew there wouldn't be a *Folk* magazine if it wasn't for Allira's agile response to the magazine's nosedive soon after he took up the helm, much less the handful of underpaid and overworked part-time staff huddled in the old dance hall. 'But I still think the price we pay for the paper stock is exorbitant.'

That old chestnut. He still hadn't let it go. When the decision was made to shift *Folk* from a free bi-monthly to a larger format subscription publication, Allira had convinced him to upgrade the pages to a thick, porous paper you were compelled to stroke like expensive linen.

'Hey, the dollars are doing the talking. People are loving it, or they wouldn't be subscribing, right? And we've got advertisers lining up!'

Justin grunted, picking up a copy of *Folk* to fan through the pages.

Allira knew she should be happy. Working here was what she wanted, she reminded herself. Delving deep into the richness of story rather than the rapid-fire who-what-where-when-why-how of the tabloids and online news sites. The breeze produced by the magazine's pages rustled Justin's hair and the motion reminded her of her father: Saturday mornings when she was an eager pre-teen, hovering at the breakfast table as he thumbed through inky news, his head lifting as he squinted into sun dappling through lace terylenes and beckoned. 'Al, listen to this.' She'd scramble to sit beside him, relaxing into that wonderful place of his whispery voice unravelling stories that she tucked into the furthest recesses of her mind. That was before university stripped it of all romance.

Allira forced herself to smile at Justin, trying to swallow the bitter taste in her mouth. One of the first lessons she learned as a cadet journalist at the *Tas Herald* was to know your people. She knew Justin.

No one knows Nora Gray. The thought was like a stone dropped into water, and the old woman's door rippled in her mind. Mint green, standing ajar. No family, no one knocking for a visit. Maybe she would go back . . .

'In truth, I think the spike in subscriptions has more to do with that story you wrote about the life of Simon Kelly's beard. What a hoot!' Allira said with a tad too much enthusiasm. It was true: it had been a great piece. The well-known marathon runner had allegedly never trimmed the beard in his life. Even Allira could admit that every so often Justin came up with a page-turner and readers caught a glimpse at the talented writer who'd once won a Walkley Award and boasted by-lines in all the top Australian magazines and broadsheets.

Justin laughed good-naturedly as he walked towards his corner office, forgetting the whole reason for the conversation.

Allira shook her head. *I should add ego-stroking to my CV.* Rae watched her with a smirk and a wink. They'd been comrades since school. Rae flicked her black bob and turned back to the phone and filing, while Allira pulled the spiral notepad from her handbag to look at a page that was blank but for the name of her intended interviewee. She picked up a pen and scratched a line through the name before writing another beneath it: Nora Gray. What was the story of the old lady with the doll?

Chapter 2

At first the room seemed empty, devoid of movement or sound. But as Allira's eyes adjusted to the dim light, she saw her.

Nora Gray was enveloped in a relic of a chair, with florid upholstery of pink peonies and oversized lemons, prancing ponies and dancing women, now bled of colour. Depleted. The music gone. Nora's angular frame hinged inwards, her feet swallowed by navy velvet scuffs, her body gobbled into the folds of a blush pink dressing gown. Her neck hung to one side, the yellowed lace of her singlet revealing a hollowed chest. The whole room seemed to slump towards the old woman, the wall behind her markedly devoid of trimmings. The only personal items in the room were on a wall shelf as wide as a ruler above her bedside table. A brown gift box tied with twine. And a curiously lifelike bird carved from dark blond wood.

Did the bird cock its head? Did its pinhead eye query her presence here?

Allira crept further into the room, found the air conditioner controls and pressed the button with the little snowflake icon.

It was at least ten degrees hotter in the old woman's room than in the hallway, enough to make anyone limp with fatigue. Cold air hissed through the stuffiness. The room, like a lethargic lung, took a deep breath of arctic air and awoke.

Nora looked up and her grey-green eyes swam out, beckoning. *Please*, they pleaded. *Please*.

The room swirled. Everything leaned into the floral armchair. The carpet and walls and ceiling and furniture and rug and windows darkened and pressed toward Nora, pointed at her, propelling Allira towards her. *What is happening?* The room was prising something from the grey stranger of a woman, laying it bare for Allira to see.

Allira's head was humming the familiar rhythm of migraine onset. Massaging her temples, she finally stepped forward, three purposeful strides to Nora's chair, and knelt in front of her. 'Hello, Mrs Gray. My name is Allira Ambrose,' she said, her voice gravelly, strange. 'I'm here visiting today.'

The rheumy eyes remained fixed on Allira, leaking but unrelenting, like she already knew. Allira reached to straighten Nora's quilted dressing gown and, as she pulled the collar into place, the woman's quavering hand gripped her wrist.

'Are you okay? Can I get you some help?' Allira asked.

Nora tightened her grasp, squeezing with brute strength.

'Please let go, you're hurting me.' Allira tried not to allow the panic she felt into her voice.

Nora's gaze remained unrelenting. Allira tried to pull her hand free, lifting one arthritic finger at a time, worried that too much force would bruise or break Nora's fingers. Her own fingertips flowered deep purple-red, blanching to white at her wrist where the old woman's hand was set like a vice.

'Where is my baby?' Nora's voice was a scalpel, blindly slicing.

Allira groaned and sucked her cheeks. The hospital room flashed. Red on white. Wrist tags. Bare feet. Flash. Flash. Flash. And then Nora let go, her grip suddenly slack and Allira's fingers slipped free, falling, sending her staggering backwards. Pins and needles ran up to her elbow and her hand throbbed. Allira ducked from Nora's bunched eyebrows and pursed lips, slung her handbag across her back, and practically leapt towards the door. Straight into Sally.

Sally looked from Allira's hand to Nora and back again. 'What's happened here?'

Allira rubbed her wrist while shaking her throbbing head, trying to continue out Nora's door.

'Easy does it, easy,' Sally said slowly, like she was coaxing a runaway horse. She held Allira firmly by the shoulders. 'I see you've met Nora then.'

Allira opened her mouth, but a boulder had rolled into her throat and her eyes were stinging. Sally frowned and continued towards the old woman's chair, a bulging calico wash bag tucked under one arm. Nora's hands were a knot in her lap, tying and untying, her face unyielding.

'Nora, I hope you've been kind to Allira. You know she chose to visit you today, out of all the others?'

The anger flew from Nora's face and her features were suddenly as innocent and inviting as a picnic spread, her hands flattened on the folds of her dressing gown. She leaned forward, eyes hungry.

'It's a real treat to have a visitor, Nora. Maybe she will keep coming back if you're good to her.'

Allira wanted to run from the nursing home and never come back, but she hesitated. Nora was holding out her arms, palms upturned, a gentle smile lifting the corners of her mouth. Sally fiddled with the drawstring of the calico bag and placed something in Nora's hands.

Allira gasped. A baby? No. A doll. Lifelike though, from a distance. The size of a newborn, swaddled in pale blue muslin.

Nora's hands were spiders spanning the doll's body, crawling around its length until it was settled into the crook of her arm. She rocked the doll, her cheeks slack, gazing at the unblinking face and crooning an unfamiliar lullaby. She kissed the plastic forehead and smiled.

Sally scooped up the wash bag and joined Allira at the door.

'Does she think it's real?' Allira asked.

'Yes. Nora treats that doll better than many mothers treat their own children.' Sally's eyes creased tenderly. 'Like I said, she doesn't have any family to speak of, no visitors, so it's her whole life.'

Nora slowly stood up, balancing the doll in the crook of her right arm, and walked to the bed with its frothy apricot cover. She lowered the doll and removed the swaddling to expose a white fabric mid-section joining the flesh-coloured plastic limbs and neck. Nora opened the drawer of her bedside table and selected a tiny, green-checked romper. She carefully manoeuvred the doll into the cotton garment, finishing the outfit with a hand-knitted beanie pulled tight onto its head.

13

'Before we found her the doll, she'd barely move from that chair all day long,' Sally said. 'In fact, for her last birthday – her eighty-first, it was – we set it up like it was her baby's first birthday instead. You should've seen her face when she saw the bunting and streamers and the blue cake in the shape of a number one.'

Allira was trying to decide if the doll charade was a kindness or a deception. When Allira was six, her parents had relented to a long campaign of convincing them to buy her a puppy. Brandy was a Jack Russell terrier cross. No one quite knew what the cross part was, although family friends had their opinions. Staffy, one said, because of its muscular shoulders, or beagle, because of its inquisitive nature. Allira didn't care. All the drawings of puppies with smiling faces and perky tails that she'd tucked under her parents' pillows had paid off. She had chattered about Brandy like she was already a member of their family, long before her parents decided that if they couldn't give their daughter a sibling, the least they could do was to give her a pet. Then, a year later, Brandy mistook the neighbour's arm for a bone. Allira was told that Brandy had to go live on a farm. Somewhere too far to visit.

'Who gave the doll to her?' Allira asked.

'One of the nurses brought it in. It belonged to her daughter.' Sally glanced sideways at Allira. 'We've got sixty-eight residents here and fourteen employees are on duty at any given time. There are only two leisure and lifestyle carers. That means there's plenty of help with bedpans and medication and cooking and cleaning, but not so much for keeping them occupied. Our residents with dementia are hard work, I'm afraid. I could dress it up and make it sound PC, but that's the simple truth. It makes the whole place run smoother if they have a distraction.'

'Why do you do it – work here, I mean?' Allira shuffled her feet.

'For all their foibles, the people we care for here are you and me with the clock wound forward.' Sally blinked rapidly before dropping her voice. 'My father had dementia – early onset, poor soul. I wouldn't wish it on anyone.' She scraped at an invisible mark on her black skirt and sighed. 'Now. Let me see your hand. What did she do?'

'It's fine,' Allira said, crossing her arms to hide it behind the opposite elbow.

Nora opened the doors of a built-in wardrobe. In the cavity where clothes would usually hang there was a bassinet on wheels. The shelves around it were filled with baby boy necessities. Nappies. Bottles. Tiny shoes. Neat piles of bunny rugs and rompers. Rattles and teddies.

She wheeled the bassinet beside the bed and then lowered her baby gently within. She selected a yellow and white crocheted bunny rug and laid it across the doll, tucking in the edges with fumbling, gnarled fingers. 'There you go, my sweet.' Her voice wavered. 'Off to sleep now.'

'It doesn't make sense, does it?' Sally whispered at Allira. 'She treats a doll like royalty but gives a Chinese burn to her first and only visitor. Last week she was telling me about the undertaking business – graves and dead people's faces and stitching the lining into coffins. Who knows where her memory was taking her, or maybe it was just something she read once.' Sally stopped abruptly, as though she'd said too much.

Allira couldn't hide the curiosity from her face, the sixth sense for a deeper story that had served her well in her writing career. There was something about Nora's interaction with the doll . . . It wasn't a doll to her. It was the way of a mother with her child, the tenderness that could whip into a highland squall at the slightest threat. For that fierceness, she instantly forgave the older woman, the bruised wrist forgotten.

Allira's ears rushed with a sound like wind carving into a mountain plateau. If she closed her eyes, she would be at the top of one of Tasmania's many majestic peaks, the ocean winking in the distance and the earth between them a patchwork of mysteries. Her pulse hammered. She knew this sensation. It was the feeling of knowing she had caught the tail of a ripper yarn.

Chapter 3

Caveside, Summer 1953

'Evelyn Grayson! You'd better have a couple of buckets full of apples by now or I'll be having words with your father about that horse!'

Evelyn had daydreamed her way home from school, adding an extra fifteen minutes to her journey to stop and watch bees on the flowering gum lazily load their cargo, to linger at Mrs Winspear's fence and squeeze nectar from honeysuckle flowers onto her tongue, and to generally delay the military call to action that dear Mother would inevitably bleat.

At the letterbox, she'd quickly smoothed her wayward ponytail, taken a deep breath and pedalled her bike as fast as her legs could manage down the gravel driveway, sunshine sprinkling her bare arms and legs like confetti. Mercifully, the back door off the verandah was wide open, and she'd been able to slip up the stairs and into her bedroom unseen. She was tearing off her school dress and jiggling into overalls when Mother's command reached her ears. Surely other fifteen-year-olds didn't have to put up with such demanding overtures on their return

17

from school each day, she thought. But she knew that resistance wasn't worth the upset. Once downstairs again, Evelyn grabbed a bundle of buckets from the cupboard under the stairs on her way out the back door, dashed along the front lawn and through the gate into the orchard, careful to duck beneath the kitchen window.

Evelyn loved the orchard. When Mother was in a mood, her older, belligerent brother David was home to sap his parents of money, or if she needed space to let her thoughts run around without their clothes on, she grabbed her journal and slid into the orchard, Marmaduke trotting at her heels, purring with anticipation of a warm lap to curl up in.

Daddy had just spread netting across the fruit trees as he did every February and Evelyn still felt a little thrill each time she stood at the end of the apple row and walked like a bride down the aisle, white billowing overhead and trees standing with their arms aloft, applauding her beauty and grace. In her mind, she was wearing silk spun of pure moonshine, her hair was swept into a chignon at the nape of her neck and a crown of scarlet flowering gum circled her head.

She scrunched her eyes shut as she relished this otherworldly scene, one that blocked out reality. The reality of her ghost-skinned face framed with a mane of unruly auburn hair. Of startling grey-green eyes that were always wide with searching, watching, noticing, tucking morsels of information away to chew on later. Eyes that appeared wild and brazen for their curiosity. A broad forehead, obstinate chin and flat nose that rubbed against the milky, blue-eyed mildness that she was so certain her mother would prefer. And holding up this face was a strong and wiry body with long yet muscular limbs, a straight waist and the womanly softness of breasts only getting in the way of her adventurous heart.

Birds chattered. Leaves rustled. A horse whinnied.

Evelyn's eyes flew open and she glanced up at the kitchen – *coast clear* – before dashing to the horse paddock bordering the orchard, plucking an apple on her way.

'Daphne, my lovely,' she whispered, stroking the palomino mare's caramel nose before placing the green apple on an open palm. Daphne crunched and snuffled the juicy offering as her ears were rubbed vigorously, just the way she liked. Her tail flicked at flies.

Evelyn looked towards the house. 'I must go,' she breathed into Daphne's velvet ear. 'But I will be back, and we can ride down to the creek after tea.'

Daphne snorted and nuzzled Evelyn's shoulder, smearing spit and apple juice down the sleeve of her shirt. Evelyn stifled a squeal and ran back to the line of trees, Daphne turning on her neat little hooves and dancing a canter around the paddock. The palomino pony had been a gift from Daddy on Evelyn's thirteenth birthday. 'The best birthday present ever!' was her delighted response. The truth was that a local family had failed to come good with the bill on their pa's funeral and had suggested a barter. The sweet little mare was the perfect offering for Stanley Grayson in the lead-up to his daughter's first teen birthday, even if it did stir up a storm with the wife. In the end, he'd put it like this: 'It's the pony or no payment. Besides, she's worth something. We can always sell her if Evelyn gets bored.'

Thelma Grayson's defeat had been marked with a terse nod of her head and an Irish stew for that evening's dinner with vegetables better described as murdered than diced or julienned with her usual scientific precision.

Evelyn hung a bucket on her elbow and climbed a wooden step ladder at the first tree in the row. Since Mother had decided it was Evelyn's job to harvest the fruit each day after school, she was determined to pass the time as pleasantly as possible and had named her favourite trees. As her teacher Mrs Pike always said in that kettle-whistling voice of hers, 'There are no uninteresting things, only uninterested people.'

Each tree was named after a character in Evelyn's books. Mr Darcy was an obvious first choice, and the others in his row had a similar theme: Mark Antony, Casanova, Edmond Dantès, Edward Fairfax Rochester, Heathcliff, Sir Lancelot and of course, Romeo.

Plonk, plonk, plonk. The apples echoed into the bucket as Evelyn began. *Thwack, thwack, thwack.* The sound deepened as she picked until there was barely a dull thud as the apples climbed to the bucket's rim. She was an efficient picker, and Mr Darcy's crop was generous.

'Thank you, Mr Darcy.' Evelyn curtsied and moved down the row.

The persistent breeze carried the sound of a wood plane zipping along the sinuous grain of a slab of freshly sawn timber. Tasmanian Oak, perhaps, or Blackwood. If Daddy was still in the workshop this late in the day, it meant one of two things: a furniture order had come in from Hobart, or someone had died. Jenny's pop? Jenny hadn't been at school today because her pop 'had a turn' on the weekend, Mrs Pike told the class and refused to answer any further questions. Or maybe that awful Clancy Dalton fell off his bike and cracked his skull on a rock. Evelyn immediately felt bad at the thought and shooed it from her mind. But how she yearned to run to the workshop door, where the dust clouds carried the exotic scents of each woodgrain that she'd learned to distinguish. The sweet, musky heaven of Huon pine, the cinnamon pang of Sassafras, the wistful otherworldly aroma of King Billy Pine. But mostly she wanted to be enveloped in one of Daddy's dusty hugs and tell him all about her day. Her horrid day.

'Evil-lyn!' they'd ribbed. Over and over. 'Evil-lyn, Evil-lyn!'

As the undertaker's daughter, she was an easy target, and it didn't help that Charlotte Marshall let slip that Evelyn hand-stitched the lining into Stanley Grayson's famed coffins. *Why did she do that?* Evelyn had shared the detail in the secrecy of her bedroom one afternoon before Christmas, explaining how she had the money to buy a new summer dress. The one all the girls had been eyeing in the shop window of Browns' Store.

'It's not my fault you're all so weird about death!' she'd snapped at the mean-mouthed boys. 'We're all going to die someday, and who's going to stitch the lining into your coffin? Not me, that's for sure!' She'd picked up her lunch tin and run back to the schoolhouse.

Nobody followed. Not even Charlotte.

It always came to this. There was a great chasm between her own, everyday experience of death and the mysterious otherness of her classmates'. If she ever let her guard down and described the process of preparing a body for burial, the group of listeners would grow larger yet quieter, their eyes wide. And then in the weeks to follow, the girls she had built trust with would extricate themselves from visits to the cinema and exclude her from after school treks to the ice cream shop. They would say things like 'Mummy said it's unhygienic to touch dead things,' and 'It's disrespectful to speak of the dead like that.'

She would love to let the tears she'd been biting back all day run down her face as Daddy listened and nodded and soothed her worries. But that would get them both in trouble. Mother wanted her apples, and Daddy must work. Evelyn dropped two more apples into the second bucket. Full, time to go. She gave Mark Antony an affectionate pat on his rough trunk and made her way out the gate towards the kitchen door, buckets swinging against her denim overalls.

Turning to push the door open with her back, she paused to relish the silence and gather her nerve. The crags of the Great Western Tiers were shadowed in the deepest hues of violet and indigo, Mother Cummings Peak holding a peach-smeared sky. A wisp of smoke hung like an exclamation mark as night encroached.

A family's choice of fabric for lining their loved one's coffin was like peering into their bank book. The rudimentary blue-and-white-striped seersucker cotton with its slight pucker was far more economical and the preference of most in the greater Caveside community. But on occasion, Evelyn had the opportunity to lift a bolt of ivory or rosebud satin from the storeroom and let her scissors glide through, like a black swan across the

Meander River. The satin-lined coffins were magnificent, and Evelyn always felt a thrill when she stepped back to admire the lustre of freshly polished timber against the satin's slippery glamour. But from a purely practical vantage, she would have chosen seersucker over satin any day. The plain cotton was obedient to her stitches, whereas the satin was forever sliding and its oily veneer showed up the most minor of flaws.

She held the needle to the window and threaded its eye. Deft fingers knotted the strands firmly and she pulled a length of crisp cotton fabric onto her lap, angling the needle towards the pinned seam.

Already completed beside her was a matching pillow to prop the deceased's head in the coffin, then she would stitch the trimming around the coffin's edge. Daddy was outside, painting the simple pine box and lid with a watered-down lacquer. He would affix the old brass handles he kept for such families who could not afford all the adornments. They gave just the right appearance for all the ceremonial aspects of the farewell, though Daddy delicately stipulated that the coffin must be already within the ground when guests arrived for the 'burial'. That way they didn't tend to notice that the beautiful, polished brass handles had been removed and there were screw holes in the coffin's sides. They generally agreed gratefully, thanking him for his discretion.

Daddy had gone to give his respects to the Roberts family promptly after little Tommy arrived with news of his grand-mother's death. He'd come bouncing on his pony, Tyrone, and while Tommy steamrolled Daddy with an account of Nanna's death (pneumonia), Evelyn calmed the spooked animal with handfuls of oats and whispered lines from *Jane Eyre*. She walked him in slow circles until his breathing slowed and then tied him to a gum tree, rubbing his ears, neck, and flanks with long, firm, fluid strokes, her pink hand against the wiry black-grey fleck of his coat.

Tommy delivered the details in one long breathless sentence and then slumped like a deflated balloon in the waning light. Mother appeared in a waft of bergamot perfume, holding a tray with a glass of milk and a biscuit, which Tommy hoed into like he'd not eaten all day. Perhaps he hadn't.

Daddy would follow him the short two miles in the mourning car to the Roberts farm. It was as good as waving a skull and crossbones flag at the poor family's ramshackle farmhouse, such would be the stir when people pulled back their curtains to see Tommy galloping on Tyrone with the local undertaker close behind in that gleaming black Buick. Better than taking the hearse, though.

'Do you want me to come?' Evelyn asked.

'No, you need your sleep,' Mother replied. 'Your father can do this one himself.'

Daddy pressed his lips together and winked at Evelyn. He hurried to the workshop, but Evelyn raced ahead and was already packing his black leather case when he caught up.

'Measuring tape, sterilised suture needle, catgut, timber samples and your pocket notebook and pen,' she said with a grin.

'You're really something, my girl. Go grab a jar of your mother's cherry preserve, will you, and write condolences on one of those fancy notecards? Then I'm good to go.'

Evelyn followed his instructions and then watched him climb into the Buick. She gave Tommy a leg up onto Tyrone and he twitched the reins with a sad smile in Evelyn's direction, then rode back the way he'd come, the tunnel of oaks a foreboding gullet.

Daddy was always thoughtful like that. These weren't merely clients to Stanley Grayson, they were neighbours, friends. When he made that first call at each bereaved family's home, his fist was heavy with sorrow as he thumped it against their door. Hat in hand, he expressed genuine sympathy and there were times when those country folk would comment to a friend or a neighbour that they could've sworn they detected a watering of old Stan's eyes. But surely not – he was an undertaker after all, and worked with the dead as a matter of vocation. They wrote it off as the waft of onions from the kitchen, or his missus turning him soft.

'It's not the sting of death that gets stuck in my throat, bloss, it's the grief written so painful like in the faces of the family,' he said to Evelyn after her first time dressing a body for burial, aged thirteen. She had hugged his thick stomach then, partly because she couldn't agree more and partly because it had been a heavy day.

Evelyn had been stitching fabric coffin linings since she was seven or eight, but this was the first time her father had encouraged her to pick up one of the large, hooked suture needles and thread catgut through its eye. When he visited the home of the deceased, there were three things he wanted to do promptly to spare the family, and himself, unpleasantries. The body was often laid out in a bedroom and the family usually knew to pull the eyelids closed over their unseeing eyes. Left too long, the membrane across the eyeball dried and there was no closing that eye without lubrication, time and gentle massaging. Sometimes the family also knew to cross the arms across the chest and overlap the legs at the ankles. Her father then tied a discreet string or bandage around their wrists and ankles to ensure the body stayed in place. 'It's to keep them neat and tidy, and saves the family some money too,' he explained to Evelyn. 'If their elbows are hanging out like a scarecrow, poss, they're going to need a mighty big coffin. That or I'm going to need to spend time wrestling their limbs into place after rigor mortis has set in.' He laughed at his daughter's wide eyes and ruffled her hair.

The last job was always done behind closed doors. Her father would usher any family from the room and assure them he wouldn't be long, explaining that he needed to take measurements and wanted to preserve the dear deceased's dignity.

This time he'd told her, 'The human jaw is a hinge, like a door. And when the breath goes out of them, the door's always left ajar.'

Evelyn had looked down into the greying face of someone's aunt and, true enough, the woman's jaw was hanging open, revealing stained teeth and a tongue like a purple sea sponge. Someone had tied it shut with a bandage wrapped around her chin and the top of her head, but that wouldn't do for the people who would shuffle through the house, bringing sympathies and homemade pork pies.

'We need to stitch it shut so these people can say their goodbyes without the last picture of her being from the set of a horror film. You understand?'

Evelyn nodded and picked up the suture needle and length of catgut Daddy was holding out for her in his hand. She threaded the needle. Daddy gently cupped her right hand in his own and guided her to push the needle high under the old woman's lip, inside her mouth into her right nasal cavity, through cartilage to the left nostril and back down to emerge within the mouth. Evelyn breathed out. It was not how she imagined – there was no blood, and while the procedure required a certain amount of muscle, the needle and catgut pulled smoothly through the flesh. Apart from the tail of thread hanging out the right side of the woman's mouth, there was no trace of where that needle had been.

'Ready to go again?' Daddy asked. 'We're nearly done.'

Evelyn jerked her head rigidly up and down, and he took her hand in his. This time he guided her to push the needle within the mouth, down behind the bottom lip, so low that it came out beneath the chin's cleft. He turned the needle, leaving the tiniest stitch, to take it back up through the soft hollow beneath the chin, behind the bottom lip and into her mouth. He pulled the needle away from the thread and placed it on a tray beside the bed.

'There. We just need to tie it up. I'm going to close up the jaw now if you can hold her lips open?'

As her father pulled the two loose threads tight, the jaw acquiesced and closed with a dull tap of teeth on teeth. Evelyn's fingers fumbled to lift the woman's lips, pulling them open like a laughing clown on Sideshow Alley. She watched as he tied a firm knot and snipped the tailing catgut neatly with stainless steel scissors, then let go and allowed the lips to settle back into place. She stepped back. The woman's face was calm, her lambs-ear cheeks settled. Searching for evidence of what she'd just been party to, all she could see was the tiniest dimple beneath the chin.

Her father was watching her. 'You all right, bloss?'

'Daddy . . .' Her eyes hadn't left the dead woman's face. 'I don't understand. Why do you use cat's guts to stitch up the cadavers?'

His laugh was so loud it could no doubt be heard ringing down the hall, through the living area to the kitchen, and he had to stuff a fist in his mouth or he might have severed any future business with this particular family on account of his inappropriate discourse with the dead. Evelyn realised later that his laugh was more relief than humour. It hadn't been his idea to involve her in the morbid task of dressing the bodies, but his arthritis was only getting worse, and no way was Mother getting her hands dirty with the dead.

'Catgut isn't cat's guts, love. It's a swell story though, something you can tell your friends when they're plucking a violin or playing tennis.' He beckoned her to sit beside him at the foot of the bed. 'Catgut is made from the intestines of pigs or cattle, usually. Lovely stretchy stuff. Strong too. I get mine from the butcher in Mole Creek. Long, long time ago, in medieval times, there was a mini violin that travelling musicians used to play, called a kytte. Spelt k-y-t-t-e but pronounced kit.'

Evelyn said it out loud, rolling the sound on her tongue.

'These wee instruments were played with a horsehair bow on strings made from cow gut – cow intestines. And the string product for the kytte got to be known as kytte gut. You're probably guessing the rest, but over time through the foibles of language, kyttegut became catgut, even though it's got nothing to do with old Marmaduke's feline friends. Catgut is used for all sorts of things, including stringed instruments, tennis rackets and suturing folks' jaws shut.'

Evelyn finished the last stitch of the seam, smiling at the memory of Daddy's eyes sparkling above the upward curve of his whiskers that day. How she loved that about him, the way he brought the mundane to life so that when she pulled out that mean-looking needle and prepared it for the familiar procedure, her thoughts naturally flowed backwards in time to dusty roads trodden by medieval minstrels, who pulled pocket-sized violins from within their colourful velvet jackets and charmed those in their midst with ballads of their wanderings. As she pulled catgut through human skin, she danced to tunes of beautiful maids, daring stallions and glittering kingdoms.

Chapter 4

Summer 2019

Rae and Allira hadn't asked permission, they just bought brushes, rollers and a four-litre tin of paint. Kamikaze Yellow, the colour swatch said. A bold yellow with the hum of butter-scotch and homemade mustard. They spent a whole Saturday rolling it onto the one wall in the *Folk* magazine office that wasn't pocked with windows and doors.

'Now that is an improvement!' Rae said, stepping back after finishing the first coat. 'Let's just hope Justin agrees.'

While waiting for the paint to dry between coats, Allira tried to finish a long-overdue project plotting the magazine's journey from inception to present day, destined for the revamped website. Her red pen hovered over the draft pages.

'I had no idea *Folk* dated back to 1948,' Rae said while sifting through a folder of clippings and articles.

'It was more like a church bulletin back then – did you see what it used to be called?'

Rae held up a limp leaflet. '*The Good Folk of the Meander Valley Parishes*,' she chirped. 'Bit of a mouthful!' She drained a glass of pinot and reached for another of Allira's legendary pork and fennel sausage rolls.

Rae held up a weathered leaflet dated 1951. 'I think this is the first one in the bundle that has a photo.' She flicked past face after unsmiling face against featureless backdrops of weather-boards or brick. If the subject blinked or the wind blew hair across their face, the shot remained. 'It seems the cameraman for *Folk* back then was a one-shot wonder, minus the wonder,' she said, holding up one particularly unfortunate portrait of a woman scratching her nose. She tapped her foot. 'Would the paint be dry yet, Al?'

Allira looked at her watch. 'Better give it another twenty to be safe.'

'Okay, give me that then,' she said, gesturing to the draft Allira had been scrawling on. 'Let me read it out aloud, a verbal proof *à la Raelene Benedetti*!'

Allira handed Rae the paper, just as she'd done with countless essays and short stories through high school, college and uni.

Rae cleared her throat and proceeded in a stage voice: 'The Anglican minister who held the reins until 1985 brought to light the kind of details that created hunger in readers. It became so popular that café owners, laundrette operators and even the museum manager started asking for copies as reading material for their customers.' She started pacing theatrically with the pages held aloft, like she was practising lines for a Shakespearean play. 'When the Launceston-based *Tasmanian Herald* took over, *Folk* was given a masthead and style guide that brought it in line with the paper's own branding. It adopted a more pleasing aesthetic from a marketing perspective and the photos finally changed to marry with the article's subject matter.' She feigned a yawn. 'This is a bit beige, Al.'

'*Folk* was pretty beige back then. They tore its heart out.'

'And you call me dramatic!'

Allira gave Rae a soft shove, taking the pages from her and tucking them back into the folder with the clippings and historical copies of *Folk*. She couldn't explain why her emotions were high. She'd stayed up late playing eight ball with Hamish last night. That was probably it: fatigue. Ever since Hamish had agreed to mind the eight ball table for a friend who'd moved overseas indefinitely, it had become their hobby, a way to unwind together. Sometimes they would talk, but mostly they would play in silence, the garage walls echoing with each clack of ball against ball. Hamish taught her how to play, but she had long outstripped him. She was a natural; it came easy to her and every game ended with Hamish's evocation of 'You really should compete, Al!'

Her response was always the same, a gruff 'nope'. Besides loathing the spotlight, Allira loved the immersive rhythms of the game, the way it engaged muscles and mind, dexterity and calculation in exploration of Newton's law of action and reaction. It felt personal, and she wanted to keep it that way.

'Let's keep painting,' she said to Rae, and they once again dipped their brushes, nervously anticipating the response it might elicit. They settled into a comfortable silence or, rather, Rae turned the music up so loud that there was no space for chatter, just hapless singing and swaying hips.

Allira remembered the tense conversations with Justin in those early days after he'd bought the magazine. 'We have to have a point of difference,' she'd argued. 'It still looks like a *Tasmanian Herald* lift-out.'

It was something the Anglican priest had written in *Folk* before handing it over to the *Tasmanian Herald* that had given Allira the idea for the overhaul. 'We are more than what we have, what we do and what is said or thought about us. We are humanity.'

Sure, the stories built a framework for understanding who a person was based on their experiences, accomplishments and connections. But Allira felt challenged to push back against this social conjuring of identity, of measuring a person's value by what they exhibited. 'A person is valuable because they are a person,' she said as she summed up her reasoning for the new pared-back approach to the magazine's photography. She wanted the reader to see the person simply as they were. Unadorned. No copious make-up or airbrushing. A moment of honesty. A moment when the reader could connect with the sadness in an eye or the joy in a smile or the nostalgia in a faraway glance. Then, after reading of the person's accomplishments or hardships, perhaps they would still be able to return to the knowledge that they were kin – fellow humans sharing the experiences of this innately valuable life.

Justin had rolled his eyes at her, muttered something about sentimental trollop and said she had three months to trial it. That had been three years ago.

Allira and Rae spent the whole day rolling, cutting in, eating sausage rolls, waiting for paint to dry. Finally, by mid afternoon, they added the finishing touches. The *Folk* magazine logo on the far left was the starting point, leading into a mosaic of wooden clipboards, one for each of the magazine's pages. It was a visual planning aid, a place where the magazine's contributors could gather and dream up the next edition. Rae propped a stepladder nearby to reach the highest boards. For now they were blank, but they wouldn't be for long. Allira smoothed a removable sticker onto the right-hand side of the arrangement, a quote she had ordered online in a bold, block font. It had the same ring to it as the minister's statement: 'We are humanity . . .' Choose your own ending.

Rae stepped back and nodded approvingly. 'No matter how harebrained!'

'No matter how mischievous!' Allira chimed.

'No matter how under-appreciated – Justin doesn't know how good he's got it,' Rae said, then pressed her lips together. 'And for the pleasure, we'll either be fired on the spot or we'll never have to shout rounds of work drinks again!'

As it turned out, Justin was on some kind of bender and didn't set foot inside the office for several weeks, by which time the creative approach to managing the magazine's content was a fixture. The *Folk* wall was a living, breathing piece of art with its revolving display of portraits, headline ideas, cover shots, notes outlining article themes and so on. When Justin finally clapped eyes on it for the first time, he froze, scanning the wall slowly from left to right. The bright yellow bounced warmth into the room's austere corners and he could see Rae absorbed in conversation with an advertiser, pointing to a clipboard where their full-page ad would sit alongside the story of a respected Aboriginal Elder. He walked to his office and never said a word about the kamikaze wall. Until he did.

*

Allira sat in the Mercy Place car park sucking big gulps of air into her lungs and waiting for the puffiness around her eyes to subside. The air was thick with smoke. She could use it as an excuse: 'The smoke wreaks havoc with my allergies.' Something like that. Allira turned on the radio in time for the hourly news report.

'Two bushfires are burning in native forest bordering Launceston's southern suburbs. The Tasmania Fire Service has advised land- and homeowners in the area to remain vigilant. You can help protect property from flying embers by clearing gutters and debris and keeping up to date via the TFS website. Weather conditions are expected to worsen over the next fortnight with a heat wave and strong winds forecast for the state's north. However, a TFS spokesperson said they were confident the two fires would be controlled in the next few days.'

Allira flicked off the radio. Nothing to worry about. She looked at her reflection in the rear-view mirror: much improved. She scraped her long chocolate hair into a high ponytail, pulled some fresh mascara through her lashes and smeared her lips with tinted lip gloss. Her fingers involuntarily moved to the constellation on her right cheekbone, following their downwards path. *It was just the alcohol talking. Don't be melodramatic.*

Justin's breath had been riddled with whisky this morning, his eyes veined like a roadmap. It should have been a great start, the day every two months when the crew put another edition to bed. She'd just about skipped up the steps of the second-storey office, humming as she opened blinds to a view of the mall. She could see Jim handing out lattes to bleary-eyed office workers from his hole-in-the-wall café, Marg powering towards the optometrist in joggers and suit, and the moody busker with her mandolin already singing with her eyes closed.

It was the day Allira relished most, when the months of interviewing, transcribing, writing and editing came to a brief pause and there was time to get caught up in the excitement of creating something new. The cheery *Folk* clipboards were full – a collage of photos and clippings – and the new edition of *Folk* would be in the hands of readers by week's end.

'Where's the story on your dementia woman?' Justin's voice whipped the back of her neck.

Allira turned quickly, hugging her waist and clearing her throat. How she wished Rae hadn't let slip that she was visiting Nora. Not that it was secret, but she wasn't sure what would come of it. She'd pitched it to Justin as a tender portrait of a woman's dusk years, of the way dementia unwittingly revisits the past on its victims. But she had a feeling this story was going to write itself outside of any structure or plan she had devised. 'It's not . . . ready yet. We talked about this, remember? We were going to run your story on the guy who's just started a—'

'Well, I didn't do it, all right!' Justin was pacing, his fingernails scraping at his scalp, the golden links of his watchband glinting.

'That's okay . . .'

'Deadline's today, Allira. You should be on top of this!' His voice was peaking, the veins in his neck pulsing like earthworms.

'I'll pull something together, Justin. It'll be fine.' Allira sank into her chair and tapped at the keyboard, pulling up a directory of articles in progress. 'Katy's already done the photos for these two, so I'll just tee up a phone interview this morning. I can have it done by lunchtime.'

Justin licked his lips and nodded. Suddenly his clammy hands were on Allira's shoulders, heavy, pressing her down like he was trying to contain her. Her stomach flipped and in one seamless movement she swivelled in her chair, avoiding Justin's grasp to stand more than a metre from him.

'I need to start this now,' she said with steel in her voice.

'It's all right for you,' Justin said, his brow glistening. 'You get all the fun without the responsibility. You just go around painting everything sunshine and buttercups!' His hands were now balled into fists and he was eyeing the *Folk* wall like it was graffiti. His voice lowered. 'But when something goes wrong, it reflects on me, you see?'

Allira bit back the retort that told him it was about time he stepped up and learned what responsibility was, rather than leaving her to lead the magazine without the title or pay grade. She took a deep breath and instead steadied her voice to gently respond, 'It will be fine, Justin. Often our best work comes under pressure.'

After that, she couldn't stay. When Justin closed the door on his corner office, she told Rae she was feeling sick and that she'd finish the story from home. And she did. But she couldn't shake the feel of Justin's long, sweaty fingers on her skin and the insinuation that she was little more than a dispensable employee. And strangely, Nora's face kept interrupting her thoughts.

So she drove and found herself in the nursing home car park, wondering if she'd gone a little mad. Minutes passed as she sat there, thinking. A flock of black cockatoos screeched overhead, their shadows slipping across the car's bonnet. A Mazda wagon pulled up and a couple with two pre-school children emerged with flowers and chocolates, a nappy bag and excited chatter.

Ping! It was her phone. Justin: '*Where are you?*'

'*Interviewing Nora,*' she messaged back before grabbing her notebook, slinging her handbag across her shoulder and run-marching to reception. The smoke was so thick she could have been swimming through a cloud.

'She's not in a good way.'

Allira had hoped to visit Nora undetected, just slip into her room for half an hour. But Sally had spotted her on the way in and joined her in the corridor.

'What do you mean?' Allira asked.

'She's physically fine.' Sally paused, searching for the right words. 'But she's struggling mentally. You will probably find her unresponsive, or incoherent.'

'That's okay. I'm happy to just sit with her.'

'Of course. Just don't expect anything of her. Days like this are difficult.'

Allira nodded and continued towards Nora's room.

'Oh, and Allira, a word of advice. Just play along.' Sally smiled patiently as Allira tilted her head. 'A few times a week there's a gentleman here who thinks I'm his younger brother,' Sally continued with a laugh, a staccato note from deep in her throat. 'He thinks I'm his real-estate agent brother, visiting to put his shack on the market. I just go along with it. It's what the researchers and studies recommend, and it actually makes sense.

It would be far more distressing for him to be told every few days that he can't tell the difference between a woman and his own brother.' She started walking away. 'I haven't sold the shack yet!'

Allira smiled despite herself, watching Sally's departing figure. She could appreciate how an old bloke with dementia might mistake Sally for his tall younger brother, especially if she was wearing the smart suit and shirt she had on today. But playing along with it?

Nora's door was closed, and Allira rapped a knuckle loudly before pushing it open. The old woman sat at the end of her bed, thighs and back at a right angle, alert, like she'd been waiting for her. She looked up at the sound of the door opening, face expectant.

'Hello, Nora.' The older woman looked beyond her, like she was hoping for someone else.

'Are you waiting for someone?'

'Well,' Nora said, pulling her hand back to her lap, 'yes. Daddy has some new timber arriving tomorrow all the way from Strahan. Jimmy Abel, he drives the truck and always stays the night. Mother told me to prepare his bed.'

'This one?' Allira pointed to Nora's own bed, realising that all her sheets were torn off and strewn across the floor.

'Yes. It's not becoming for a delivery man to sleep in the house with us, so the pallet bed will have to do. Hopefully he's not allergic to dust.' Nora smothered a mirthful chuckle with a hand. Her eyes were alight with energy, and she suddenly stood upright, her back a rigid line from her hips to her crown.

Allira noticed for the first time how tall she was. Long, slightly bowed legs led to narrow hips and shoulders. Slender arms hung like trailing vines, and broad hands were half closed, clawed. Her hair was shoulder-length with thick natural waves sitting in an unruly yet attractive mass around her square forehead, flat nose and determined chin. Even with deep lines like parentheses around her mouth and splaying from the corners of her eyes, her skin was glowing. She was beautiful, Allira realised. And once, she had surely been stunning.

Allira lifted one of the discarded sheets from the ground and started smoothing it across the mattress.

'No, no!' Nora's voice clapped. 'They're filthy, can't you see? Daddy takes his naps on that day bed with every sawdust you can imagine still clinging to him!'

Allira peeled back the sheet and threw it towards the door. 'You're right. What was I thinking? I'll go grab some fresh sheets from down the . . . er, from the linen cupboard.'

With Nora's nod of approval, she hurried to the nurse's station where she was directed to a storage room with rows and rows of fresh sheets. She selected two starchy flat sheets, a pillow slip and, as an afterthought, a Vegemite jar from a box of vases and glassware she could only guess was to cope with the steady flow of floral arrangements in and out of the facility.

Nora was plumping a pillow when Allira returned with the sheets, thumping it with great gusto but little effect. Her hand quavered and she barely managed to hold the pillow still. Allira sat the sheets on the bed and handed Nora the Vegemite jar.

'I thought we could pick some flowers and put them beside the bed.'

Nora grasped the jar and closed her eyes for some time. As she swayed gently, clouds scudded across the sky outside her window and footsteps amplified and receded. Allira remained completely still, taking mental snapshots of every detail, including the way that, despite the serene smile smoothing Nora's lips, tears leaked from the creases of her eyes and wove like silver ribbons down her cheeks.

When Nora opened her eyelids, her irises were flamed with memories. Her hands encompassed the jar, fingers overlapping, and she peered down into the vessel as if to catch her tears. Those once-copper waves fell across her face as she slumped onto the bed, her spine curved like a sickle. 'Yes,' she sighed. 'That's just what I did.'

Chapter 5

Summer 1953

The Vegemite jar was one Daddy used to wash his brushes in. Evelyn arranged three yellow dahlias and a few sprigs of foliage neatly in the jar, which she had carefully scrubbed of any residual turpentine. Hopefully Mother didn't notice the absence of the flowers in her garden. Evelyn pushed the arrangement to the centre of the bedside table, which was actually a turned-over wooden fruit crate with a blue-and-white-checked tea towel smoothed over top.

Daddy would receive delivery of his specialty timbers tomorrow from Jimmy Abel, all the way from Strahan in Tasmania's rugged west. Evelyn had never been there, but her imaginings sculpted scenes of impenetrable forests, creatures lurking in bone-strewn dens, black rivers and Indigenous people bare-skinned and beckoning. The trip took Jimmy nearly six hours in his rumbling Bedford truck, so Daddy always offered him a bed for the night in the workshop.

Jimmy was the sort of person you could listen to for days. There were stories in his Nordic blue eyes, in his leathery hands, in his long scruffy beard and stained work boots. If Evelyn was lucky, the stories made their way to his tongue after a few brandies when Mother had gone to bed. Jimmy and Daddy sat in companionable silence until Evelyn crept out of bed to join them with a mouth full of questions. Sometimes he answered with nothing but a wry grin. Other times he shifted in his seat, knocked back the dregs of his cup and started on one of his ambling tales of life out west. They were never short, but always ended abruptly, even mid-sentence sometimes. Hearing them lit a fire in her belly that kept her warm for days. *There is adventure out there.* Her imagination zinged and snapped with possibilities beyond her world of the weatherboard house and acreage across the road from the Caveside church, and the eighteen-minute bicycle ride to the Chudleigh district schoolhouse.

Evelyn turned to the bed, hands crossed in front of her aproned chest. An annoyingly full chest, in Evelyn's measuring. The girls at school were agog for bosoms and bras. They wouldn't shut up about the new 'Make-Believe' Berlei bra that supposedly added two inches to the bust. Shirley's mum bought her one and she pointed her breasts around the place like she was offering a box of assortments. But then, she was all curves and eyelashes. No wonder the boys were 'honeycakes' and 'sugar' with her.

Evelyn sighed. Would a boy ever notice her? Evelyn Grayson with her gangly white legs, flipper feet, no bum to speak of, rusty red hair that behaved like a blackberry bush, freckled face with eyes like duck ponds and a mouth that blurted unmentionable social faux pas. Like how to sew a cadaver's jaw shut. A grin tugged at her dimpled cheeks. *The look on their faces!* And anyway, what boy would want a wife with such spangled dreams? *I want to explore the world. I don't want to darn socks and make green tomato pickles.*

Daddy knew. He let her in. Like with Jimmy. His mouth was rough, and Daddy winced at some of his descriptions of women and brawls; he would place a firm hand on Jimmy's arm for a moment before the deliveryman continued. But Mother? She put up walls. Mother *was* a wall. As far as she was concerned, Evelyn was in training to be somebody's housewife, and it didn't matter a jot that there was some kind of flame burning in her.

Evelyn pulled up the comforter, folded the sheet down and fluffed the pillow. Jimmy would sleep soundly here. The Lord only knew what his sleeping quarters were like back home.

The moment that class was dismissed for the day was like the crank of a Jack-in-the-box finally triggering the lever. Evelyn jumped from her desk and collected her books in one scrambling movement, shoving them into her school bag as she dashed for her bike on scarecrow legs. She was already pedalling away from the schoolhouse as most of the children were just making their way down the front steps.

It was a glorious summer day, the kind that would normally entice her to linger in the syrupy light, to jump the fence and run along the creek, through thigh-high grass as curtains of butterflies lifted like a net, brushing their wings against her cheeks and neck and unfurled fingers. She would have liked to lie there in the grass, making an indent on the ground, eyes closed and listening to the creek gurgling, a tractor's hum, and the chirp of crickets. She would have rolled onto her stomach and watched the swallows carving the sky with their crescent wings, sending up wishes for some of their agility and freedom.

Today, however, was the day Daddy's timber would be delivered, the day Jimmy would stay, the day she might glimpse some more of the wide world beyond Caveside. Evelyn's feet pumped the pedals of her blue Malvern Star, David's old bike, so hard that her face flushed red with effort and excitement. She quickly put distance between herself and the smattering of houses that made up the township of Chudleigh, bumping along a mixture of dirt and sealed roads through lush green pastures freckled with sheep. Across the creek, around the corner at Mr Byard's shed and then she could see the little weatherboard church in the distance, across from the line of oaks that marked her driveway and the sign swinging in the breeze:

S & T Grayson

Carpenter | Undertaker

As much as Evelyn's focus was on getting home, she couldn't help but slow ever so slightly and lift her eyes to the right where the Great Western Tiers dwarfed the little church-yard, and Mother Cummings Peak stood sentinel. They were moody today. The sun's glare cast deep, ruinous shadows down the ranges' flanks, and Mother Cummings was creased into a thousand furrows, like an origami warning.

Evelyn's chest thudded a little louder, a little faster, but she kept her feet pumping their circular rhythm until she reached the driveway and swung her handlebars left, elbows lifted, tyres skidding on gravel before she corrected and pushed on through the flickering leaf light.

The old forest-green Bedford was backed up to the workshop door and she could see stacks of timber in its tray, some already unloaded. Jumping off her bike and dropping it against the fence, she shrugged off her school bag and ran towards the sound of men's voices.

'Daddy! Jimmy!' she yelled.

They were at either end of a piece of Huon pine, lifting it onto storage rungs along the walls of the carport. Daddy's face broke into a smile. 'Hey kitten,' he said as a man who was not Jimmy stepped out of the shadows, brushing sawdust and splinters from his hands.

'You're not Jimmy,' Evelyn said flatly.

'Jimmy hurt his arm, dislocated, so he sent me to deliver.'

This other man was not much older than Evelyn herself, muscular, with high cheekbones, heavy brows and cropped dark hair. His skin was the colour of a jersey caramel, and he looked at Evelyn through piercingly blue eyes with the intensity of one who hasn't yet learned the rules. He frowned, absently rubbing his right earlobe.

It was barely a breath's length, this moment of them taking the measure of each other. Of him seeming to notice the unruly wildness of her hair, the river-green eyes and the ready-to-run energy surging through her. Of her replaying the lilt of his tongue, the meshing of man and boy still evident in his face and the stillness of his spirit. They noticed each other, and then flailed to un-notice, swimming back to the surface of benign pleasantries.

'I am Michał Friedrich,' he said softly, extending a hand.

'Evelyn,' she replied quickly, shaking his warm, work-roughened hand.

Daddy dumped a length of timber against the Bedford's tray with a loud *thwack*. 'Why don't you go help your ma with the afternoon tea, poss?'

Evelyn wordlessly swung her school bag across a shoulder and headed through the rose garden, up the sandstone steps with their timeworn grooves, across the verandah and down the hall to the staircase.

'I'm just getting changed, Mother,' she called towards the kitchen as she jogged up the carpeted treads, her right hand skimming the Blackwood rail that linked downstairs to upstairs like an artery.

The house had six bedrooms. Downstairs were two modest bedrooms used as private studies or extra space for boarders or visitors. The master bedroom was downstairs also, across from the music room, where a solitary upright piano occupied a corner beside a large open fireplace. This was also where Mother relegated the obligatory Christmas tree in December, so the smell and droppings didn't assault her in the home's main living spaces. David was the only one who played piano, so for Evelyn it was a room of pompous symphonies and stinging comparisons. How talented he was. How generous his gifts. How he brought life to the house. How successful, how handsome, how sweet. All bundled in that week of Christmas. She spent as little time as possible in the music room.

But since David had left, the upstairs of the rambling home had become her sanctuary. There were three attic rooms, one with an adjoining study that still smelled of David. Each had dormer windows that allowed Evelyn views in all directions. In the second bedroom, the back panel of the built-in wardrobe was loose, and when she jimmied it free, she could crawl into the triangular void of roof space once used for storage but long forgotten. Evelyn had found all manner of treasures there: a love note penned in almost illegible script, a hand-knitted baby bootie and an ornate tortoiseshell hair comb among them.

She had chosen the south-facing bedroom once David had left. Yes, because of the outlook to the Great Western Tiers, and because she could see the property's comings and goings, but also because the dormer window was positioned so she could hoist herself onto her elbows and climb out onto the grey corrugated iron. She had always been careful to choose her time. She knew that if Mother, or even Daddy, found her balancing on the highest part of their two-storey house, there would be no chance of attempting it again.

So she had waited for special conditions. A full moon. A birthday. A good report. The anniversary of something. The day Daddy returned from war. She would wait until the sound of soft snoring wended upstairs from her parents' bedroom and the day had turned black before gingerly creeping onto the rooftop to lay under the bowl-of-porridge moon, counting stars and imagining their light was sliding down to her. She had taken an imaginary straw and slurped them down like a frothy vanilla milkshake, all while marvelling at the magnitude of the canopy stretched above her, at the wonder of it. *Surely this is God*, she had pondered. She certainly hadn't glimpsed him in the narrow pews and hawk-eyed gaze of parishioners on Sundays. And she hadn't even seen him in Mrs Pike's textbook description of the celestial bodies. But lying on the roof with the Southern Cross winking like diamonds on a bed of velvet, she thought there must be a god. A god who was more wild than she was, to think up such baffling things as whole galaxies and stars and planets, and life itself, and that they didn't collide and explode and implode. So many questions the textbooks left unanswered.

Shaking off the thought, Evelyn stepped into the custard-yellow dress Mother had bought her for Christmas. She hated it. Hated the flouncy skirt that skimmed just beneath her knees, and the bunched sleeves, all the fuss. But she knew Mother would appreciate seeing it on her, a sure-fire way to begin the rest of the afternoon in her good books. As Evelyn entered the kitchen, Mother looked up from arranging lamingtons on a plate and, sure enough, a terse smile stretched across her face.

'You look like a real young lady in that dress,' she said, and Evelyn didn't miss the implication that she didn't look like a 'real young lady' any other time of day. She thanked her anyway, and loaded a tray with sugar lumps, a teapot brewing Bushells, cups, saucers, cream, and teaspoons, and followed Mother to the little wrought-iron settee on the paved area among the roses. The sun came and went like a nervous guest, and a chill breeze stirred off the Tiers. Evelyn wondered what stories the new boy, Michał, might share with her and Daddy tonight.

Chapter 6

Summer 2019

Allira pulled on her running shoes, pushed her phone into her sports bra and stashed the house key under a pot plant. She reached for earphones but dropped them again, leaving them strewn on the bench. There was too much noise in her head already – no space for music or a podcast today.

She jogged down the hill towards the Gorge and found her rhythm. The comfortable, metronome thrum of footfall, breath and blood. It was a mild afternoon and the light golden. Her muscles loosened with every minute of fresh air and silence. She needed this.

Allira picked up her pace and skirted around a huddle of Korean tourists taking photos of a peacock with his tail fanned. Even after twelve years living in Launceston, the presence of these extravagant birds amongst the Australian fauna struck her as peculiar, comical. The pademelons and native hens and possums in all their browns had been well and truly shown up by the introduction of this mardi gras of a bird. So typical of nineteenth-century thinking, when the Cataract Gorge was first opened up as a tourist attraction. The Gorge's deep bowl and rugged ravines needed to be improved, they said. Needed to be made more like England; Anglicised. The man with the pet shop on Balfour Street had said it when she interviewed him about his family's migrant background: 'Our history is of improvement rather than acceptance. Is it any wonder we are not content?'

She took the gravel track towards Duck Reach, the site of one of the first hydro-electric power stations in the world. Blackwood and wattle created a leafy wall on her left while the ground dropped dramatically to the right, a cliff face down to the river's steady rumble.

The tracks were so familiar that her feet found their route subconsciously. The rock that needed to be scaled, the tree root tripping hazard, the path's sudden veer right. And in the familiarity and rhythm, Allira revisited her afternoon. *Oh Nora, what secrets are you holding?*

The Vegemite jar had transported Nora and given her words to describe that fragment of time, but Allira could see that there was more, and that the truth was a heavy burden. The old woman sat at the end of her bed and retold that day when Michał Friedrich, a mysterious young European man, delivered specialty timber to her father's coffin-making workshop in Caveside. Nora's eyes were focused. There was no stumbling over details. It was a definitive description of something bright and clear, like she had stepped outside of her ageing self and given a full-colour snapshot, where until now the pictures had been smeared, black-and-white negatives.

And then a nurse had walked in with Nora's medication and the connection was just as quickly severed. She rushed to her doll's cradle and started cooing and rocking the unchanging plastic face and those frozen hands and feet. 'Tell me about Michał,' Allira prompted after the nurse left. But Nora's face was a blank page. There was no recognition, no spark.

'Hold him for me,' she said, lowering the doll into her arms.

Allira held the doll stiffly, its glassy eyes staring relentlessly while Nora fussed with a bottle and bib. *Did something happen with Michał? Where is he now?* Allira wanted to hammer her with questions to fill all the gaps, to pull out that spiral notepad and scribble everything down, to map out some hypotheticals that were emerging.

But she said nothing. Found herself absently rocking a fake baby, like she was rocking Nora's wounded spirit.

Allira doubled back, retracing her steps to the First Basin. Its green-black waters were only ventured into by teenagers hurling themselves from boulders in the height of summer and the occasional soul in a swimming cap and Speedos, arching slow, steady strokes like they'd been doing it their whole life. The man-made pool with its aquamarine paint job, safety fencing and lifeguard was where the crowds gathered. Toddlers paddled in the shallows, older children splashed and duck-dived, parents hovered at the edge, and girls sunned their bikini bodies alongside families with picnic spreads on the expanse of lawn maintained by the council, running from the murky basin to the pool, the playground and the toilets beyond.

Something else Nora had said was playing on her mind. 'No one calls me Nora – except Daddy,' she had replied to Allira's usual chirpy greeting. When Allira had delicately asked what she should call her, Nora's response had been quick, laced with incredulity. 'Evelyn, dear,' and she had patted Allira's leg sympathetically, like it had been *her* losing her memory.

'Hey, gorgeous!'

Allira spun around, shaken from her reverie. She recognised that voice. 'Rae! Um . . . what on earth are you wearing?'

They hugged and Allira stepped back to take the full measure of Rae's outfit. White linen pants and a fuchsia floral kaftan were paired with a wide-brimmed hat, bum bag, thongs and a camera hanging around her neck.

'Eww, you're sweaty, girl!' Rae laughed.

'Resort wear meets outback Australiana? Is that an Akubra?'

'Yep, got it from an op shop for five bucks. Do you know how much these are new?' Rae tilted the rim of the brown felt stockman's hat, dispersing shadow from her perfectly made-up face. She wore fuchsia lipstick matching her nails and kaftan. 'I'm working on a freelance job, a travel feature about holidaying at home. Don't tell Justin.'

Allira nodded. 'But that still doesn't explain the bum bag, Rae.'

'Sure it does, I'm in character.'

Allira laughed and shook her head at the same time, her glossy ponytail swishing. A soccer ball bounced along the grass near her feet and she scooped it up, throwing it back to a shaggy-haired kid still in his school uniform.

'Justin got pretty intense on you the other day.' Rae was suddenly serious, scrutinising her friend's face. 'It's not fair, the way he treats you.'

Allira's eyes darkened. She shifted her weight to her other leg, adjusting the waistband of her running tights.

'Oh, it's nothing,' she said, trying to make light of it. Rae crossed her arms, waiting. 'He's just messed up. I wish he'd get some help or something, you know? He's not a bad guy.'

'He's threatened by you, that's what he is. Have you told Hamish what he's like?'

'No, it's really nothing, Rae. I've known Justin forever, he's just in a funk.'

Rae's flamboyant kaftan lifted in the breeze, flapping and billowing behind her like she was trying to compete with the peacocks. 'Can you keep a secret?' she asked.

Allira tilted her head.

'I bumped into this guy who's chummy with Justin. Real tight. They're members of the same golf club. And he asked me if we'd found a new office.'

'What?'

'My theory is that Justin's not keeping up with the rent, Al. And that means he's probably not keeping up with other bills either.'

Allira groaned.

'You up for some sneaky business, like old times? Let's make some calls, find out what's going on. I reckon if I can pull off this tourist thing, I can play the boss's PA, no worries!' Rae bunched her fists and swung her hips to bust out her signature hip-hop-inspired choreography. Allira was doubled over laughing at Rae's spontaneous dancing, the curvy hips swinging, boobs bouncing, her face exuberant.

'You sure can,' she agreed, joining the flash dance for all of five seconds before noticing the attention they were attracting. 'But Rae, you kinda are his PA.'

Rae pouted.

'And everything else!' She knew Rae desperately wanted to write for the magazine, but Justin wouldn't look beyond her admin proficiency. 'Right. I'm going home.'

'Don't worry, babe, we'll get to the bottom of this.' Rae smiled, her Akubra askew.

As she jogged home, Allira couldn't help replaying the conversation. Could it be true? Justin wasn't keeping on top of bills? The magazine had never been better financially, so it didn't make sense for him to be struggling. Of course, his recent behaviour suggested profits could be draining out in another direction.

Her stomach churned. There was too much to lose. The number of times she had stepped up to take charge in Justin's absence was too many to count. Lately, staff had been coming to her first. They knew she was the unofficial editor, the get-things-done person at *Folk*. She actually loved it. She was always energised by the troubleshooting. She enjoyed calmly talking a colleague out of overwhelm or working with a contributor on a different story angle, brainstorming new leads, new revenue streams, new advertisers. Like the time she'd agreed to have a work experience student with her for a week. Or the time an interview subject felt they had been misrepresented, and she shouted the old man lunch and listened to him as he shared his anger first, but then the loneliness he felt after his wife's death the year before.

As her feet pounded the footpath, she realised that she was far more invested in this job than she'd ever intended. She pushed herself to run harder, faster. Just a few kilometres home now. The uphill burn. What would she do if *Folk* magazine folded?

Allira's arms were pumping, her breath laboured. *It can't fold.*
It can't. She was thinking of Rae and the other employees, of the
faithful subscribers, and all the stories still waiting to be told. Her
calves were burning. She passed the house with the gnarled old
lemon tree laden with fruit, the unmown lawn reaching its lowest
branch. Justin had been handed the magazine on a silver platter,
and what improvements had he made to ensure its survival? She
didn't mind the lack of recognition for her ideas and management, but she certainly would mind if, despite it all, Justin ground
the magazine into the dirt. Allira could feel her face was red,
and wet with sweat. Her legs were screaming. She couldn't let
this happen. Rounding the corner, she sprinted to her letterbox
and stopped, folding at the waist, hands on knees, heaving. She
checked her smartwatch – a new PB for the last three-kilometre
stretch. As she panted and mopped her forehead with the hem
of her top, she made herself a promise to do everything within
her power to keep *Folk* alive. And as she went to walk down the
driveway to start cooking dinner, she realised something bigger.
Folk was already hers. In her heart, it belonged to her.

I want to be the editor and manager of Folk. The words
aligned unbidden in her mind, catching her breath and her step.
Yes, her whole body agreed, sending tingles down her spine. *Yes.*

Chapter 7

Summer 1953

'Michał. Michał.'

Evelyn was lying in bed waiting for the light to drain from the sky, waiting for Mother to fall asleep so she could slink out of the house and down to the workshop to join Daddy and Michał, who were no doubt nursing mugs of whisky and sharing tales into the night. It wouldn't be the same without Jimmy, but she was intrigued by this younger delivery man with his thick accent and brazen eyes. How did he pronounce his name?

'Mee-how. Mee-how.'

That was it. With a rasping, back-of-throat sound linking the two syllables. She practised in whispers as the wind swirled outside, gently rattling her attic room windows. The lights were off downstairs, the house quiet but for the whisper of wind slipping under doors, between weatherboards and under eaves. Evelyn waited another half-hour. Finally, she pulled her overalls over her cotton pyjamas and hurried downstairs on light feet, avoiding the creaky treads with the deftness of someone who had done this many times before. She went through the kitchen, not daring to exit past the master bedroom, grabbing a handful of Mother's rock cakes and wrapping them hurriedly in a tea towel as she went.

There was light under the workshop door, but no voices. She often wondered if Daddy and Jimmy talked much at all when she wasn't in the room, or if they mostly sat in companionable silence. But Michał seemed different, like he'd want to know about things . . . She rapped on the door, three firm knocks. She heard the rustling of paper, the scraping of wood against concrete. The door swung open.

'Yes?' Michał Friedrich stood before her, confusion darkening his face. He wore work pants and an undershirt, the white cotton fluorescing against his bronzed arms.

'Is Daddy here?' Evelyn pushed past him into the workshop.

A single lamp threw a warm glow across the room so that everything had a soft double of itself leaning against the walls. A blanket was a makeshift curtain, crudely nailed to the architraves. Michał's rucksack sat at the foot of the pallet bed, its mouth gaping open, and letters were strewn across the sheets. Daddy was not here.

Michał shook his head, eyebrows furrowed.

'But we always . . . Daddy always comes and . . . Jimmy . . .' She was glad for the rock cakes giving her hands something to hold onto. Michał's stare was almost as bad as Mrs Pike's when she caught Evelyn daydreaming during class. Piercing. But sparkling a little with something like mirth. And that colour, deep and storied as the patterns on Mother's Blue Willow china set. She fiddled with the tea towel and instead of bundling up the cakes more tightly, the contents tumbled out, one-two-three-four, onto the hessian matting at her feet.

Evelyn dropped to her knees, collecting up the crumbs, keeping her head dipped to cover the flush of red swarming from her forehead to her neck. 'I'll get out of your way. I'm sorry. Daddy and Jimmy always had a whisky and talked up late. I crept out once Mother was asleep and joined them. Mother doesn't like me listening to men's conversations. I brought rock cakes . . .' She talked fast and breathlessly until all the crumbs were cleared, then abruptly stood.

Michał had stepped closer, his hands still in his pockets, a lazy smile playing with the contours of his buttery face. 'How old are you?'

His English was good, Evelyn realised. The accent, something European – Austrian? German? – only rounded off his words in the same way Daddy sanded the sharp edges off his beautiful chairs and sideboards.

'I'm in my sixteenth year.' She lifted her chin. He didn't need to know that she was only a month into her sixteenth year.

'My sister is fifteen too,' he said with a gentle smirk. 'She wants to be a famous singer.' Michał's voice trailed off.

Evelyn sensed sadness lurking, the same sadness that crouched in the shadows of farmhouses nestled in bucolic Caveside, where strong men railed and then wept into the aprons of their wives, where young men limped, and where lovers replayed the day there was a knock on the door and a telegram.

'Swell! How glamorous. Does she sing at church or any of the dance halls where you live?'

Michał shook his head. 'She doesn't live here. Sabine is with Mama in Berlin.'

'You're German?'

'Mama is from Poland but, yes, my Papa was German, and we lived in Berlin mostly.'

'So your name is German?'

'Polish. It was my grandfather's name, on my mother's side.'

Evelyn glanced at the letters on Michał's bed, fiddling with the thick plait of auburn hair hanging across her left shoulder.

He followed her gaze. 'They are from Mama. She tells me all the detail. The snow is melting, spring coming. She tells me the cost of a pound of sausages and how her neighbour, Herr Schuster, will marry a woman half his age soon, and that Sabine grows more beautiful by the day, and she sings only in French or English.' He gathered up the letters gently, folding and tucking them back into their envelopes. The paper was yellowed and crude, not the kind of stationery Mother used to send letters to her sisters in England. But the hand was refined, the looping words leaning forward in elegant anticipation.

Michał put the letters into his rucksack. 'I miss them.' He sat on the bed, rubbing the back of his neck.

Evelyn took a step backwards. She suddenly felt like an intruder, like she was peering through a keyhole into someone's bedroom as they undressed. At the same time, there was an urge to reach out and touch him, to hold his face and listen to the painful things that he carried on those stiff shoulders.

Michał looked up, his face a masked smile. 'Did you bring those for me?'

'No . . . I mean yes. For you and Daddy.'

'Can I?' He reached out a hand and Evelyn acquiesced, depositing the bundle in his palm.

'Mind, I probably collected sawdust with the crumbs when I cleaned them off the floor,' she said, eyes lit. 'It might be an improvement!' She turned on her heel, throwing a 'goodnight' over her shoulder to make the careful retreat back to her room.

Evelyn woke to the sound of an almighty mechanical wheezing and spluttering. She tore the bedcovers aside and was at the window in two strides. Jimmy's Bedford truck was sitting where it was yesterday, to the side of the teardrop-shaped turning circle, but with its bonnet unhinged. Daddy and Michał were leaning in, heads nodding together, poking at its innards with oily rags and fingers.

'Give her a try,' she heard Daddy say, and Michał swung up into the driver's seat. He turned the key, pumping the accelerator pedal, but all Evelyn could see was a gentle shudder of the dark green truck's bodywork, like it had just swallowed a brussels sprout on Mother's orders. She was down there too, standing at the gate in the rose garden, watching. Her hair was still in rollers, and she held the collar of her dressing gown to her throat. She said something and the men looked up and nodded before she marched back inside.

Evelyn pulled on her school dress and ran a brush through her hair before racing outside.

'Hey Nora-girl,' Daddy said from beneath the truck's bonnet. It was the name that only Daddy called her. That affectionate name he had managed to instate, by increments, behind Mother's back. Evelyn was such a prim name. Her middle name suited better, like something the highland winds sang in a squall. And while she loved the way it was wrapped in fatherly fondness, it reminded her that it was the only time he had pushed back against Mother's iron will.

Before she could so much as smile in return, Mother was calling her back into the house. The kitchen was full of frying bacon and coffee smells.

'The truck has broken down, so it looks like that German boy will need to be staying on a while longer, until your father can get the spare part,' Mother said, without looking up from scrambling eggs at the stove. 'Set the table for breakfast, Evelyn, with an extra place for *Michael*.'

'Mi— Yes, Mother.' She fairly skipped to gather plates and cutlery, her insides vibrating, her head tingling. Michał would stay longer. Probably a week. All that time to learn about his adventures. Berlin to Strahan. A sister who sang in French.

She was setting the coffee pot on the table in the dining room when she heard Daddy at the back door, taking his boots off and then stomping down the hall. *The phone.* She crept through the adjoining lounge to press her ear to the door. Daddy was speaking loud and slow, articulating each word carefully. Static on the line, probably.

'Tell Jimmy . . . truck . . . ordered part . . . at least a week,' Evelyn made out through the door.

So it was true. A whole week. Evelyn's heart thumped faster than she thought possible. She pulled away from the door and spun a pirouette, eyes closed, her hair coming loose and flailing like a flag behind her. She opened her eyes, still spinning, watching the room blur; mantelpiece, brass doorknob, wallpaper, floral cushions, books, pot plant, Michał. She stopped. Swallowed.

Michał was leaning against the doorway to the dining room, arms folded. Evelyn felt suddenly exposed, like he was the one peering through the keyhole this time. She ran clammy fingers across her lips and looked straight into his face, challenging him. *Is this how Elizabeth felt under Mr Darcy's gaze? What is he thinking?* Evelyn's mind reached for the line she would most desire him to utter in this moment: 'I have been meditating on the very great pleasure which a pair of fine eyes in the face of a pretty woman can bestow.'

She dipped her head to catch herself from snorting at the absurdity of her romanticising. This was the bloke who dropped wood to Daddy in a big old green Bedford truck. And German too. But then he smiled, just the slightest curve of his lips, and she smiled too. Her heart thumped loudly in her chest and blood roared in her ears. It felt like the longest time that they stood there in silence, receiving each other. And then he was in front of her, reaching for her hand and bringing it to touch his lips.

His eyes hadn't left hers.

'Breakfast's ready,' he said.

Chapter 8

Summer 2019

'*Nooo!*' Hamish Ambrose's finger was still on the light switch as Allira pulled the sheets over her head in protest. 'It's too early.'

'C'mon, babe, this is our first day off together in weeks. Let's make the most of it.'

'What time is it?'

'Time for an adventure!'

Allira groaned. 'Seriously? Can you be more annoying?'

'Challenge accepted!'

Hamish launched towards her in one athletic leap, ripped aside the doona, and dived straight for her weakness: her incredibly ticklish feet.

She writhed and squealed somewhere between laughter and pain. 'Stop it,' she gasped. 'You win! I'm getting up.'

Hamish wrapped his arm around her waist and hoisted her to stand and face him. There were just a few centimetres of height difference between them. He dipped his head to kiss her on the mouth. 'Love you, Lira-girl.'

His thick mop of dark blond hair stood on end, and those

easy, inky blue eyes creased with contentment. He had always been the one to set the tone in their relationship, and Allira marvelled all over again at how he managed to lift and energise her. She loved this farmer's son and sports nut, who invested himself into every responsibility and activity with the gusto of a five-year-old on a sugar high.

By the time Allira had thrown on a cotton gown and padded barefoot into the kitchen, there were omelettes on the table and Hamish was handing her a latte. 'Oh look, it's a rabbit.'

'Mine's an old lady with a big hook-nose.'

They peered into their coffee froth, Hamish's latte art. What started as a jab at his amateur barista ranking in their home became something of a ritual. Like finding shapes in the clouds as a kid.

'You visiting Nora today, babe?'

Allira looked up from her mug. *Has she become that much a part of my life?* She mentally tallied how many times she'd visited in the last two weeks and realised it had become a part of her routine.

'No, I wasn't planning to. But you said adventure . . .'

'I know what you're thinking . . . eight ball tournament!' Hamish was still hounding her about taking it up competitively, and she was still stubbornly refusing.

'It's too beautiful outside for that, Hame. How about we go on a research adventure?' Allira suggested.

'Keep talking.'

'There are a few things Nora said that I'd like to look into. She asked me to call her Evelyn the other day. Said that only Daddy called her Nora.'

'Sounds like a mystery to be solved. We'd be like private detectives for the day.'

'Have I mentioned how wonderful you are?' Allira kissed him on the cheek.

The town library was a dead end, a case of too many books and not enough information to know where to start. Allira wanted to speak with Dale, her contact at the Community History Branch at the museum, but he was on long service leave for another few weeks yet.

The sun was high and relentless as they retraced their steps back to the car. Hamish's thongs flip-flopped and the hand that wasn't linked with Allira's shook the dregs of an iced coffee before he slurped the last drops. He flung it at a bin and tugged the peak of his cap lower over his eyes. 'What's our next move, Sherlock?'

'Maybe this is premature. I don't really know enough about her.'

'Let's see about that . . . People know her as Nora, but she asked you to call her Evelyn the other day when she relived something from her childhood. Did you get a sense of how old she might've been in the memory?'

'Old enough to be making up a bed for a visiting timber supplier.' Allira slurped on her own iced coffee, still half full. 'Young enough to still be at school . . . I'd guess in her teens.'

'Good. And you said she's eighty-one now, so that would make her . . . twelve in 1950.'

Allira nodded slowly. Post World War Two. Some rationing

would've still been in place. Cars weren't widely available. No telephones or television until the mid fifties for most households, although Tassie would have been a few steps behind the uptake, particularly in rural areas. Robert Menzies was prime minister. European migration was climbing. 'I think she was a bit older, fifteen maybe.'

The traffic zipped by as they continued along the street, past the terraced boutique shops with their cashmere throws and scented candles.

'What else do you know about her?' Hamish asked.

'Her dad was receiving a truckload of specialty timber from Strahan when she had that flashback the other day.' Allira fanned her face. 'I need to get out of this heat. Let's check this place out,' she said, pulling Hamish through the glass door of an antique shop. A brass bell chimed as they entered and a woman's voice rose in sultry song, a cacophony of keys and brass carrying her notes through the cavernous space's cool air. They paused momentarily, relishing the temperature change while trying to make sense of the voice, husky and bruised. Allira spotted the record player, its black eye spinning, just as a white-haired man wearing a bow tie and houndstooth slacks appeared.

He peered over spectacles propped halfway down his craggy nose. 'Nina Simone. Best female jazz singer of all time, in my humble opinion.' The little man folded into a deep bow, flourishing his right arm in an extravagant arc that nearly knocked an oriental vase from its shelf.

Allira jumped to steady the ornate porcelain, but the shopkeeper didn't notice.

'One of the few contralto voices of her time,' he continued, his piercing eyes darting between the two of them, back and forth like a tennis match.

'Ah—'

'It's the lowest female voice type. Nina reached vocal depths that most female singers could only dream of.' He straightened his spectacles.

Hamish grabbed Allira's hand and opened his mouth—

'Sadly, her life plunged to great depths also. She faced a lot of prejudice on account of her being Black.' He picked up the record which was spinning soundlessly, and flipped it over, gently dropping the stylus onto the outer lip. He closed his eyes and his ruddy cheeks twitched, hinting at a smile beneath the shaggy overhang of a moustache. His hands danced in the air, conducting dust as it agitated from bone china tea sets, the gappy teeth of a Bösendorfer piano and a one-eyed marionette doll.

'We're just—' Hamish made a move towards the back of the shop.

'You can hear her torment, can't you, Nina Simone's?' The man's eyes were still shut, and the couple didn't attempt a response as the strains of her voice rose to fill the space again. 'Of course, that wasn't her real name.'

'It wasn't?' Allira's interest was piqued for the first time.

'She was born Eunice Waymon,' he said, opening his eyes to study Allira. He rubbed his moustache.

'Why did she change it?'

'Eunice! I would've changed my name too.' Hamish laughed.

'To escape the ire of her family,' the man said, pointedly ignoring Hamish and directing his reply at Allira. 'She disguised her name when she started singing in nightclubs. Her family would have called it the devil's music. Nina became her stage name, although it was initially to escape shame.' He eyed Hamish ruefully with the last word.

Nina. Nora. Changed names. Family shame. *Maybe Nora was born Evelyn and she changed her name to escape . . . something*, Allira thought. Hamish squeezed her hand.

'Well, she has a lovely voice. We're actually here to look at the, uh . . .' She glanced past the wizened faces of clocks, of cut-glass perfume bottles, an RAAF officer's cap from one of the world wars, a rusty juice press. Past a junkyard chandelier of hanging flotsam, a tricycle, two red Bentwood chairs, a legless shop mannequin, cast iron pots and pans. Down the narrow aisle, she spied the farthest reaches of the quirky man's shop. 'Books. We're here to look at the books.'

'Go on then, they're right down the back. You just holler for Clancy if you need anything.' The funny man sauntered away, humming with his Nina.

The books were like wallpaper and ceiling paint and carpet in the little room at the back of the shop, stacked vertically and horizontally, on shelves, in crates, in piles on the floor. There was no obvious order, the spines revealing no particular criteria for earning their place, with everything from *Eat, Pray, Love* and *The Girl with the Dragon Tattoo* and lines and lines of Jeffrey Archer titles to Rudyard Kipling and copious volumes of *Encyclopedia Britannica*.

Hamish whistled through his teeth. 'At least it's quiet back here, but I hope you weren't actually looking for a particular book.' He hung an arm around her shoulders and then brushed her hair behind her ear, tracing the contour of her cheek and jawline before leaning in to kiss her: a long, wanton kiss.

Over his shoulder, Allira spotted a black box with its glaring red light and imagined Clancy watching them on a monitor somewhere. 'There's a camera, Hamish!'

'We could give him something to really look at,' Hamish said, his arm dropping to Allira's waist, but she wasn't listening. The shelf below the camera was labelled with black marker on masking tape in spidery block capitals: *TASMANIAN HISTORICAL*.

'What year did you say Nora would've been in her teens, Hame?'

'Early fifties.'

Allira pulled a red book from the shelf and read the title aloud: '*Walch's Tasmanian Almanac*'. The cloth cover was ornately embossed with delicate filigree in each corner framing a coat of arms above the title script. She gingerly flicked past pages of ads printed on red paper, to the index. 'No way! This book is like a doco on 1953 in Tasmania.'

He peered down at the book, resting his chin on her shoulder, arms still wrapped around her waist.

'Look – all different clubs and societies, laws, licensing information, train fares, and . . .' she paused, flicking towards the back, 'there's a section on all the different municipalities, too. Look, it lists the names of police, coroners, ministers of religion, MPs, state schools . . .'

'Might be a clue in there about your Nora. Let's get outta here though, look at it over lunch.'

Allira handed the twenty-five-dollar asking price to Clancy, who was now standing behind the counter, dwarfed by an enormous moose head mounted on the wall above him. Its shaggy brown neck and head alone must have been as tall as him.

'Goodbye!' she called over her shoulder as she walked away, the moose's sad eyes following her out the door. Clancy fluttered a hand in her direction, already back with Nina, eyes closed, swaying. The lyrics were about a willow tree weeping, its branches stretching out in sympathy. Wind and night and starry light. Sighs and shadows and aching. The words snagged, coiling around Allira's heart like the scribbling vine-limbs of the shaggy tree. A stride from the door she was suddenly breathless, her hand hovering at the handle. Her head spun and her eyes were scratchy. It was like the willow in the song had reached out to push on her pain, to say, *There, that's where it hurts, isn't it?*

Hamish swept the door open and Allira stepped through on autopilot. The lyrics replayed in her ears as they continued. Nina. Nora. Shame. The heat. They stopped at a set of traffic lights, waiting for the green man and Hamish lifted her chin, worried eyes searching hers.

'You okay, babe?'

'That song.'

'I know.' He laced her fingers between his before the green man flashed and they were walking again. 'It's two years this week.'

Warmth filled Allira's belly. *He remembered.* Her throat was sore. She couldn't speak.

'We have to be gentle with ourselves, right?'

She nodded again. They reached the car, climbed in. Hamish turned over the engine and then turned it off again, gathering Allira's hands from her lap.

'It wasn't your fault.'

Chapter 9

Summer 1953

'You ride my bike and I'll take Daphne.'

It was Saturday morning. Two whole days since Michał's truck broke down. Evelyn's hopes of long conversations with this mysterious person about his connections to far-flung places had not eventuated. There was school, and then Mother filled every spare moment with chores and women's nonsense, like cross-stitch and making beef stock. And Daddy was clearly relishing the male company, holed up with Michał in his workshop; all Evelyn could hear was the sound of hammering, a hand plane scudding against timber and the occasional murmur of male voices.

Daddy had been working since dawn on a Huon pine dining table commissioned by the Devonport mayor, and since Mother had a croquet association meeting in Deloraine, he suggested Evelyn show Michał some of the local sights. Mother huffed that Evelyn would do 'no such thing', but it seemed upon picturing her gangly, wild-haired daughter sitting beside the genteel croquet ladies and then mingling at the luncheon afterwards, she relented on the proviso that they take a chaperone. 'That Roberts boy, Tommy,' she said. And that was that.

Michał pedalled on the road while Evelyn trotted atop Daphne on the grassy verge beside him. The palomino snorted and pranced, as excited by the freedom as her rider, even if they did have to enlist a tag-along for the sake of propriety. The Roberts' place was situated at the point where farmland connected to bush in deeper and darkening density on its way to the jumbling crevices of the Tiers. It was the route to Evelyn's favourite place, the place she wanted to show Michał.

Evelyn slid down from Daphne, straightening the tweed cap she'd borrowed from Daddy. Her hair hung in a loose plait down her back over a white, short-sleeved shirt scattered with tiny yellow buttercups that she wore tucked into biscuit-coloured riding trousers. She smiled at Michał before walking the path to Tommy's front door.

'Is Tommy there?' she asked the tired woman who answered the door with a screaming baby on one hip.

'He's helpin' his Pa cut firewood t'day,' she said, then hollered his name over her shoulder. Tommy was at her side within five seconds, his eyes darting between his ma and Evelyn. Mrs Roberts walked away, warning that he must pull his weight.

'We're going up bush and Mother said I have to have a chaperone,' Evelyn explained.

'Sorry,' Tommy said, eyes on his big toe poking out of a holey sock. 'They won't let me today. I'll say I was with ye if they ask though, if that helps.'

'Thanks, Tommy.'

The younger boy grinned and shut the door as she jogged away from the falling-down, weatherboard farmhouse.

'Where's the boy?' Michał asked as she leapt up onto Daphne's back, clicked her tongue and gave the mare a gentle nudge in the ribs with the heel of her riding boots.

'Busy,' Evelyn said.

'But your mother said—'

'She won't know any different.'

Daphne set off at a canter, leaving Michał to beat at the blue Malvern Star's pedals with greater gusto. His heavy-duty work pants weren't really sunny-day bike-riding apparel, Evelyn noticed, but she supposed when he agreed to Jimmy's request to deliver the timber, he couldn't have guessed that he'd be balanced on some girl's bicycle, riding in lush countryside hemmed with hawthorn hedges where red robins flitted amongst the branches. As they headed along the straight piece of road that would soon propel them into the shadowy foothills of the Great Western Tiers, Michał unbuttoned his shirt down to his undervest and tucked it into his waistband at the small of his back. He returned his thick hands to the handlebars and pedalled again to keep up with the pony's agile gait.

They continued for another twenty minutes on a little-used road that steadily ascended, and the tall trunks of bluegums to their left and right were a crowd of pale onlookers. The road became a narrow track and then a dead end, or so it appeared. But Evelyn steered Daphne to the left and, ducking beneath the branches of an ancient blackwood tree, continued along a path overgrown with bracken and vines.

'We're nearly there. You can leave your bike here,' Evelyn said, and Michał gladly propped the bike against the dappled grey-white trunk of a gum and followed Daphne's tail, flicking sporadically at flies.

The sun was high and bright when they emerged from the trees into Evelyn's secret place. The clearing was carpeted with soft, mossy grass except for a pile of crumbled bricks, a stack of charred beams and the edge of a slab all but reclaimed by the earth. Someone had lived here once. The clearing nestled in the bush wasn't large, but it pointed to largeness elsewhere. Downwards to the farmland of Western Creek and Caveside, the paddocks and crops laid out like colourful blankets. Upwards to Mother Cummings peak, her lofty cliffs like a signpost to the skies.

Evelyn watched Michał's reaction as she jumped lightly from Daphne. His neck craned as he turned a full circle, breathing the eucalypt, moss and mountain air deeply. His eyes were closed, thick paintbrush lashes resting on the chiselled landscape of his face. Dark hair shaved at the temples revealed the softness of his ears and a neck thickened by hard work. Bristled cheeks creased, boomerang-shaped around his mouth. Finally he opened his eyes, turning his startling blues towards her. They were shining with more than light, like the sheen on a leaf after rain.

'Piękna, as Mama would say.' His voice was soft. 'It means beautiful.'

'Pee-ay-kna,' Evelyn tried.

He looked at his hands. A blue wren chattered nearby, darting and shimmying its luminescent feathers at several females. A shadow slid across the clearing, a lone cloud rowing towards the highlands. There was a dull *thud-thud* against the earth, the sound of a wallaby retreating.

'Well, let's have some lunch.' Evelyn scurried to fill the yawning silence with egg sandwiches and slabs of butter cake. She unbuckled Daphne's saddle and saddlebags, eased the bridle over her head and slapped her rump. The palomino snorted and pranced to the far end of the clearing to chomp on fresh grass while Evelyn spread out the saddle rug and arranged lunch, pouring black tea from a thermos into tin camping mugs. They ate and stretched lazily on the grass, Evelyn giving a long stream of information about all the families that crammed the pews of the Caveside church across the road each Sunday. Michał listened intently, asking questions in all the right places, prompting her to share more and more. When she started to describe how she helped Daddy with the undertaking business, he asked no more questions. His skin paled and his eyes were far away.

'Are you okay?' Evelyn asked.

'Just makes me think of the war.'

'Please tell me. If it's not too hard to talk about . . .'

Michał squinted at her through his thick lashes. 'It was April twenty-fifth, 1945, what you celebrate as ANZAC day,' he began. 'That was the day that my suburb in Berlin was *liberated* by the Russians. They pounded on the door of our beautiful home in Dahlem that afternoon and told my poor Mama that the residence was required as a command post and first-aid station. She was a widow who'd just lost her son, and now they wanted her house. She bundled us into her bedroom, Sabine and me, telling us not to come out as we listened to soldiers' boots stomping on our Persian rugs as they brought in stretchers of wounded men, laying them out on our beds, on our sofas, even on our kitchen table.'

Evelyn tried to imagine living at the very centre of the war in the final days before Germany's overthrow. The constant boom and rattle of firearms, shells, and grenades. Knowing the next sound to rattle the windows could be your death knell. Armoured vehicles rolling through empty streets. Fearing for the safety of loved ones.

The war barely touched Tasmania's landscape. The Great Western Tiers were in the same place every morning she looked out her window, as was the smattering of farmhouses below. No, the change, even to a little girl, had been marked in the absences. Brothers, fathers and uncles gone, or returning somehow depleted. No sugar for baking, and no musk sticks or sherbet. Worst of all, no Daddy. A hazy memory of him in uniform, kissing her cheeks and forehead, then a gaping void until his return when she was seven.

'I didn't realise you had a brother. What was he like?' she asked.

'There was a nine-year age gap between Dominik and me. He was strong, ambitious, a leader. Mama said he was like Papa. I have no memories of my father, but Dominik . . .' Michał's voice floated away.

Evelyn brushed crumbs from her lap and played with the tail of her plait, waiting for him to continue.

'I think he must have despised us because of the connection through Mama to Poland. He wasn't a full-blooded German. He took the first opportunity to join the army, but Mama said nothing of it. Every time Dom spoke of the war or his training or uniform needs, she changed the topic or left the room.' Michał's voice stopped and started, as if he was making the discovery for the first time. His mama didn't like her own son. 'He had a temper that turned him into a monster, but she did love him. He was her son . . .' Michał shook his head. 'Dom died in 1944 while fighting with the German army against the Russians in Poland. How do you grieve your own blood when he loathed that very lineage? It was a sorry business.'

Michał's hands balled into fists beside him. Evelyn wanted to reach out and touch them, to dispel the tension. Instead, she waited. Allowed the silence.

'I wanted my bear,' Michał began again. 'I was eleven, but I still slept with this scruffy brown bear, and it was in my bedroom. Sabine was asleep and Mama was in the kitchen, so I tiptoed down the hall to my room, slipping through the door without anyone noticing. There, lying on my bed, was a soldier.'

Michał's right forearm was flung across his brow, shielding his eyes from the glare of the sun as he spoke. His gaze was fixed on some undetermined spot in the sky, like a ballet dancer maintaining a focus point as he flung his body in dizzying fouetté turns.

'His leg was blown off at the knee and I could see that the blood had already soaked deep into my mattress. My sheets were drenched with it and one end, trailing over the edge of the bed, was dripping onto the floorboards. He had a bandage around his waist and his breaths were gurgly. Shallow. I stood there, pressed against the wall, frozen to the spot. I didn't know what to do. It seemed wrong that he was lying there alone.

'After a while, I crept up beside him and held his hand. He stirred a bit. There was a flicker of something across his face, already grey with death. He knew he wasn't alone. Mama said I must've sat there for an hour until one of the soldiers came to check on him. The man was dead by then, and I was asleep with my head on his arm, his blood on my sleeves.'

Michał stopped to gulp air into his lungs. He wrenched a fistful of grass from beside him and threw it at the sky. 'The world is cruel, Nora.'

The sound of her special name on his tongue was like a kiss, and she blushed but didn't correct him. He must have heard Daddy using it.

'We shared Mama's bed that night, clinging to one another, and then left the next day. One of the Russians said it would be safer. He escorted us to a suburb on the outskirts of Berlin and we stayed in the cellar of a ruined house. I lost track of the days. It was weeks, maybe a month.'

Michał dropped his arms beside him, let his head and spine fall into the earth, giving his weight to the dirt. Evelyn sensed his exhaustion, sensed that he'd never spoken like this before, about the soldier that bled to death on his bed. The blood that haunted him. Not even to recall it to his sister or mama. She watched how the lightness of relinquishing that shard from the flesh of his past brought relief. His breath lengthened.

Evelyn reached for Michał's hand and curved her fingers between his, warm and soft against his leathered palms. He was suddenly present, she saw. Her stomach leapt, her nerves snapped, but she dared not move. The world receded around them, the visceral sensation of spinning, of their context smeared like an abstract painting while their own bodies sharpened.

Chapter 10

Summer 2019

Allira shuddered. The dream was rolled out, brightly coloured and steeply contoured. Every minute detail bright and clear. No escape. No crawling back into the warm womb of sleep. Like wet hair after a shower in winter, she was going to have to dry this out before a chill set in. To separate the strands of thought and allow understanding's warmth to penetrate. Stepping out onto the front deck, the fresh night air tightened around her. Allira tied her dressing gown firmly around her waist, pulling the collar up to her chin. It was a clear night. Stars competed impotently with the glare of streetlights and taillights. Even at 3.15 am, the city's embers glowed stubbornly.

This was where the dream began. In fact, didn't they all start here? Whoever directed her dreams tended to use this front yard as the set, she realised. She took a deep breath and pushed herself to walk through the dream's landscape, through every sequence, because she knew that, grisly as it might be, there would be no sleep until she performed this autopsy.

Allira hugged her stomach and closed her eyes.

She was holding a little girl's hand, guiding her off the deck and onto the lawn. It was warm. They were barefoot, the grass springy beneath their soles. Their loose cotton dresses billowed in a warm breeze that lifted their hair and made the trees whisper. *Were they whispering her name?* Yes – a sweet, sing-song sound repeating her name again and again, not calling it so much as taking joy in the articulation of each syllable and watching the effect of the letters sprinkling the air like petals from a cherry tree. She was happy. The little hand was warm in hers as she walked on, down the incline of the front yard, following the curve of the garden edging, sunshine on cheeks and eyelashes. They came to a tree shaped like a goblet, with leaves as big as her hands. As she looked closer and reached out, she realised it was a fig tree.

'Darling, look,' she said, plucking a plump fig, pregnant with flesh and juice, and breaking it open so that the magenta insides were bared.

It was at this point that she looked at the face of the little girl for the first time. She must have surely gasped in her sleep because she knew instantly to whom she belonged. Hamish's intensely blue eyes were framed with her own chocolate brown hair, only silkier and flicking at the ends, spiralling the way a toddler's hair does before their first haircut. But none of this made Allira stop in her tracks so much as the cluster of beauty spots on the child's right cheekbone. Three small dots, barely more than freckles. *They will darken as she grows older*, Allira thought as she stroked the girl's cheek.

Chubby fingers reached for the fruit. 'Some?' she asked, and took it, biting the sweet flesh, the juice running down her chin. She munched on the fig, licking her fingers and enjoying the sticky sweetness, wiping her hands down her front. The red-pink juice painted the white cotton of her dress, flowering momentarily, before dissolving, disappearing completely. The white glowed.

Allira was relishing the moment, watching the beautiful child, when she sensed a presence behind her. She turned around slowly and froze, sucking in a sharp breath and pressing her elbows into her sides. Reared up behind her, with a head the size of a basketball, was a python, its enormous body coiled less than a metre from them.

Allira knew that the next part of the dream needed her careful dissection, for her to weigh up the thought process of her subconscious self. A possum screeched somewhere but otherwise the night was unaccountably still, the waft of wood-smoke from the neighbour's chimney and the wink of city lights the only movement.

Indecision was never a feature of Allira's dreams. The little girl had just about finished her fig and would look up at any moment to see this monster waiting for the right moment to embrace its prey. There was nothing else to do. The serpentine creature was bigger and stronger; there was no overpowering it. There was only this: ensuring it chose the right meal. Allira leaned down and whispered in the child's ear, 'First one to the house wins a lollipop!' and watched as she giggled and didn't hesitate to race away on short legs, hair streaming, white dress billowing. And just as she'd hoped and perhaps knew, because dreams endow a particular knowing, Hamish was at the door to gather the child into his arms and usher her behind his stocky frame so she couldn't see the horror coiling around her mother. He loitered at the door, leaning out, his body tense. His mouth opened to form a battery of words. Soundless, transparent words. She couldn't make them out, hard as she tried to read the shape of his lips as they opened and closed around the sentence, over and over. And he was pointing, aggressively pointing to – what? To the ground? To her feet? It wasn't to the snake. Its breath was warm on her head, and she knew it was bearing down on her.

That's when Allira had woken with a jolt, the sensation of cold scales against the skin of her neck chilling her instantly. Hamish was asleep on his back, open-mouthed, a forearm marooned on his forehead. He hadn't stirred when she slipped out of bed and padded from their bedroom to the living room.

Allira stood on the deck as if rooted there in the crisp early morning air. The day was yawning, slowly waking. Cars drove by, workers commuting. Windows lit up. Newspapers thwacked on doorsteps and a slow-moving vehicle hummed and squealed with the stop-start dance of accelerator and brake. She rubbed at the tightness clamped across her chest.

It had been two years now. Two years on Friday since they lost him. Moments from that day played on repeat, memories flickering like flames that licked and spat but never warmed her. Hamish sobbing. Fluorescent lights on white walls. Blood marbling with water in a toilet bowl. A tiny hand splayed on her fingertip. A clipboard hanging at the foot of the bed with her name in the space beside 'Mother'.

They called it miscarriage. He was too early at eighteen weeks to be called stillborn. 'Babies born not breathing after twenty weeks are stillborn,' a nurse had gently corrected her as she added another white cotton blanket to Allira's bed. She had nodded, too numb to ask who it was that decided that a young woman who gave birth to her dead son could not have the liberty of calling the experience what she liked.

'It's just a paperwork thing in the end,' the nurse continued, as if sensing the questions. 'Unfortunately you won't qualify for all the benefits.'

'Benefits?'

'I'm sorry, that's the wrong word. I mean assistance, the still-born payment and that sort of thing,' the nurse said, rubbing her arm.

They gave him a cradle. One of those perspex-walled things on wheels, with a tub underneath for the nappies and onesies. The nurses discreetly positioned an ice pack beneath his limp little body and changed it every few hours. They encouraged Allira and Hamish to hold him, take photos, 'build memories'. Hamish held him first. Wrapped him up in a flannelette blanket and laid him in the crook of his elbow. Instantly, he was a giant. A barefoot, blue-jeans, tousled-hair giant against the little sparrow he'd scooped into his arm. Hamish's body automatically rocked and swayed with his weightless son, and he spoke to him tenderly in choked whispers.

'Hey there, little man. I'm sorry we didn't get to meet properly. I'm Hamish . . . your daddy.' He stood at the window where the clouds boiled grey and white and a flock of starlings swarmed like flies before lighting on powerlines. 'We would've looked after you real well, you know?'

From her position on the hospital bed, chained with an intravenous needle and a plastic tube, Allira crumpled, pushing palms against eyes, heaving with the burden of that scene. Of Hamish and her little son.

Now Allira shook her head to disrupt the familiar trajectory of thoughts. *Has it really been two years?* She closed her eyes and rested her chin on her chest, tears slipping down her cheeks. *Poor Hamish.* Her stomach churned as she thought about his yearning to be a dad, of how he had patiently waited for her to be ready to have a child.

The little girl's face from the dream. So real. The softness of her cheek beneath Allira's fingertips. Her generous mouth, wide with delight and discovery. The flash of gappy teeth. Brazen blue-fire eyes, thickly rimmed with dark lashes and luminescent with . . . Allira's stream of thought halted abruptly. She rewound the scenes. Warm little hand enveloped in hers. The child running beside her. Dress billowing. Face upturned. Light. Carefree. Trusting.

The word slipped into her mind like a gift: the child was utterly *trusting* of her. And Allira was utterly devoted. There were no hesitations, only fluid love carrying them.

It's just a dream! Allira moved her arms and legs, realising for the first time that they were numb, pins and needles flushing her left foot. *Just a crazy dream.* Yet for the first time, there was the gentlest warming of hope at the site of an injury that had been too tender to touch. She saw a fierce, renewed version of herself. Sure, it was a dream, but it was exquisitely real. *Could I be that Allira again?*

A new day poured into the sky's bowl, pale blue dispersing the black, blowing it like ash to the ether. Allira exhaled. She just had to figure out how to cut that monstrous dream snake into little pieces.

Chapter 11

Summer 1953

Mother returned from the croquet association luncheon in a temper that Saturday afternoon. Evelyn had only just unsaddled Daphne and was brushing down her sweaty coat when she heard the crunch of tyres on gravel. Michał sat with his back against a fence post, smoking a cigarette and listening to Evelyn mollycoddling the horse, Marmaduke curled in his lap.

The car door slammed with the force of fury and Evelyn stopped mid-stroke, her hand frozen on Daphne's twitching flanks. She threw the horse brush to Michał, who only just caught it in his free hand, and jogged towards the house. She could hear rummaging in the kitchen, pots clattering and paper bags rustling as she approached with a cheery, 'Hello, Mother. I was just giving Daphne a brush-down. How was your luncheon?'

Mother didn't seem to hear. She was muttering under her breath, a long string of incomplete sentences as she crouched in front of a cupboard. 'Claudia this, Claudia that . . . cherry jam best in show, my arse . . . little tart . . . how dare they . . . bunch of uppity inbreeds . . .'

Evelyn bit back a giggle and reached around her mother to fetch the jam pot from beside the sink. There were bags of cherries in brown paper bags on the bench and she could guess what Mother was trying to find. 'Is this what you're looking for, Mother?' she asked.

Mother leapt to her feet, sending her handbag sprawling, lipstick and coins rolling in different directions on the vinyl floor. A wide-blade knife was in her hand, and her eyes were bloodshot, make-up gone to smears. She'd enjoyed one too many sherries, Evelyn thought as Mother smoothed her dress against her wasp-thin waist. The navy-blue button-front dress with a fitted bodice accentuated her petite, angular lines. She swayed on matching court shoes, ankles so thin they could snap, and straightened a bobby-pin in her once immaculately coiffed hair.

'What are you doing sneaking up on me like that?' she barked.

Evelyn quickly apologised and dropped to her knees, scooping the displaced items into Mother's black patent leather handbag before fastening the gold clasp and sitting it on the bench. She asked once more how the luncheon went.

'Oh fine, fine. I was voted treasurer again. The wonderful Claudia Vanguard stepped up as secretary. She's that snooty sod Jerry or Terry . . . you know, from your school . . . his mother.' Mother waved the knife around like she was conducting an orchestra.

'And the cherries?'

'They're from that bovine Jan Hood, who seemed to think I don't know how to make a good cherry jam. Sodding cow!'

Evelyn snorted. Coughed. Laughed. She couldn't keep it in. She clapped her hand across her mouth, but her eyes creased with mirth, a dead giveaway. Mother's own titter erupted into uproarious laughter, and she slapped an arm around her daughter, tears rolling down her face until they were both gasping.

'Oh, my head hurts. I'm going to pour a bath. Be a darling and do us a batch of jam to knock the coy look off Mrs Hood's face, will you?' She wandered down the hall muttering, 'Late for cherries, the poor trees were probably too scared to fruit.'

At that moment, Evelyn would have done anything to please her mother. She had the feeling that this carefree doppelganger sashaying to her bedroom to find her silk pyjamas and robe was the woman who had first met Stanley Grayson at a dance hall in Hobart on New Year's Eve. It made Evelyn wonder if they had more in common than height and hair colour. But she knew that once she'd bathed and slept off the grog, Mother would be the sharp, severe-tempered commander of the house once more.

Still, Evelyn was buoyed by Mother's playful mood. She lifted an apron from the hook behind the door and flicked on the wireless, tuning it to a station playing light-hearted swing and pop. She hummed as she lifted the cast-iron cherry pitter from the cupboard beneath the sink and screwed the clamp tightly around the bench. It was such a laborious task. Even with the top-of-the-range equipment Mother had bought last summer, it took a lifetime to remove the pits, placing cherries one by one beneath the contraption's spear, then winding the handle so that the ruby flesh relented and gave up its innards. The pit dropped one way and the hollowed cherry and juice were caught in a bowl.

Evelyn found a rhythm, plucking the stems, positioning the fruit, winding and repeating. Pluck, position, wind, repeat. Her arms swung and her hips swayed. Her ears were full of music and her fingers stained an ever-deeper shade of red. The repetition was mindless, a motion her muscles learned quickly, unbridling her thoughts to gallop back to the mountain clearing where Michał's skin was warm against hers. His pulse in her hand. The comforting rumble of his voice softening to a strained thread of sound. Her shuffling closer, leaning in to hear brutal recollections of things no child should see. And how he lay there afterwards, utterly spent, as if he'd hauled lumber uphill in driving rain.

'There's a better way, you know.'

Evelyn flinched. It was Michał's voice, smooth and confident. Her face flushed and her pulse quickened but she resisted the urge to turn around. There was something about his cocksure manner that grated, like he'd walked in and leaned over her shoulder to pry as she wrote deeply personal ponderings in her diary. Did he always have this effect on girls? Was it so commonplace to him? She imagined girls like Shirley with their pointy bras and puckered lips fluttering around him, dazzling him. They would do it to scorn her, if not for genuine interest. Evelyn clenched her jaw and rammed another cherry under the spear, yanking the handle with more force than ever. Michał lingered as if waiting for permission to enter, his shoulders nearly filling the doorway.

'What, you're an expert on cherry jam now?' Evelyn fired back. Her neck was hot. She wished she hadn't pulled on the pale blue cardi when they'd returned from the ride.

Michał rubbed his forehead, trying to decide whether to step into the kitchen or not. 'An expert? I, ah, I helped Mama is all. My job was always pitting the cherries. Wasn't allowed outside to play till it was done, so I got real quick at it.'

Evelyn turned around with her hands on her hips. 'Well, I already have a cherry pitter, thank you,' she replied, pointing to the clunky device clamped to the bench.

Michał let out a long, low whistle. 'Now there's a sturdy contraption. Looks like it belongs in your pa's workshop!'

Evelyn didn't respond. Her hands were still on her hips. *Is this a game to you?* she asked wordlessly as Michał dug his hands deeper into his pockets.

'Show us how it works then,' he said.

Evelyn rigidly chose a cherry, placed it beneath the spear, wound the crank and watched the hulled fruit roll down the metal tongue into the half-full bowl beside. She turned to Michał, who ducked his head to hide a lopsided grin. 'What?' she demanded.

'It's just that . . .' His voice rose at her steely gaze. 'Gosh, Nora, it'll take you an age to have enough fruit for your jam if you use that hulking thing.'

'Oh, and I guess your way will have it all finished in a blink?' Evelyn snapped.

'Maybe?' he said, showing his palms and shrugging.

She scrutinised his face. Heavy brows overhung those ludicrous eyes, a shadow running from high cheekbones to the sides of his wide mouth and angular jaw. A deep cleft divided his bottom lip and chin, and his hairline had a slight widow's peak, squared at the sides. She couldn't read her own feelings;

they were so foreign. The swooning girls at school leered at her again, and she swatted them from her thoughts. She was not some air-headed housewife-in-the-making. She would not be swept off her feet and away from her wiles. She stomped her foot and Michał flinched. 'I'll race you.' She shoved a paper bag of cherries at his chest and plonked another in front of herself.

He stepped up to the bench beside her, picking up the knife that Mother had waved in the air earlier, and reached for a heavy wooden board. 'I'm ready,' he said.

'First to finish the bag wins,' Evelyn replied stoically. 'Go!'

Michał poured half the cherries onto the board, quickly pulling away any stems. He lifted the knife and laid it flat against the firm red orbs, pounding the heel of his hand against the broad blade. The cherries underneath were instantly macerated. He continued around the board's surface before deftly picking out the pits and scraping the limp cherry flesh into a bowl. Juice dripped from his fingers.

Evelyn furiously cranked the handle of the cherry pitter, threading fruit beneath its sharp spear as fast as it spat the hollowed cherries into the waiting bowl. But it could only take one at a time, and she quickly fell behind. As Michał tipped the last of his cherries onto the board, Evelyn guessed that she still had three-quarters of her bag to go. She turned the handle faster, her muscles complaining. The music from the wireless popped with saxophone and keys, a merry instrumental that rubbed against Evelyn's tenacious grip on her pride.

'Done,' Michał shouted, throwing the knife onto the empty board with a clatter.

Evelyn fronted him suspiciously, checking the brown paper bag, poking her finger through the bowl of pitted cherries and then wiping her hands on her apron. Michał watched her with a smirk on his cherry-splattered face. The red juice was sprayed across his shirt, up his arms, freckling his otherwise unblemished cheeks and forehead. Without thinking, Evelyn brushed a finger across his lightly bristled chin and then put it in her mouth, sucking the juice between her lips. He dipped his head, stepped towards her and plunged a hand into the thickness of her hair, pulling cherry-stained lips towards his own. She didn't resist, all the ripples of worry smoothed in a single movement.

A door slammed down the hall.

Michał and Evelyn jerked back from each other as if burnt. Mother had probably finished her bath and was walking to her room to get dressed.

Evelyn cleared her throat. 'You're the fastest, but I'm the cleanest. Mother would have kittens if she saw this.'

Michał looked around at red-splattered walls, cupboards, floor, all fanning out from where he stood. He turned a slow circle until he was back facing Evelyn. 'Looks like a crime scene.'

Evelyn's solemn face cracked open and she laughed heartily, throwing a dish cloth at the unnerving man in her kitchen. 'Clean it up, then do the rest of the cherries. Actually, the other way 'round.'

'I'll help with your jam if you let me cook you something.' Michał was already pouring cherries onto the cutting board.

'You can cook?' Evelyn could feel her face was flushed pink in the warm afternoon light.

'Mama used to make Kołaczki with our cherry jam.' He groaned theatrically, clutching his stomach with his eyes closed. 'It's the most delicious thing you'll eat, Nora, a Polish delicacy, like a biscuit or pastry, with jam filling and sprinkled with icing sugar. I will make them for you.'

The kitchen was soon filled with smells of fruit and sugar, lemon zest and hot oven trays. They worked side by side for several hours, until finally Michał handed Evelyn one of his pastries. She turned the pastry in her hand, noticing the lightness of texture, the browned edges, the jam running out, caramelised to a blood red slurry. She allowed her teeth to cut through its middle, her tongue to weigh the buttery texture before it dissolved in her mouth. Evelyn savoured the tang of cream cheese against the sweet, oozing cherry jam and the sprinkling of icing sugar. The balance was perfect. Not a cloying sweetness like the tarts and pavlovas baked by most of the women this side of Bass Strait.

Mother slinked from the bedroom to the kitchen to reheat a side of corned beef for supper. A tray of Kołaczki sat enticingly on the bench. She eyed the kitchen scene disapprovingly, turning from Michał's cherry-splattered shirt to the foreign pastries and the icing sugar around her daughter's mouth. But there were eight jars of jam in a neat row beside the hob. She smiled tersely before taking a Kołaczki and walking into the dining room to set the table.

Evelyn grabbed Michał's hand and they tiptoed to the doorway, peering at Mother who was standing at the table with her eyes closed, slowly devouring the pastry. Was that a smug smile on her face? Did she just chuckle as she licked her fingers?

Yes Mother, Evelyn conspired. *We'll not only give you prize-winning cherry jam, we'll give you a delicacy that'll make Mrs Hood's scones good for pig slop.*

Chapter 12

Summer 2019

Allira's phone jangled beside her bed and she fumbled in the dark to stop the clamour. Hamish rolled away from her, groaning. He'd just come off a twelve-hour shift and must've only been home a few hours. She held the phone, about to jab the reject call button when she noticed two things. It was 1.16 am, and the caller ID said Nora's Nursing Home. Allira swung her legs over the side of the bed and cleared sleep from her throat. 'Hello?'

'Thank you for picking up!' Sally sounded genuinely relieved.

'It's pretty early—'

'Nora's gone missing.'

'What? How—'

'We've been searching for her since midnight. The police are helping too. Maybe the SES soon. But I'm worried that she's got no one to calm her down when we do find her.'

'And you want me to—'

'Yes. You're good with her, Allira. I know that her dementia means she can't properly know you, but there's a softness with you that we don't see when she's with others.'

Allira didn't need further encouragement. Her stomach had already plummeted to somewhere near her heels. She threw on a pair of jeans and joggers before scrawling a note for Hamish.

When Allira arrived at Mercy Place Aged Care, Sally was bent over a map of the city divided into sections with a thick, pink highlighter. She handed a middle-aged couple a sheet of paper and told them to call in immediately if they found her. Her tone was upbeat – in a forced, mildly desperate way. Allira felt sorry for her. This must be a worst-nightmare kind of situation, even if you were as fiercely capable as she.

Sally spotted Allira and straightened, coming out from behind the reception desk, bringing with her a slim man half her volume who looked as though he was from somewhere north of the equator. India or Pakistan perhaps.

'Allira, this is our executive director, Steve Shenoy.' She swallowed hard and nodded curtly. The man looked at Allira through narrowed eyes.

'Good to meet you,' she said, shaking his outstretched hand awkwardly over the reception desk.

'Thank you for coming in to help, Allira, it is most kind.' English was clearly his first language. His neatly trimmed beard was greying, while the hair on his head remained glossy black, long salt-and-pepper sideburns merging with his beard. Well-manicured hands gesticulated elegantly as he continued. 'Sally tells me you have a special connection with Nora and that you would be happy to spend some time calming her when she is found.'

'Of course. I'll do whatever I can to help.'

'Thank you. Sally, I'll leave it with you to explain the rest. I have some phone calls to make.'

As Steve walked into an office and shut the door behind him, Sally looked up from the map, exhaling through her teeth.

'Are you okay? What happened?' Allira asked.

'She was sundowning at dinner time and it just kept getting worse. Nothing seemed to help. I flagged it to the nurses, but they were busy with all the bedtime meds and didn't get to her in time with something to help her sleep.'

'What's sundowning?'

'People with dementia often get restless and anxious in the late afternoon, early evening. It's like cactus hour with kids. But we can usually distract them with some lively old-time tunes or a cup of warm milk. For Nora, it's that blasted doll that calms her right down.' Sally leaned on the reception desk and sighed. 'My new leisure and lifestyle girl thought she'd go the extra mile and take Nora's doll home to sew up a loose seam when she thought Nora was asleep. Her plan was to stitch it up and bring it back first thing. But Nora woke up and went hysterical when we told her, then cried herself to sleep. At least we thought she did. One of the nurses noticed her gone when doing her half-hourly checks. She's on our AWOL register, which means someone has to check her every half-hour. The laundry door was wide open.'

Allira nodded, deep in thought. 'Do you remember what she said when she realised the doll wasn't here?'

'I do, actually. She said, "I saw you digging the hole." She was looking at me like I was a gravedigger. There was something else too . . .' Sally shut her eyes. 'It was something about

Mr Darcy and some other character from a book. Sorry, that's as much as I can recall.'

'Where's the doll now?' Allira asked.

'Right here.' Sally opened a shoebox on the desk. The doll lay staring at the ceiling. Neat stitches raced up its naked mid-section, plastic hands and feet curved in mock contentment.

An idea was forming in Allira's mind. 'I know where to look.'

Sally locked eyes with her. 'Go,' she said. 'Don't worry about any of this'—she waved an arm at the volunteer search register on the desk—'I'll put your name down, just go find her!'

Allira grabbed the doll and a throw rug from the sofa in the waiting area and jogged towards the glass automatic sliding doors, her heart thumping.

Allira had been sitting in Nora's room reading a book when the old woman woke from her sleep with a start.

'I picked the apples, I did,' she'd blurted. 'Buckets and buckets of them. You'd think Mother would be pleased . . .' Her voice trailed off.

Allira had marked her place with a bookmark and leaned forward in her chair. 'You had an orchard?'

'Oh yes, dear, we had a lovely big orchard alongside Daddy's workshop. Full of fruit trees.' Nora's voice dropped to a stage whisper. 'I named the apple trees, because they were my favourites, all in a row with their arms in the air, cheering me on.'

'What were their names?'

'Well, let's see. There was Mr Darcy – he was prolific. Mark Antony and Romeo had the smoothest trunks, best for leaning against to read, you know? Then there was Casanova, Heathcliff, Edmond Dantès, Sir Lancelot and Edward Fairfax Rochester.' She counted them off on her fingers. 'The last one, he remained unnamed.'

Allira recognised the characters from the classics she had studied in English literature classes. She couldn't help but smile, imagining a country girl naming the apple trees in her family's orchard after literary heroes – if what Nora had said was indeed true. Allira had looked long and hard at Nora then. The old woman's eyes were bright and clear, her body animated as she continued recalling events with such lucidity that Allira couldn't help but be carried along in the current. She couldn't imagine how an expiring mind could fabricate such exquisite detail.

'I imagined a whole other world in that orchard, one where I was free to come and go as I pleased, and the apple trees were my friends.' Nora's face had been slack with joy. 'That was until Heathcliff died. His leaves curled and fell, no buds came in the spring and Daddy dug him out. Replaced him.'

'With another apple tree?' Allira had asked, but Nora had pulled the blanket up to her shoulders, her eyes staring at a blank patch on the wall opposite. She hadn't spoken another word that afternoon.

Where would Nora have seen apple trees nearby? Allira pulled out of the nursing home's long drive, pocked with speed humps, and motored along slowly in her rattly VW Polo, peering at the circles of light under each streetlight. She passed a police car and then an SES vehicle going the opposite direction and imagined

Nora huddled out there in the dark somewhere. *Please let it be me that finds her.*

Allira strained to see some detail in the streetscape, but it was all shadows and silhouettes beyond the glaring wash of her headlights. She pulled over to think for a moment. Apple trees. It was there, a shimmering clue swimming just beyond the reach of her memory but no matter how hard she tried to clutch its slippery tail, it wriggled away. The famed orchards on the banks of the Tamar River were too far. There were probably apple trees hanging over the fences of neighbouring houses, but she felt certain Sally would have coordinated a door knock of those already. The school had a small orchard . . . but the gates were locked each afternoon when the teachers left.

Then she remembered: the church. It was the church where she'd walked down the aisle into the arms of her scruffy-haired husband-to-be, his eyes red from crying, the big softie. The tiny church crouched at the end of a driveway lined with poplars, sweeping towards the arched doorway with its wrought iron hinges. Everyone agreed it was Launceston's most photogenic church. And standing in a line, within easy view of the road, were four old apple trees. In a few months' time, the Reverend would throw nets across their branches and use the church's message board to invite the community to pick the fruit. One year the sign had controversially read, *Help yourself to the apples. We'll blame Eve.*

The church was a five-minute drive away, which meant it would be a brisk thirty-minute walk for most people, much less an 81-year-old with dementia. Surely she wouldn't have walked all that way, Allira thought as she pulled out into the road, picking up speed and navigating the quickest route. The roads were empty, and this part of the city was only lit sporadically with streetlights.

When Allira pulled up outside the church gates, there were no old-woman-shaped shadows slipping into the night. She yawned and checked her phone lying on the passenger seat. A message from Sally: *Call me as soon as you find her.* She turned off the car lights and sat for a moment, allowing her eyes to adjust to the black, her ears to become attuned to subtle night sounds. She wrapped the doll in the throw rug, a pale-yellow plaid, and tucked it into the crook of her arm before stepping outside. The pebble driveway to the church's door was lit by the moon. The row of apple trees was still there, just as she remembered, their crooked branches heavy with leaves and swelling buds of fruit.

The church's message board displayed a verse: *The Lord is my shepherd, I lack nothing. He makes me lie down in green pastures, he leads me beside quiet waters.* The words trickled through Allira's veins, strangely calming, and she picked her way to the trees. At first she noticed nothing but the wet spray of dew on her shoes, the whiff of fertiliser and the scratch of a possum scrambling up a gumtree. But as she walked closer to the apple trees, she heard the faintest mew of exertion and scraping. And there she was. Found. Hunched at the base of one of the trees, Nora clawed at the dirt with bare hands. Her throat rang out a lonely note of effort with each handful of dirt extricated from the roots, her dressing gown rolled up at the sleeves, arms coated in dirt, her bare knees leaving deep grooves in the ground. A hole the size of a butternut pumpkin had opened beneath her hands.

Allira hesitated. *Oh Nora, where is your family?* For her to be so completely alone after eighty-one years on this earth pressed on her painfully. A woman kneeling in dirt in the middle of the night, and nobody worried aside from those who earned a wage for it. Allira shook the thought from her head and focused on how to approach Nora without startling her. The old woman must be back in her youth, back when only Daddy called her Nora. Allira stepped forward.

'Hello, Evelyn,' she said warmly, as if finding her beneath an apple tree in the small hours of the morning was the most normal thing in the world. 'I heard you were looking for this.' She squatted down beside her, offering the doll wrapped in its yellow blanket.

'But I saw him . . . wrapped in that towel . . . I saw him do it . . .'

Nora's face tilted upwards. Moonlight filled every line and crevice, like they had been plastered over to leave an expressionless orb of white, blank as paper. And then, just as quickly, she dipped her chin and the shadows slunk back into their familiar hollows, her eyes shimmering green with confusion. Her hands reached out, quivering, as her face concertinaed into a caricature of herself and she wailed. One long, wretched cry as she took the doll into her arms and rocked him wearily. 'Why did they take him from me?' Nora demanded, her voice high. But she didn't wait for an answer, just continued rocking and sobbing. 'There, there. I thought I'd lost you.'

Allira sat down in the dirt beside Nora, shimmying closer to see if she was hurt. The dressing gown was tied tightly around her waist but gaped at the neck to reveal a thin nightie. Her bare legs were tucked beside her, feet in quilted satin slippers. A small scratch on her leg was bleeding, but she seemed otherwise okay. Thank goodness it was a mild evening.

'Who are you?' Nora asked.

Allira smiled sadly. 'I'm a friend. We thought we'd lost you, Evelyn. There are a lot of people looking for you, worried about you. I'm just going to send a message to let them know you've been found, and then we'll slowly make our way back. How does that sound?'

She pulled out her phone and quickly punched a one-word message through to Sally. *Found.* And then another. *Give us 20 mins.* She wanted to allow Nora some time to gently come to terms with what was going on around her, before the bright lights, questions and prodding back at the nursing home.

'But why are you here? You don't look like the others. I don't know you.'

Allira put her phone back in her pocket, ignoring its aggressive vibrations as responses from Sally hammered through. She couldn't help but think of her grandmother when she'd died, surrounded by loved ones. When her end had approached, the family agreed to a roster so there wouldn't be any chance of her dying without someone by her side. Allira remembered the two times she'd sat in her gran's room, reading as the older woman slept. The blip of a monitor, the laboured breathing, the jangle of trolleys wheeled down hospital corridors.

'I lost my baby too.'

The words fell like rope unknotted. Allira clapped a hand to her mouth, realising it was to stop the emotions from tumbling headlong out, rather than a mien of shock. She had never voluntarily uncovered this wound to anyone before. Her mother happily avoided the topic. Hamish had his own pain and, while he had been attentive and caring when they'd lost their baby, she knew it was too difficult for him to linger in the past. He needed to move forward. Rae had asked questions early on but received only stoic, one-word answers and thin 'everything's fine' smiles.

'Al, I care about you too much to shut up and pretend everything's rosy, okay?' Rae had said, confronting her about six months after. 'I know we're both wired differently and all that enneagram stuff, but I'm worried about you.'

Allira had had no words to meet the kindness of her friend's heart, and she had just nodded.

'Right. Well then, I'm going to make it my business to ask you at least once a month how the heck you're processing all this and you can say nothing, like you've just so beautifully demonstrated, you can tell me to shut up, or you can go ahead and tell me what's really going on in that pretty head of yours.'

Allira had thrown her arms around her friend then, knowing that one day she would be able to talk about it.

Nora dropped a heavy hand onto Allira's own and squeezed. She didn't offer sympathy or condolences, just settled into the silence and closeness. Her head nodded gently, watering eyes fixed on a branch's elbow. She knew the sanctity of this pain, most sacred of things. And she knew not to shatter it with mindless platitudes.

'I stabbed myself once.' Nora coughed and laughed dourly at the same time, the sound reverberating in her chest cavity. She was still squeezing Allira's hand. 'I was learning to whittle.

I picked up the knife and did just like he told me, shaving the wood away a tiny scrap at a time. I always picked things up quickly. Didn't take long and there was a pile of shavings on Daddy's workbench.'

'Who was teaching you?' Allira couldn't help herself.

Nora looked through her. 'The knife lodged in the lump of Huon pine I was holding . . . Have you smelled Huon before?'

Allira shook her head.

'It's sweet, musky . . .' She drifted. The memory of the perfume had carried her away, floating, weightless.

Allira squeezed Nora's hand, encouraging her to continue. 'Evelyn? How did you stab yourself?'

Nora looked blankly at Allira.

'You said the knife lodged in the lump of Huon pine you were whittling?'

'It did!' she said, suddenly lively. 'He told me never to put my hand in front of the knife, but it was wedged tight. It all happened so quickly. Such a sharp little blade. I thought it'd gone right through my palm. I pulled it out and hurled it to the ground.' Nora loosened her grip on Allira's hand and lifted her palm into the moonlight.

There it was. A tiny, triangular scar, embedded like a sliver of precious metal.

'Beautiful, isn't it?'

Allira looked again. The silvery scar was pearlescent, snagging the moon.

'It bled a lot,' Nora continued. 'He felt terrible. There he was, teaching me to whittle, and within moments his student had stabbed herself. He held a handkerchief to it for at least twenty minutes, until the bleeding stopped. Told me about Berlin and Sabine . . .'

Allira gripped Nora's hand again, trying desperately to anchor her. 'It is pretty, isn't it? Did he do anything else, this mysterious man?'

Nora ignored her. 'The pain means I always have it, right here in my hand. I don't ever want to forget it, you see, so I'm happy for the way the knife cut me.' Her fingers curled, nails pressed into her palm like it held something precious.

Allira's throat hurt. *How can she know?* There was no moving on, only acceptance and carrying. Becoming the woman who could wear the pain like a cherished piece of heirloom jewellery and not a backpack full of bricks. Holding it with poise, dignity. She wound an arm around the old woman's waist, rested head on shoulder. 'It's a part of your story, Evelyn. You're not you without it.'

Allira drank her own words in. *Where did that even come from?* The truth of it rendered her weightless with a deep sense of peace that she hadn't experienced in a very long time. She fingered the smattering of beauty spots on her cheekbone, absently running her finger along them as she always had. Finally, she spoke. 'We'd better get going.'

Nora was rocking the doll again, making soothing noises and stroking its cheek. She stopped and looked at Allira. 'Who are you?'

'I'm a friend, come to take you home for a big hot chocolate and a bath.'

'That sounds nice. I like chocolate. Turkish Delight is a personal favourite.'

Allira helped Nora to her feet, brushing dirt and leaves from her dressing gown and unrolling the sodden sleeves down to her wrists. She walked with an arm protectively around Nora's waist, braced to catch her if she stumbled on the uneven ground.

'What's your name?' the older woman asked.

'Allira.'

'You seem to be a very nice girl, Allira. I'm Nora. Now, if I give you some coins, can you run along and buy me some Turkish Delight?'

'I'll get you some Turkish Delight, Nora, don't you worry.'

In five minutes, they would be back at the nursing home with its security keypads, intercoms and visitor sign-in sheets. There would be police officers and a doctor to give official statements. Steve Shenoy would be hovering between calls from the Department of Social Services, and he might even have a word with Sally later about why the rogue volunteer took so long to bring Nora back. But once Nora was in safe hands, Allira would slip away. No doubt she would need to give a written statement, but that could wait. First, Turkish Delight from the all-hours supermarket and a hot chocolate from Maccas, Nora's orders. And perhaps tomorrow, when she visited to check up on her, Nora would talk some more.

Chapter 13

Summer 1953

A hush fell across the Grayson house on Sunday afternoons. Mother came from a long line of Sabbath-keepers, and despite her seemingly unquenchable appetite for productivity, between the Caveside church's last benediction and supper time, she disappeared into her cavernous bedroom with a stack of *Women's Weekly*s and a big pot of tea. One cup.

She allowed very little to disrupt this ritual, ordering her week so that the hours were hers and hers alone. She baked bread and biscuits so that lunch and afternoon tea were serve-yourself. The wash house was a flurry of activity every day excepting Sunday. If there was a funeral, she prepared flowers or luncheons or pleasantries ahead of time. The family knew that to interrupt her would invoke a wrath beyond their placating. Even visitors like a Polish-German worker from Strahan must capitulate to this custom.

Mother's strict adherence to her Sabbath afternoon created a little oasis of deliverance for the other family members. Stan often wandered down the road to share some ales with a neighbour, a rough, returned-soldier sort who Mother had never approved of. Evelyn usually saddled Daphne and they clip-clopped up the driveway to explore, finding new places to read or daydream the next instalment of her life.

Mother and Daddy had sat between Evelyn and Michał in the church pew that morning, and she found herself strangely relieved. She still felt tingly and odd where Michał's hand had curved against her own, their fingers locked together like a dovetail joint on one of Daddy's furniture commissions. She feared she would spend the whole service flushed a hideous shade of pink if he was pressed in the pew beside her. Mother might've thought she had a fever and put her on bed rest for the remainder of the day. Still, they'd stolen furtive glances at each other as Michał recognised some of the people Evelyn had described so evocatively the day before, during their picnic in the clearing. Frank Hardy the baker, seated in the back row, pointedly looked at his watch every five minutes and cleared his throat noisily the moment the sermon exceeded thirty minutes. Mr Herbert the beekeeper, with his bulbous red nose, heartily belted out notes to every hymn despite being utterly tone deaf. Mrs Byard sat up front in her beaver hat, the furry chestnut tail trailing down her back. Tommy was there, sullen, exchanging a wan smile with Evelyn before his ma shoved the baby into his arms and grabbed the ear of a sibling.

Reverend Green had delivered his message, as predicted, to the rhythmic rocking of his hips against the lectern, pro-viding a tempo for his words. Slow as molasses. She couldn't look at Michał. She'd told him of the time the older boys had wiped chalk dust along the edge of the lectern. Poor Mrs Green had fumbled at the front of his crisp black suit slacks, trying to remove the bright white stripe across his pelvis, setting the whole country congregation a-titter with observations of Rev. Green's crotch. Michał had laughed until tears ran down his face.

Later, when Evelyn heard the click of Mother's bedroom door and the crunch of gravel under Daddy's boots, she hurriedly changed out of her Sunday dress with its fussy, blue-checked sateen and matching gloves. She chose a pair of black linen shorts with pleats up to a belted waist and a sage-green shirt that reflected the vibrance of her eyes. She looked at herself in the mirror. Long white legs and arms. Straight hips. Bony shoulders. Freckled nose. She did up the top button of her shirt. Plaited her hair and then undid it again, let it fall in waves around her shoulders. Bit colour into her lips.

Michał's back was turned when Evelyn stepped through the doorway of her father's workshop. Honeyed light gilt the walls and carried dust motes in slow spirals through the air. A broom was leaning against the wall beside a pile of Huon pine wood shavings, the dregs from Daddy's latest project, still spreading sweet aromatics that competed with the acrid stench of glue and shellac. The central workbench held the mayor's tabletop commission, clamped tightly around its perimeter. It was a puzzle of Huon pine, the sinuous blond lines contrasted with knots and whorls of birdseye timber, like wind flurries and draughts had been captured beneath glass. The pattern was exquisite, a riddle of natural and contrived markings. They should never put a cloth on this table, Evelyn thought as she gently ran a finger across the joins.

Michał was perched on a stool against the far workbench, his right arm flexing as he drove some kind of tool against a piece of wood. The windowpanes in front of him were thick with dust beside Daddy's shadow board of tools mostly in their right places. A handful of nails poking from the wall held sketches and scribblings that flapped lightly in the breeze. Daddy's filing system.

Evelyn scuffed her shoe deliberately against the concrete floor and Michał turned around.

'What're you doing?' she asked, a smile in her eyes.

Michał wore one of Daddy's leather work aprons over his shirt. His eyes sent her stomach to sea as he grasped her hand like he had just a few days ago in the lounge, pressing his lips into her palm.

'Stop it!' She laughed, her cheeks on fire.

'I'm making something for you,' he said, then led her by the hand to the workbench. There, a scrap of Huon had sprouted a wing. The crude motion of steel against timber was forming the spread of a wren's wing, its feathers like long splayed fingers. A beak and head were also emerging from the chunk of rough wood.

Evelyn turned the carving over in her hands. 'Show me how you do it.'

Michał picked up the pocket-sized knife from the bench and, cradling the bird in his left hand, shaved tiny slivers of timber away. He worked slowly, patiently, one curled ribbon of Huon at a time. The knife was razor sharp, sliding through the pine like butter. Gradually, Evelyn saw that he was whittling texture into the bird, each cut mimicking the delicate fringes of feathers that make a wing.

'It's beautiful,' she said.

He stopped, his hand hovering above the creation, looking at her as if she were a mystery to solve. He gulped. 'You have a try.' He set the knife and a chunk of wood in front of her, pushing the stool behind her knees. 'Small strokes, just cut a little bit at a time. And keep your other hand behind the blade.'

She could feel his breath on her neck. At first she hacked at the wood with the knife but, after a few cuts, found the right angle to shave pieces away so they fell like confetti on the bench as she curved off one corner of the block to a dappled round-ness. With each stroke she built confidence. But then she angled the knife too deep, only by the smallest degree, and it wedged stubbornly into the timber. She wrestled with it a moment, shifting her hands for better grip.

'Careful—' Michał said. Too late. The blade dislodged, only to plunge into the soft flesh of Evelyn's palm. The knife clattered to the floor as she ripped it aside and jumped to her feet, clutch-ing her hand.

'Oh fudge!' Blood flowed down her wrist.

Michał pulled a crumpled handkerchief from his pocket and pressed it into Evelyn's palm, the same hand he'd held on the grass beneath Mother Cummings. 'I'm so sorry,' he said. 'I'm so sorry. Do you feel sick?'

Evelyn snorted, 'It's just a little nick, I'm fine.' But she didn't mind him holding her hand like that, his warmth and tender-ness oriented towards her. Her hand may have been throbbing, but her heart was on a bull ride at the Chudleigh Show as she noticed his glossy dark hair and breathed deeply of the spiced, earthy smell of him. 'How did you get that scar?'

Where Michał's hand held the hanky to Evelyn's palm she'd spotted a silvery line running from the knuckle of his left thumb down the outside of his hand reaching nearly to his wrist.

'Boarding school,' he said. 'I caught it on a nail pulling myself out of a rowboat onto a jetty.'

'You went to boarding school? How awful!'

'Everyone did. Everyone I knew, anyway. It was safer than home.'

'How old were you?'

'I was nine when my school in Berlin was evacuated, early in '43. We said goodbye to our mamas and set off for a village about two hundred kilometres east of Berlin. There were sixty of us boys and three teachers, all relocated to a Polish chateau by a lake.'

'Sounds fancy!'

'It was beautiful. While the bombs were falling and Hitler's tea party was being dismantled, we rowed on the lake, fished, played hide and seek in the halls of that immense castle. No air raids. No tankers or soldiers marching by our windows. Just silence. That's where I learned English too.'

Michał remembered those two years of his childhood like a dream, he told her. The teachers were hard, quick to snatch the riding crop from the hook on the back of the kitchen door for any misdemeanour, from talking after lights out to failing a spelling test. But he was used to hard. And they were three greying teachers, quick of wit but slow of movement, against sixty energetic boys full of country air and mischief. There was an unspoken solidarity among most of the rabble; they looked out for each other. Gave alibis, shared cigarettes and alcohol pilfered from Lord-knows-where, sounded the alarm when a teacher was on the prowl.

The greatest threats were the aspiring Hitlerjugend. Bullies like their older brothers, mostly. Their noses were out of joint for having had to relocate to a pretty house by a lake in Poland, of all places. They considered it a kindergarten, a babysitting service, when they could have been out on the streets fighting for Hitler.

It was one of them who'd reached a hand out to Michał that day on the lake, hoisting him halfway out of the boat onto the jetty before letting go. Michał had flailed backwards, snagging his thumb on a protruding nail before hitting the boat and then sinking into the waist-deep, muddy pond water. It had needed five stitches, much to the ire of the moustachioed schoolmaster. 'Clumsy lout,' he'd muttered, his wiry eyebrows joined in frustration as he made arrangements for a doctor to visit.

'Schloss Steinbockshof,' he said. 'That was the name of the grand house – more of a castle, really – that we stayed in until early 1945. It belonged to a Polish aristocratic family and was taken over by the German army to run our little school. I often wondered about them, where they went, who they were.'

They'd had daughters. The chateau's eastern wing was out-of-bounds, which was like hanging a welcome sign in its halls for the boys from Berlin. Dust sheets were draped over two beds in one room, a doll house in a corner, two pairs of red buckled shoes sitting beside a blanket chest. The other room was wallpapered with forget-me-nots, had books stacked beside the bed and a wardrobe heaving with starchy cotton dresses, skirts and blouses, mostly in white, blue and yellow. The garments would have been too big for him at nine, ten and eleven, and he couldn't help but wonder what teenage girl had been commanded out of her home in such haste that she didn't collect the book with the dog-eared page halfway through, or the faded favourite dress, still strewn across a chair? Michał used to think of his sister when he remembered that room, and now he thought of Evelyn too.

He lifted the handkerchief from Evelyn's palm. 'The bleeding has nearly stopped. Just a little bit longer.'

'Why did you come to Tasmania?' she asked.

'I started a woodworking apprenticeship with my uncle. Uncle Hans was like a father to me, although he isn't technically my uncle, not by blood. I spent so many hours as a child building jewellery boxes and toys in his workshop. After the war, hunger forced me to quit the last year of my studies and get a job in Uncle Hans' workshop to look after Mama and Sabine. The wages weren't good, but he also paid in bread that Auntie Charlotte baked us once or twice a week. We got by. But when I finished my apprenticeship, Uncle Hans couldn't afford to keep me on.' Michał looked out the window and cleared his throat. 'Every fortnight I would go with my friend Joseph to collect our dole from the unemployment office. One day there was a poster on the doors as we walked in.' He lifted his free hand to frame the poster's headline in the air: *The Hydro-Electric Commission of Tasmania wants you!*

'I had no idea where Tasmania was. Thankfully the next line of the poster said something like, "Applications to the Australian Military Mission in Berlin". So Joseph and I came home with application forms and made a beeline for Mama's world atlas. It didn't take us too long to find the little scrap of land at the rear end of Australia.'

'Hey!'

Michał grinned. 'I went on down to the Australian Mission Office in West Berlin, and I figured out quick-smart that they were only taking blokes that were twenty-one years and up. So I lied about my age. My big shoulders helped with that!' He flexed a bicep comically. 'I had no papers anyway. Lost them when the war invaded our house. So I signed up for a job with Tasmania's Hydro-Electric Commission. My English helped a lot, and they liked that I was good with the tools. It was July 1951, over two years ago, when I boarded a DC4 plane at Tempelhof Airport with about fifty other Berliners and flew from there to Sydney via Rome, Cyprus, Bahrain, Calcutta, Singapore and Darwin. That bit took five days. Then from there to Sydney and on to Launceston.'

Evelyn's unblinking eyes glittered. So many places. Her whole body leaned in to be close to Michał's story, her free hand splayed beneath her throat. 'Keep going.'

'Well, there's not much more to say. I was sent to the Butlers Gorge station and heave-hoed there for the two years of my contract. Mama and Sabine were distraught at first, but the money I've been able to send back has given them the comforts they deserve. I want to bring them here in time.'

'Would they like to come here?'

'I sent Sabine postcards of Cradle Mountain and some of the white sandy beaches on the East Coast, but her reply said, "It's no Zugspitze!" That's Germany's highest peak. She's like that. Takes a while to warm to change.'

'What about Jimmy? How did you end up working for him in Strahan?'

'Jimmy was delivering timber off and on, told me there was plenty of work out his way if I wanted it. Truth is, I really missed woodworking, so I took him up on his offer as soon as the Hydro contract ended a few months back. He's a good boss, and I love working with the Tassie timbers.' Michał lifted the handkerchief from Evelyn's hand once more. The bleeding had stopped, the wound reduced to a red puncture mark and a few ragged petals of skin. 'Make sure you wash it well, and put some antiseptic on it and a bandage until it's healed up.'

The sun glared through the window at Michał's eye level. Evelyn gave him no warning, no time to gather his wits. When she stood up and pressed her lips against his in one seamless movement, he staggered backwards first before quickly regrouping to enclose her waist in his hands. She'd been thinking of this the whole time he held her hand, playing nurse. He reciprocated the gentle passion of her mouth, and she tasted his salty-sweet freshness. Her strong neck and chin pressed forward. Defiant almost. Then she slipped from his hands and was at the door where she could see the sun still dazzling his view.

'I'd better wash this,' she called over her shoulder, injured hand aloft.

And she was gone.

Chapter 14

Summer 2019

Rae stood at the door with a bottle of Jansz in one hand and a New York cheesecake in the other. After a suitably long pause to allow Allira's full appreciation of her tableau, she chirped, 'Bet you're glad to see me. When the hubby's away, the girls get to play!'

Rae's brand of effervescence was always welcome, as far as Allira was concerned, especially on the lonely nights when Hamish worked night shift. She hadn't been known as 'Lemonade' in high school for nothing: bubbly, and the personification of the 'when life gives you lemons' adage.

Allira gave her a tight hug. 'I've been hanging out for this night so bad!'

'Can't get enough of me, hey.' Rae winked, then walked through to the kitchen and helped herself to two champagne flutes from an overhead cupboard.

'I'm bursting to hear what you've found out about Justin,' Allira replied. 'I wish you'd just tell me, cut all the theatrics.'

'You know that's not my style, Al.' The cork popped like an audible exclamation mark and Rae expertly filled their glasses.

Bright pink resin hoops dangled from her ears and a sequined rainbow stretched across her white t-shirt, reflecting colours across the room. Allira always felt the urge to strip down after a day at the office, like a costume change to signal a change in roles. And the swap over to home always favoured comfort. Lounge pants were her go-to, the kind that could be pyjamas or track pants.

Allira cut generous slabs of cake and carried two laden plates along with a punnet of raspberries to the couch. Spotify played a mix of nostalgic '80s rock, and birds were chattering in the magnolia tree outside. She loved this spot. It was this sunken lounge with a wood heater to cut through Tasmania's icy winters that Hamish and Allira had fallen in love with the most in the house, prompting them to make an offer a year after their marriage. The original house plans stated the build date as 1957, but the design had a nobility to it, like it had borrowed from future decades. Tasmanian oak-lined ceilings were held up by windows that stretched floor to ceiling, giving sweeping views across the Tamar River. Wide eaves kept the living space cool in summer and warm in the cooler months when the low sun cast its rays all the way to the opposing walls. Kookaburras alighted on the same eaves, their staccato cackle competing with lawnmowers and rubbish trucks some days. Wrens flitted in the shrubs and splashed themselves indulgently in a marooned pot saucer that provided a makeshift bird bath.

The views of the Tamar were different to any Allira had witnessed before, capturing the industrial shipyards and factories of Invermay. Standing at the windows of an evening, nursing a steaming cup of rooibos, or a glass of red, she would watch the tea trees lining the riverbanks bent backwards in fierce squalls that tunnelled down the water. Stately old pelicans landed on piers, and black swans arrowed through brown tides. There was the slow decay of boats left to die, their hulls riddled with rust. Forklifts manoeuvred busily, like yellow worker ants stockpiling the nest. Flashing lights met thick river fog. Bulrushes met joggers and kids walking home from school. Faraway mountain ranges met the twinkle of a city's slumber. All witnessed from these windows.

Allira had enjoyed giving the home, with its white walls, raw materials and neutral tones, her own stamp. Earthy hues and objects that connected her to the outdoors were what made it feel like a sanctuary to her. Allira had never been able to introduce bold colours into her home. Perhaps it was because she was so often immersed in other people's narratives, attentive to their personalities and the way they painted their lives, that when she came home, she just needed clean space and sumptuous textures. Linen, woodgrains, brown paper, shells, pinecones, clay, and buttery leather. Rae was easily the brightest thing in her house.

'What's with the flowers?' Rae said with a mouth full of cheesecake. She knew that Allira would never choose sunflowers. Leucadendrons or proteas were more her vibe. But they did look stunning, standing tall in the centre of the salvaged timber table, their golden faces turned towards the windows.

'Hamish bought them to "brighten my day".' Allira gulped her wine.

'I know . . . two years, hey?' Rae was suddenly sober. 'It's kind of why I suggested we meet tonight – didn't want you alone with Hame having to work. So are you okay?' Rae's voice was confident, but Allira could tell she was nervous. She hadn't intended it to be a taboo subject between them, especially for this long, but she was also grateful that Rae had let her set her own pace.

'Actually, I'm good. I feel like I've turned a corner or something. That sounds so naff.'

'Who cares how it sounds. You're talking. This is literally the most we've ever spoken about your son, you realise.'

Allira's eyes sheened. 'My son . . .'

'He was your son, Al! He was your son, and you are his mum.'

Allira smiled through tears. 'Yeah, you're right.' She took another mouthful of cake. 'Gosh, Rae, I had the strangest conversation with Nora. She's really helped me see the bleeding obvious in this. She went missing the other night and I found her five kilometres from the home, digging a hole where she thought someone had buried her baby. Something awful happened to her, I know it.'

'Some people with dementia dream up entire other realities, Al.'

'I know, but this is different. Her grief is so real. It's hard to explain.' Allira rubbed her thumb over her palm, the same place where Nora showed her the silvery scar. 'Nora told me the story behind a scar she has on her hand. It was sketchy, but I think it happened while her boyfriend was teaching her to carve a piece of wood. She went from child to Gandhi in a blink.'

Rae laughed, trying not to spill champagne on the sofa.

'Seriously, it was this moment where I could've known her forever, like she was my mum or aunt dispensing wisdom.

Next minute, she's asking me who I am. She said she loves the scar because it reminds her of the pain but also the context of the pain. I think she was talking about her sweetheart, Michał. He must've been worth remembering all these years.'

Rae's lips pressed together, and she slowly nodded, chewing over what Allira said. 'I like that. And for you, that means treasuring the context of your own pain?'

Allira looked down at her hands. 'I'm a mum. I have a wonderful husband. I had a son.'

Rae wrapped her arms around Allira, pulling her into a tight hug. There was nothing half-baked about Rae's hugs; squishy, warm, and fragrant with a heady mix of hairspray and perfume. Allira wasn't a hugger, not really, but she'd never turn down a Rae hug. When they pulled away, Rae removed a long piece of Allira's hair from her mouth, and they dissolved into laughter. Bono was singing 'I Still Haven't Found What I'm Looking For' in the background and they poured another glass of bubbles while singing along.

'Tell me what you've discovered about Nora,' Rae said.

Allira held up an index finger before jogging to her office nook. She returned with a black leather satchel, which she laid on the coffee table, clearing their empty plates to one side, and pulled out a manila document wallet with *EVELYN* written in block capitals.

'Evelyn?'

'Yes.' Her voice came out louder than she'd expected. 'I think her real name was Evelyn Grayson, not Nora Gray.' She opened the folder to a spiral notebook with lines of her own precise hand and duplicates of Working with Vulnerable People forms, then lifted out a vintage, cloth-bound book in fire-engine red and unwrapped it from white tissue paper.

'Oooh,' Rae said, reaching to touch its cover.

'I found this at that quirky antique shop in town. It's like the Google search engine for Tasmania in 1953.' There were three sticky notes hanging like errant tongues from its pages and Allira thumbed to the first. 'An undertaker by the name of Stanley Grayson lived in the Deloraine municipality, specifically in Caveside. Nora has spoken about coffins and funerals quite a bit. She even explained in full detail how to stitch a person's jaw shut when they've died.'

'Eww! How do you know his name is Stanley though? He's just listed as S. L.' Rae tapped the page.

Allira turned to the last tab in the book. The pages had been red in this section, the colour aged to a pinky-apricot, delineating a section of paid advertising. They were mostly ads for solicitors and insurance companies, all framed with a rudimentary black line and drop shadow. *Birchall's for Books is almost a Proverb*, an ad for the Launceston bookseller lauded. It had closed just last year. *Tourists should see—the West Coast of Tasmania!* proclaimed a full-page ad for the Emu Bay Railway, which beckoned with a timetable of departures from Burnie at 7.35 am daily. But wedged between ads for a wine and spirits merchant and a sawmiller was a line drawing of a dining table and chairs. The headline read 'Custom Furniture', and below, 'Stanley L. Grayson' with an address on Western Creek Road, Caveside.

'Nice sleuthing,' Rae exclaimed. 'That makes sense too, that an undertaker would also be a carpenter. I don't imagine there'd be enough deaths in a little backwater like Caveside to support a family. What's the other tab?'

'That's another Grayson.' Allira turned to the tab where T. E. Grayson was named as the treasurer of the Deloraine Croquet Association. 'Could be another relative, maybe even her mum. I'm convinced this Stanley guy is Nora's father. But I'm left with the mystery of why Mrs Nora Gray of Mercy Place Aged Care at some point distanced herself from her family by changing her name from Evelyn Grayson.'

'Look at you getting your Miss Marple on. I haven't seen you this energised since . . .' Rae left the line hanging.

Since two years ago, Allira finished in her head.

But Rae had recovered. 'It's going to be one of your power reads, I know it. It'll be long, and Justin will rant about that. But then he'll finally sit down at his desk one day and read it with the door closed. Half an hour later, he'll rip the door fair off its hinges to declare that it's the best thing he's read all year, and make it the cover story. That's my prediction. You're welcome.'

Rae's face was smug and Allira knew she should be chuffed at the compliment but she squirmed, hugging a cushion to her stomach. Nora had become more than the subject of an article to her. She hadn't been visiting for the past three weeks simply to glean information – so why did she go? It was hard to say. Was it because she felt sorry for her? Maybe she couldn't stand the thought of someone coming to the end of their life completely alone, but Allira sensed it was something simpler than that, less honourable. She liked Nora, enjoyed spending time with her. There was a magnetism in learning more of her story, so that she might understand the woman better and, in a perplexing way, understand herself better.

'What about you, Poirot – if we're going with the Agatha Christie theme? Tell me what you know about Justin.'

Rae fiddled with a strand of her block fringe. 'I'd prefer Phryne Fisher, if you please.'

'Argh, you're making me work for this, aren't you? Miss Fisher it is. Suits you actually. Now, proceed. Or shall I gather all the suspects first?'

Rae abruptly jumped to her feet, calling 'Back in a minute' as she dashed down the hall. Allira assumed it was nature's call, but Rae announced her return with a theatrical 'Yoo-hoo!' before strutting back to the lounge, wearing a black fedora that Hamish had worn to a 1920s birthday bash, a red feather boa from the same night, and a pair of Allira's tallest heels.

'What—'

'Hush, darling. I'm thinking.' Rae paced the length of the lounge room and Allira snorted when she realised she was puffing archly on a red and white striped straw, pretending to blow smoke rings at the ceiling.

'You totally missed your calling, Rae.' Allira sat cross-legged on the couch, settling in for the show.

'First thing's first. I contacted the real estate office to check if the rent is indeed overdue, saying that I was Mr Justin Taylor's PA and he had misplaced the latest statement of overdue rent. The receptionist was more than happy to oblige this honey-voiced woman's request. She sent it to me immediately and confirmed in less than ten minutes that Justin hasn't paid rent for three months.' Rae paused for dramatic effect, taking a long draw of the candy-striped straw wedged between her manicured fingers. 'I then telephoned the printers, again under the guise of Mr Taylor's PA, to make the correct payment of overdue accounts. Last edition's print bill remains outstanding, and the down payment on the one we've just put to bed hasn't been paid either. Justin must be sweet-talking them something mighty to have them continue printing when we're so far in the red.'

Allira's stomach churned; her hands were clammy. 'I had no idea we were *that* far behind. Keep going.'

Rae paced again, wobbling on her stilettos, calf muscles bulging. 'Finally, I had a less contrived conversation, this time with Katy Driver. She's employed as a contractor, as you know, invoicing the magazine each month for her hours. Sure enough, she's not been paid for the last two months. She's only continued out of her love for the job. And that can't last forever.'

Rae stopped. She kicked off the heels, threw the boa to the floor and sat the fedora on the mantelpiece. She hadn't missed Allira's crestfallen face now propped in her hands, her elbows on her knees. 'I did encourage her to hang in there,' she said, rubbing Allira's arm.

Allira sighed. 'What are we going to do?'

'Not we,' Rae said firmly, 'you.'

Allira opened her mouth and closed it again, blinking rapidly. 'Me?'

'This is your chance! Go and make Justin a proposal that'll make all his troubles go away. This is the opportunity you've been waiting for.'

'What on earth do you mean?'

'To officially head up *Folk* mag, silly.'

Allira rubbed her cheekbone, drawing comfort from the subtle convex shapes of those spots. Always there, always the same. 'I don't think I've been waiting for this at all. I'm happy with the way things are.'

'Even if that were true, the way things are is awfully unstable. We'll probably be out of jobs before long if Justin doesn't do something about his money woes.'

'I should talk to Hamish.' Allira looked hesitantly to Rae. 'And make an appointment with our bank . . . and our lawyer?'

'Now you're talking! I'll put all my findings together in a report with the actual figures and whatnot. I'll keep digging too.'

Allira's head was swimming. She wanted this, of course she did. But she'd never thought it would involve taking down her boss.

Chapter 15

Summer 1953

Evelyn spent the whole afternoon in her bedroom. She'd pedalled home from school and told Mother that she had homework to do. Told Daddy the same.

He looked at her with creases in his forehead, stubbed out his cigarette beneath a boot on the grass and tipped the dregs of his coffee into the garden. He pulled her to his chest in a rough hug and whispered in her ear, 'Go do your homework, Nora-girl. I love you, y'know?'

She gulped, squeezed him back and ran to the house, trying to keep her shoulders straight, her step light. She sat on the edge of her bed, staring at the wall opposite. Flocked wallpaper in pastel pink and green ran from ceiling to floor, with lines of insipid flowers. The walls were short, the ceiling long, angling sharply towards the room's highest point above her bed. She loved the sloping ceiling and all the irregular shapes it created. Words from mathematics lessons tumbled around as she measured the different formations with her eyes: isosceles, trapezium, rhombus, pentagon. Words of precision, masculine words, against a backdrop of her bed's white lace coverlet and frothy pink valance.

All the decorating had been Mother's undertaking. Not a thing was of Evelyn's own choosing. Not the vase of fresh flowers that was changed every second day. Not the botanical prints in gilt frames, nor the Queen Anne desk with its matching chair that held her schoolbooks in a jumbled pile, backpack slung over carved scroll motifs. The only place she could say was entirely of her own design was a small bookcase under the dormer window. Daddy had made it for her one Sabbath afternoon when Mother was holed up in her room drinking tea and reading magazines. The simple Tasmanian oak shelving held all her favourite books, their cheerful spines making a ribbed rainbow. It was also where Evelyn displayed the flotsam and jetsam of her wanderlust: pinecones, fossils, bird nests, an echidna quill, eagle feathers and an egg-shaped rock in darkest ox blood red.

This morning, she'd added a new item to the shelf: a wren whittled from Huon pine, its wings splayed in flight. She lifted the carving from its place, her fingers tracing the intricate patterns that mimicked downy breast feathers, an inquisitive eye, a jaunty tail and a determined beak. She breathed in the musky perfume, the smell of bush, Daddy's workshop and Michał's hands, all muddled in the fragrance of the little golden bird.

Evelyn sighed and fell back on her bed, her feet still flat on the floor. Her legs made twiggy right angles and her hair was frizzy rather than wavy, a messy hash of red on white. Had it really been just this morning that Michał revved the engine of the Bedford truck, belched the horn and drove away? The spare part for the truck's engine had arrived two days early and Daddy and Michał lost no time rolling up their sleeves, digging into the guts beneath the old truck's bonnet until it rattled to life late on Monday afternoon. He was gone before she left for school that morning, Michał and Daddy shaking hands like army comrades, slapping each other's shoulders. Mother had said a curt farewell and Michał had slipped her an envelope marked *Mrs Grayson*. He'd written the recipe for Kołaczki in tiny, neat letters, after he and Evelyn had been privy to the rapturous look on her face as she bit into the buttery pastry two days earlier. And to Evelyn he just smiled, a knowing smile, one that turned her face to beetroot.

She had raced upstairs to watch the truck's green paint-work glinting in the sun as it ate up the black road, threading between fences, inching up the seams of patchwork paddocks, smaller and smaller, driving into oblivion. Would she ever see him again?

It was when the green Bedford had disappeared from her view and she slumped back from the dormer window that she saw the package on her pillow, bundled in a piece of striped cotton and tied with string. She pulled the string ever so slowly, feeling the rub of twine against twine, the friction of the fibres and their warmth. She wanted to savour it. She watched the bow unravel and fall slack before unfolding one side of the fabric, and then the other. A slip of paper fell out as she lifted the bird from its cloth enclosure, enthralled. Could there be a better gift in the entire world? Something so exquisite crafted from his hands, his mind, his heart. Heat spread from her chest out to every nerve ending in her body and she felt painfully alive, sorrow grinding against affection. She lifted the piece of paper and unfolded it on her lap.

Nora,
    You will fly one day.
    I wanted to say this to your beautiful face, but I did not know it until the opportunities ran out. I love you. I love you, Nora, although we've only just met. You surprise me, the things you stir in me. Never have I said those three words to a woman, and never has a woman made me so weak with distraction.
    I am utterly yours,
    Michał.

Evelyn folded the note along its creases again, pressing it to her heart. Her head was full of static and she felt detached, like she had exited her body and was gazing at it from afar: a red-haired girl in her floral bedroom, pressing a love note to her chest. Why was she so melancholy? She watched herself as she pulled a book from the rainbow of spines and secreted the note within the cover. *Romeo and Juliet* seemed appropriate – and melodramatic. She was fine with a bit of melodrama in the quiet of her room, where her actions wouldn't be considered gratui-tous or childish. She was none of those things. But the thought of Michał shaping his mouth around those three words, spoken for her alone, levitated her above her mundane little existence.

Evelyn swung her legs against the scratchy lace valance, stretching her arms wide. She had hoped for this. Michał's hooded eyes, the way he'd pressed his lips against her palm, the softness of those lips against her mouth. She wanted him all to herself.

Evelyn was subdued at supper. She spoke only when spoken to, chewing slowly on the roast lamb and mint sauce. She helped with the dishes, returning to her room as quickly as reasonable to watch the light ladled from the sky, Mother Cummings cloaked in layers of violet. When the sky was black and her parents' bedroom door had been shut for more than an hour, Evelyn hoisted herself, barefoot, onto the ledge of the dormer window, using the bookcase as stairs, stepping out onto the roof below. On tiptoe, she shimmied sideways and then crouched, gingerly sitting her bottom onto the corrugated iron and stretching her legs along the ribbing. She let her head fall back against the weatherboards and inhaled the pure country air. It was a clear night. Stars studded the sky's canopy and a ringtail possum scurried along the telephone wire, an accomplished tightrope walker. Rabbits feasted down on the lawn, their white tails flashing bright as torchlight with each hop towards juicier stalks of grass and Mother's lush petunias.

The stillness soothed her. Like water running over sun-warmed river stones, the night took the fever out of her. Untwined her from the heat. Carried her. Evelyn imagined sitting beside him on a train in Europe or Asia, their bags stowed in metal baskets overhead, hands clasped, her head resting on his shoulder as the carriage chugged and swayed. They would comment on the changing landscape flicking past their window like a film slide – but real. They would leave footprints in Budapest, Valencia, Venice, Santorini, Paris . . . and Berlin. She would let him lead her to all the broken places of his childhood and they would kick the ash, some to be carried away by the wind, some falling as a salve on old wounds. They would share meals with Sabine and Mama, talking until the wine ran out, sleepy with contentment, and Sabine would sing, her notes every bit as nightingale-like as Evelyn imagined. She would introduce herself to them as Nora. Kiss their cheeks in the European way and give them her name like a gift: *My name is Nora.* Just a bud of a name, a moonflower ready to unfurl and catch all the mysteries of a rich and full world. An unblemished name, spoken only with tenderness.

Evelyn swatted at a mosquito on her leg and hugged her knees to her chest. She imagined evenings by firelight in a home of their creating. None of Mother's flocked wallpaper or in-vogue prints. Just things that made them happy. A string of cowbells and a hand-woven rug from a market in Amsterdam. A miniature of the Arc de Triomphe, painted as they watched the artist's strokes by a canal in Venezia. A record player. Brightly coloured sheets of Egyptian cotton that made sumptuous cocoons around their bodies. She would come to know his skin as her own and he would teach her how to look at her body through his eyes. They would listen: to each other and the world. Their hands would know toil, productive and invigorating. And one day, their love would be productive also. Evelyn imagined a newborn babe nestled in her arms: heavy-lashed eyes, buttery skin, warm. She imagined how it must be to nourish new life, to hold a baby to her breast and watch it draw milk from her. The tug of need, little hands massaging the flow. Growing and thriving each day from the attachment of their bodies. To be so needed, so wanted.

Evelyn pressed a fingernail into the mosquito bite twice, so that the two crescent indentations formed a cross. Daddy said it stopped the itching. She wasn't sure that it worked, but it had become instinctual. She dropped her legs, felt the cool tin roof on the backs of her thighs and calves. She ran her hands down her décolletage, down the front of her cotton pyjamas where her chest swelled softly, down the buttons to her abdomen. She laced her fingers beneath her belly button and closed her eyes. For a moment, with only Mother Cummings as her witness, Evelyn imagined carrying a child, her whole body engaged to sustain the life of an entirely new being. She could not imagine anything more profound. Of all the adventures a girl could embark on in this world, she thought that becoming a mother must be the most daring. And she let the thread continue, allowed her imagining to ramble further still into wildflower fields like none she'd glimpsed before.

She had witnessed the mystery of life as a country girl, watching buck and ewe, bull and cow, mare and stallion rutting in their fields. The violence of it. The pragmatic efficiency of the act. But she also knew that it was different for people. That time she heard the breathless sounds of ecstasy from her parents' bedroom. The hunger in the eyes of lovers. Body and heart were somehow melded. Desire mingling with purpose. And the taste of it was on her tongue as she thought of Michał. To carry his child. To be mother to Michał's child. The skin beneath her pyjamas felt feverishly hot once more.

Chapter 16

Summer 2019

It was Sally who'd encouraged Allira to visit Mercy Place's dementia ward at dinnertime. 'Come when they're sundowning,' she said. 'You'll find it . . . illuminating.'

It wasn't that visiting for dinner was inconvenient. Five nights out of ten Allira ate alone, filling her evenings with Netflix, social media scrolling or an escapist novel. Sometimes there were cringy conversations with her mother who would inevitably ask *that* question, which would lead to a monologue about older mums and Hamish's sperm count, Allira having to suddenly cut the call short with some thinly veiled excuse.

Allira's relationship with her parents had become strained since they moved to Queensland to retire. Her dad was practically allergic to phone conversations. Whenever he did answer a call, he responded to questions with one-word answers and Allira could almost hear him looking at his watch, as if phone companies still charged by the minute. He was so different in the flesh. He had all the time in the world for his 'beautiful and intelligent princess', and they'd spent long afternoons exploring obscure topics, their inquisitive minds thrilling in a travelling partner of the same ilk. And her mum . . . Allira didn't know what to make of her. The distance made her keenly attentive to her daughter's life – by text message only. Gushingly so. The slightest cold and she was sending her links to chicken broth recipes, asking for daily health updates laden with heart emoticons and dropping a *Get Well Soon* card in the post. But beyond that? Well. Perhaps Allira hadn't forgiven her after all.

When she had been lying in the maternity ward wearing a pale blue hospital gown, her dead son in a plastic cradle against the wall, she hadn't wanted her mother to call from her sunny Queensland home and ask, 'Do you want me to come down?' Allira knew they didn't have the money for last-minute flights to Tasmania in peak tourist season. 'I'll come if you want me to,' her mother had said. But the question made Allira feel guilty, like it would be her fault that they wouldn't be able to afford their holiday that year. *I don't want you to have to ask, I want you to know that I need you*, Allira had replied in her head. What she actually said was, 'It's up to you, Mum,' as lightly as her voice would permit. And her mother didn't buy the ticket, didn't come to her daughter's bedside, didn't meet her first grandchild. Allira sighed. No, visiting the nursing home in the evening wasn't inconvenient so much as uncomfortable. All those people with their vulnerabilities bared. But she was determined to do the hard thing, for Nora's sake. And perhaps also to prove something to Sally.

Allira punched the now-familiar code into the keypad at the entrance to the dementia ward, walking towards the dining room as the heavy doors clicked locked behind her. Something was wrong. She picked up her pace. A dog yapped madly, opera music was playing too loudly and a woman's shrill voice was raised over what sounded like a schoolroom of rowdy children. Allira stepped into the room. Could this be the same subdued place she visited so frequently? She had wandered past the dining room at lunch hour and seen the residents bent over sandwiches, nurses and carers at their elbows, walking frames lined against the walls. But the scene she beheld now was like she'd gone down the rabbit hole.

Allira moved into the room, past a table where two women she vaguely recognised were deep in conversation. They spoke with great animation while spooning tinned tomato soup into their mouths, chased with white bread and margarine. Their conversation was a noisy stream of nonsense without pause for listening and responding. It was like watching two monologues at the same time.

The yapping dog stopped yapping and sat chewing a crust of toast at the feet of a bewildered-looking gentleman in a tweed hat and jacket also slurping soup. 'Can you take me home with you, please?' he said as Allira walked past. 'They treat us like animals here.' Splodges of soup ran down his tie and he carried on eating and patting the Yorkshire terrier intermittently, like he never expected a response or he had already forgotten that he addressed her at all.

The opera singing rose to a crescendo and Allira realised it was unaccompanied, that the rich baritone sounds were emanating from the throat of someone in her midst. Allira recalled one of the nurses mentioning a resident, Gilbert something, who didn't say boo aside from rare operatic serenades. She spotted the giant proportions of Gilbert's body, sitting alone at one of the dining room tables with its plastic tablecloth. His soup was untouched, the spoon cast aside. Hands the size of plough discs spread on the tabletop, anchoring him as brazen notes peeled from his cavernous chest. He had been an Opera Australia singer once upon a time, touring the world, performing to tens of thousands. Now, a room of no more than forty was impervious to his talent. The gutsy vulnerability of the opera made a slurry of Allira's emotions as she sought out Nora's dinner table.

A bird of a woman wearing a sequined dress and R.M. Williams boots balanced atop a chair, spouting instructions to 'Descend with caution, dear friends' and 'Take just your good selves, don't tarry, or the cost may be your life!' Sally was there, trying to placate the woman, who flinched at an imaginary bomb blast before succumbing to Sally's persistent encouragement to take her hand and step down from the chair.

'Oh, you came! So lovely to see you, dear.'

It was Nora, speaking in Allira's direction. Allira looked over her shoulder, but no one else was there. Was it possible that Nora remembered her? Allira took the seat across from the older woman with her tousled mass of grey hair and lipstick smeared across most of her lips. Her baby doll was swaddled and lay on the chair beside her.

'I saw you listening to Gilbert. Isn't he marvellous?'

Allira nodded, still recovering from the confusion of Nora recognising her and then speaking with such familiarity.

Nora grabbed her hand from across the table and leaned in, her head nearly touching Allira's. 'It's such a circus in here, don't you think?' she said, her eyes sparkling conspiratorially.

Allira opened her mouth and closed it again. It was stranger than a circus. It was like landing on a different planet altogether, one where her compassion was being used as a weapon against her, slicing her to pieces. 'Gilbert's voice is . . . ethereal,' Allira replied.

Nora squeezed her hand and smiled as the baritone cord of sound continued to wrap around them, bold and unfaltering as Gilbert rolled his tongue over word endings and skipped and played with the resonance of each note. They sat like that, Nora's hand over hers, the only two in the room giving Gilbert their full attention, although he didn't seem to notice. It was like the urge to sing had been percolating, then boiling and then clamouring until he had to let it out for the sake of his sanity. Not to woo a crowd, but to placate his carnal creative bent.

The aria built to a close. They sensed it, like an impending storm, when black cockatoos flew down off the mountains and decimated whole trees in suburban backyards. His voice became urgent, driving to a new volume and timbre, finally holding a long vibrato that pounded at the walls and windows and ceiling and floor. And then it was over. Gilbert lifted those enormous palms from the table, picked up his spoon and began slowly shovelling the sweet sludge into his mouth. Nora and Allira clapped enthusiastically but he didn't notice or didn't care to. He had slaked his passion and now was emptied.

Nora lifted the doll to her shoulder and jiggled it up and down. 'You liked that, didn't you?' Her face was tenderness itself. 'He's always enjoyed music,' she said, beaming at Allira. 'Your turn now.'

'What do you mean?'

Nora chortled, rubbing the doll's back. 'Don't be coy with me.' She stood to her full height and theatrically waved at the whole room which, for the first time that evening, fell into a hush. Heads turned, necks craned. Sally and Juliette, another carer, responded to Nora's beckoning, asking if she wanted more soup.

'Unlikely,' Nora scoffed, and Allira stifled a laugh. 'This dear one would like a turn at the singing now,' she said with utmost authority, pointing to Allira.

Sally raised her eyebrows and Juliette covered her mouth.

'No!' Allira said reflexively, standing from her seat. 'I mean, not here . . . er, I don't think they would appreciate my voice quite so much as Gilbert's,' she said, trying to smooth over the vehemence of her reaction. There was a good reason why Allira used to mouth the words to the national anthem at school.

'Oh, stop it, Sabine. No one's falling for this charade. Look at all these people! They'll lap you up, they will,' Nora said, her voice climbing excitedly.

Sally still said nothing. Allira's hand involuntarily moved to her cheekbone, rubbing those three spots. *Sabine, Sabine. Such a distinctive name.* She'd heard it spoken by Nora before, during one of her lapses, when she'd described the place beneath the mountain where she learned about Michał's past. *His sister. She thinks I'm Michał's sister!*

'Nora,' Allira said warmly, testing the name that was usually so sharply rejected but now seemed right. 'I strained my voice, remember? Michał had me singing for Mama late into the night, soothing her pain.' Allira's pulse raced, her face hot. Was she going along with this? 'I've been sucking lozenges all day.'

Nora stepped around the table until she was beside Allira, pulling her into a tight hug, the baby doll sandwiched between them. 'Bless you, dear. Your poor voice, of course you can't sing. You must save it for your mother.'

Sally's face broke into a smile. 'Bravo,' she mouthed at Allira and walked away.

Allira exhaled. Juliette flashed wide, gappy teeth and winked. 'Looks like you're both okay here,' she said, following Sally to another table, another confusion. Allira felt like she'd passed some kind of test.

Nora walked in circles, rocking the doll, kissing its forehead, stroking its head. She was so absorbed, she didn't notice the dining room emptying, the walking frames being filled one by one, the bowls and cutlery being cleared. Allira watched. Her phone was off; she had no pressing commitments. She imagined the doll was real and Nora a new mother. Imagined colour back into her hair, plumpness to her cheeks, the straightening of her spine. *What a mother she must have been. Pouring energy into her newborn, wrapping herself around him, lighting his days with activity.* Allira felt the emptiness of her own arms as she watched Nora, yet their song seemed so similar. They both yearned.

Nora wandered back to her chair, eyes full. 'I love you.'

Allira stammered, 'I love you too.' Her eyes were foggy, her throat tight. How this old woman played with her heart! But there it was, the truth laid bare. She loved the erratic, wounded and determined person in front of her. Enough to traipse into the night searching for her, to burrow into historical records looking for some morsel of information about her identity and to sit quietly at her bedside without searching for something unnamed. Just being.

'Now, who are you again?' Nora's eyes enquired even as her mouth curved upwards.

Allira returned the smile, wanting to reassure her. 'I'm your very dear friend.' The words came without hesitation.

'You're my friend?' Nora faltered, her grey-green eyes puffy. 'I have a friend?' She looked visibly touched: her skin lightened and glowed and her grey waves swayed as she shook her head and squeezed her eyes against a tide of tears. 'I had a best friend once, a very long time ago,' Nora said. 'But then he had to go away. Far, far away.'

Chapter 17

Autumn 1953

At the Grayson homestead in Caveside, the Great Western Tiers mountain range was a towering reminder of their smallness. Fertile farmland as flat as a tabletop met the mountain's rotund foothills, like overfed bellies pressed against a banquet table. That was how Evelyn had always imagined these giants in her midst.

Each morning she eagerly slipped from her bed to stand in the dormer window and yank the curtains open. Their form was blurry at first, through dripping condensation and some- times swathes of fog. She would push the window ajar, lifting the collar of her pyjamas as the sharp morning air needled her bed-warm skin. And there they were, the Great Western Tiers, like a family of rowdy children tugging on the skirts of their ma, Mother Cummings peak. Their dimpled forest-flesh and tangled tableau of want and greed juxtaposed with their Mother, standing sentinel to the left of her view. Poised, her lines refined, her head lifted, alert. She was protector, leader, sustainer.

Perhaps it was the influence of tales like 'Snow White and the Seven Dwarfs' or 'The Pied Piper'. Or perhaps it was the abandonment she felt from her own mother, the distance between them. But the presence of the Great Western Tiers outside her window had always been a comfort.

When David had turned eighteen and went to join their father in the war effort, leaving just her and Mother, she'd stood here, eyes transfixed as she sorted through the tumbled feelings of a seven-year-old. The mix of relief and fear. The giddy gratefulness of knowing she would not compete for affection in her own home any more. The heavy stone of knowing that Daddy and David might never return, that the family photo on the mantelpiece might become a memorial.

When she'd woken one morning, aged nine, to find that the starling in the shoebox beside her bed had died in the night, she pushed a chair to the window and climbed up to sob at the skirt of the great unmoving mountain peak. The little bird had fallen from its nest the day before and Evelyn had scooped it into her hands, promising she would look after it.

When Uncle Trevor and Aunty Philippa had come to stay with their ever-expanding brood of children, she came here to plead for happy brothers and sisters of her own. She had to weave through the sleeping forms of several cousins draped across her bedroom floor to reach the window. How she loved hearing their snuffly sleep sounds and knowing that she would wake to their warm bodies climbing into her bed, their kisses on her cheeks and their utter adoration of big cousin Evelyn.

When Mother had accused her of breaking a porcelain vase that had been balanced on a plant stand holding a bunch of bearded irises from the garden, she came here to await her punishment. The more she insisted on her innocence, the more Mother's anger avalanched.

'You dusted this morning,' she said with hands splayed across her thin hips.

'But I didn't . . . I would have told you—'

'Don't speak back to me. I will not abide a lying tongue.'

'But, Mother, please believe me—'

'Enough! Go to your room.'

Evelyn had stomped angrily up the stairs, smearing a grimy hand along the wallpapered wall as she went. She paced by that window in her room, biting back angry tears each time she stopped to look out at the silhouetted mountain range. The sky was black when she finally heard Daddy's heavy footfall on the stairs. He stepped into the room, pulling the belt from his trousers.

'I didn't do it, Daddy . . . she wouldn't believe me.' Evelyn was wretched with the grief of thinking her father believed she had done the deed, and then lied about it.

'I know, poss,' he replied and gathered her into a long hug. 'She does love you, you know. She wants you to be strong, Nora, ready for how harsh the big wide world is.'

'Feels harsher here,' she whispered.

Minutes passed. They could hear Mother washing the dishes, the clunk of each plate or bowl onto the drying rack. They knew she was listening. Daddy picked up the belt from where he'd draped it at the foot of Evelyn's bed. Thick, hard leather with a chunky metal buckle.

'Stand up, Nor. You're gonna have to help me now.'

Evelyn flinched. She slowly stood, shoulders slumped, carrying more than the weight of her wayward auburn hair.

'Six'll do. I'll swing the belt, you cry. Make it convincing.'

There was a sparkle in Daddy's eyes as he swung the belt against the foot of Evelyn's bed, not too hard, just enough to encourage a sharp thwack of leather against wood that echoed off the walls of the stately country house and reached down into the kitchen. Evelyn's first responding cry was one of surprise and a hand clapped over her mouth to catch the delighted sound that threatened to follow. They quickly found a rhythm: the belt's crack, Evelyn's theatrical sob. Thwack. Gasp. Wail. Groan. Her eyes were bright moss green and Daddy's whiskery cheeks were full of smile.

That had been last summer.

Today, from her peephole to the mountain, Evelyn's eyes were wide open to a blue-sky day, a lone wedge-tailed eagle soaring on the invisible seam of an updraft. Usually she would have been engrossed in the bird's majestic presence, the way those motionless wings carried it far above the earth. *What do you see?* She would have imagined the vista from the eagle's soaring perspective: rooftops, a patchwork of crops, a web of roads and laneways, the wink of water in lakes and ponds, and the scurry of human life feeding chickens, steering a tractor or leaning from a dormer window with eyes brimming with sky.

But today she felt unsettled.

Evelyn ran downstairs and busied herself cooking a batch of scones, keeping her mind on the flour and butter between her fingers. There was a knock at the door, and she turned down the wireless, still wiping flour from her hands as she went to answer.

It was Michał. She could hardly believe it, but there he was. His shoes were polished, a fedora in his hands. Evelyn flung her arms around his neck and he laughed into her hair, his hands circling her waist. He allowed the brief contact before pushing her gently away, holding her hands.

'Careful,' he said, and that's when she noticed that his skin was paler than normal, his eyes clouded.

'Mother's in the back garden and Daddy's reading the newspaper in the lounge,' Evelyn said.

'And what are you doing?' His tone was light but his eyes remained serious.

'Making scones.' She reached out to touch his face, ran a finger along his hairline.

'I have some news, Nora,' he said and then caught the hand that was trailing his chin and brought it to his lips, kissing her palm.

She loved it when he called her that. It felt right, like they'd known each other from infancy.

'Who is it?' Daddy bellowed from the lounge.

Michał dropped her hand and took a step backwards.

'It's Michał,' she called over her shoulder, eyes still fixed on his.

'I have to tell you,' Michał whispered, his accent thick with urgency.

But Daddy was already clomping down the hall, calling 'Michał!' with arms outstretched. Evelyn stepped aside as her father embraced Michał, slapping him on the back good-naturedly like he was his own long-lost son. A friend of Jimmy's was a friend of Stan's, he'd said that day when the timber was delivered. The two men walked their blokey banter indoors.

'Put the kettle on, love,' Daddy said.

Evelyn scurried around the kitchen as fast as she could, loading a tray with the teapot, cups, sugar lumps, milk, fresh scones and jam. What urgent thing did he want to tell her? So important that he would travel all the way from Strahan to say it? She added a bundle of freshly pressed napkins to the tray.

'Ah, well, that's great news then, isn't it, Thelma?' Daddy was saying when Evelyn entered the room.

Mother was sitting stiffly beside him, eyebrows arched, her weeding apron hanging on the door handle. The pungent tang of her perfume hung heavily in the air: patchouli, bergamot and something that reminded Evelyn of the mossy smells of an impending storm.

'What news?' Evelyn said.

'Jimmy's arm's all fixed up like new.'

Evelyn exhaled long and slow as she poured strong black tea into the delicate, bone china teacups. She always thought it odd to see the men's thick, work-roughened fingers pinching the handles of Mother's hand-painted teacups.

'What will you do now, *Michael*?' Mother asked.

'Mr Jimmy was happy for me to stay and work for him. I have worked with wood since I was a child in my uncle's workshop – although your timbers are different here. So beautiful.'

Michał drew a mouthful of tea into his mouth and gulped. His eyes slid to Evelyn and back to her mother: bulbous cheekbones, pursed lips and that same fiery hue of hair but pulled tightly against her scalp. 'But I have had news from home, from Berlin. My mother is ill. My sister, Sabine, she needs me there to help. I am on my way to sail on the *Taroona* to Melbourne, where I will make my passage back through Europe.'

Berlin. Evelyn stuffed a scone into her mouth and refused to look at Michał. She concentrated on the texture of the pillowy cake. Soft, light, a little doughy. Undercooked, Mother would say. The jam was cherry. Evelyn tried hard not to remember that it was the jam she'd made with Michał the day that Mother had returned from the croquet luncheon tipsy and with bags full of cherries. The juice had splattered on Michał's shirt after his messy, yet efficient, approach to pitting the fruit. She concentrated instead on squeezing chunks of cherry flesh between her teeth, imagining the ruby syrup oozing behind her lips.

'Sorry to hear it, fella, can't be easy news. When's the boat sail, Michał?' Daddy asked.

'Tomorrow afternoon.'

'Well, you'll stay here the night and put your nose in the manger with us. I'll drive you into Launceston in the morning.'

'That's okay, Mr Grayson. I was just going to hitch a ride to Deloraine and take the Western Line to Launceston later today.'

'I won't take no for an answer. Who knows when you'll be back on Tassie shores – we won't have your last memories of this fair isle being a dirty old train carriage and a bout of bed bugs. What would your good mother say to that?'

'Thank you, sir.' Michał's eyes were on his shoes, his tanned face flushed and his voice cracked.

'Well,' Evelyn said, slapping her hands onto her thighs, 'I have homework to do.'

'Yes,' Daddy said, 'and I have a consignment of chairs to build. Nor, would you get the blue room ready for Michał?'

She nodded mutely while gathering dirty cups and plates.

'The workshop's a right mess, dust everywhere,' Daddy jabbered on, avoiding Thelma's dagger-gaze. 'It'd be worse than the hovel you'd have bunkered down to in Launceston if I let you stay there.'

Michał was already on his feet, helping Evelyn to clear the dishes and they soon found themselves alone in the kitchen, avoiding each other's eyes. Finally, Michał touched Evelyn on her elbow, sensing their time was short. 'I'm sorry, Nora,' he said, 'I'm so sorry.'

She shook her head, shook it over and over. The green scarf tied around her hair came loose and slumped like a dead bird onto the tiles. Evelyn ripped off her apron and ran from the kitchen, down the hall and upstairs to her room where she could cry without him seeing. She propped her elbows on the deep sill of her favourite window and looked blindly to the mountains, tears falling unhindered. *How can this be happening?*

The castellated outcrops of Mother Cummings had been privy to all Evelyn's grief, but she was certain today's was the worst. To have found a kindred spirit only for him to leave. Gone to the other end of the earth. To his glamorous sister with her silken voice. And his sick mother. Her stomach lurched. *What a beast I've been! His poor mother . . . I didn't even ask after her!* Tears spilled down her cheeks.

Evelyn was mopping her face with a handkerchief when she noticed movement down in the rose garden. It was Michał, walking slow loops on the pavers, hands deep in his pockets. She wanted to call out to him, but she hesitated. *He must think me heartless.* A shadow shifted darkly across the scene, and he looked up to see the great wedge-tailed eagle riding the updrafts in elegant arcs high above him. And Evelyn, framed in her window.

Michał's face lightened. He pulled his hands from his pockets and there, fluttering in the breeze, was Evelyn's green scarf. He lifted it to his face, kissed it and tucked it into the breast pocket of his shirt. 'I love you, Nora,' he mouthed to her window, his hand still on his heart.

The eagle winged around the weatherboard house, hooked beak turning to angle curious eyes at the humans below. One high, one low. Too far to touch hands. Too exposed to call out. Turned towards each other but separated. And in a breath, the Tiers ushered clouds down off the highlands, dispersing white in straggly wisps across the countryside.

Chapter 18

Summer 2019

'Dim the lights, would you, babe?' Allira called to Hamish from the dining table where she was polishing cutlery, positioning knives and forks beside napkins and wine glasses.

Hamish scratched his head. 'Seriously? We're not romancing the guy.'

Allira stopped, raised an eyebrow and fixed a glassy stare at her husband.

'Okay, okay, dimming the lights, my mast— I mean, lovely.'

'And I'd prefer you wore the shirt I bought you last week, the one with the navy cuffs.'

Hamish shrugged and started undoing the buttons of the shirt he was wearing. 'I'd prefer you didn't wear that dress, truth be told,' he said, eyeing the low neckline.

Allira plucked self-consciously at the slinky fabric. It was Rae's choice. Last night she had come over to help Allira prepare. They'd shut the door to the bedroom and a pile of clothes steadily grew on the bedspread. Finally, Rae had nodded her approval at the bronze satin slip dress.

'Perfect. Just enough to set him off-kilter, while also flatter-ing him,' she said conspiratorially.

'I don't know, Rae. It's a bit showy.'

'Exactly. We want Justin to suddenly see you, first as an exceptionally attractive woman, but then as an intelligent leader who has what it takes to run the mag.'

'Can't I just do the second part?'

'Trust me, Al, it's all about setting the scene. Now, what are you serving for dinner?'

Allira had always trusted Rae with the finer details. In fact, Rae had always chosen her important outfits: first job interview, School of Journalism ball, first dates and even the clothes she'd tucked into an overnight bag to take with her to the hospital two years ago.

The bronze dress flirted with the light and Allira did a hesitant spin for Hamish. 'Too much?'

Hamish frowned but said nothing. He'd never had much time for Justin.

Allira tilted her head. 'The details are important on a night like tonight,' she said, repeating Rae's reassurance. 'We have to create the right scene, put him at ease, or at least maintain control of his comfort.'

Hamish was bare-chested, his shirt slung over one shoulder. 'Hate to break it to you, babe, but you sound like a sociopath.' He folded his arms, intentionally flexing his biceps, knowing that the dim lights were working wonders for his six-pack. The gym sessions had paid off. It never took him long to turn holiday love handles back to muscle, and he knew Allira couldn't resist it. Her eyes lingered on his bronzed upper half.

'Hey! Unfair. On two counts. I am simply putting my interview skills to good use,' she said as she placed two bottles of Tasmanian pinot in the middle of the table and undid the lids to let them breathe. Hopefully they would sate Justin's robust appetite for wine. Hamish was at her elbow with bedroom eyes. 'Go put a shirt on, you big hippy,' she said, shoving him playfully. 'He'll be here in ten minutes.'

Justin had happily accepted her dinner invitation earlier in the week; in fact, he seemed thrilled to be asked. Allira had felt a pang of guilt at her ulterior motives, but quickly brushed it away, Rae's firm pronouncement ringing in her ears: 'This is the opportunity you've been waiting for!' The opportunity that she didn't realise she had been waiting for.

Allira lit the elegant taper candles. Everything was just as she'd planned it. Instrumental music played in the background, the delicious gruyere souffles (her mother's recipe) were ready to slide into the oven when Justin arrived, the other courses were prepared so that she would barely need to leave the table, and Hamish looked like a Moroccan billionaire who'd just stepped off his yacht. Allira had always been a little baffled by the way her husband's rugged, surfy features effortlessly adjusted to different settings. His height, tanned skin and bright blue eyes drew more than an occasional glance and time had taught Allira that those hungry eyes – belonging to women and men alike – were less admiration or lust, but the expression of intimidation. Beauty paired with confidence was a threatening combination. Did Hamish realise the effect he had? Allira didn't think so, but he had inadvertently developed strategies to warm people to his presence. His affable personality and the way he could set a person at ease within moments were his greatest assets. And Allira intended to use them tonight.

The doorbell rang.

Allira exhaled slowly. This was it. She shaped her glossy lips into a smile and opened the door. Justin stood under the porch light, a dozen long-stemmed roses in his hands. Red roses. *The gall of the man.* His hair was flicked to one side, his posture as nonchalant as ever, but Allira could see from the slackening of his mouth that her dress was having the desired effect.

'Allira, you look . . .' He paused, whether for emphasis or because he was stumped for words she didn't find out as Hamish strode up behind her noisily.

'Justin!' Hamish reached past Allira and pumped the older man's hand enthusiastically before stepping aside. Justin greeted Allira with a kiss on each cheek, while Hamish's arm remained protectively at her back. 'Let me take those for you,' he said as he lifted the roses from Justin's arms. Allira gestured for Justin to go into the living room, then followed Hamish to the kitchen, where he dumped the flowers unceremoniously on the bench.

'I'll put them in water.' Allira narrowed her eyes at Hamish before tending to the discarded bouquet. Justin strolled the perimeter of the open-plan living space and Allira could see that he was taking the measure of her through her pared-back decorating, appraising the dynamics of the room as she'd seen him do with interview subjects. He came to a standstill at the floor-to-ceiling windows, watching the city sparkle as the sun went to bed. He commented on the view as all visitors did, how clear the night, how fortunate they were to behold this vantage of the city and river every day. And the evening carried on in benign decorum to the sound of wineglasses tinkling, muted laughter and violin strains.

Allira and Justin traded stories from the newsroom, remembering how the history-shaping events had unfolded behind the scenes and their roles in deciding how to disseminate news of shootings, celebrity deaths and political scandals. They described the unease that every journalist felt when they opened the paper the next day, having relinquished their stories to sub-editors, those nocturnal creatures who burrowed through words when all the journos had gone home, slapping headlines above by-lines they didn't own. They laughed at the typos, the inevitable 'pubic' events and 'dognuts' for sale at school fairs, not to mention the cadet who had somehow managed to have his restaurant review published with 'bon ape tit' in the first sentence. Hamish kept pace, feeding them tantalising stories of flesh injuries, near misses and domestic altercations from his paramedic rounds. Justin didn't once reject the free-flowing wine that Allira continued pouring into his glass.

While they cracked the burnt sugar of their crème brûlées, Justin asked about Nora. Allira's answer was prepared.

'Nora's been unwell, so I've shelved her story for now,' she said. It wasn't untrue. Nora had caught a terrible cold after her midnight escape. Allira had visited every day that week, lucky to be greeted with a wan smile.

'How did you know?' Nora enquired daily to Allira's gift of Turkish Delight, as she fumbled with the wrapper and then sank her teeth into the chocolate. 'It's been so long since I had this simple pleasure,' she said with her eyes closed.

Allira wasn't sure she wanted to write the story any longer. Her interest in Nora's past was only whetted more with every encounter, but their relationship had changed. When she had visited yesterday, Nora was sleeping and Allira sat beside her for half an hour, not waiting for her to wake, just happy to be there with her. For her. But Justin wouldn't understand that, so she steered him off the scent, telling him about a Dutch family she had tracked down who lived in a cottage at Government House in the state's south, tending the garden.

'My contact was the gardener's son. He speaks of growing up with the Botanical Gardens as his very own backyard, and meeting all sorts of dignitaries – or at least peering over fences at them.' It worked. Justin's interest was piqued and they talked at length about the palatial sandstone and slate house with its seventy-three rooms on the banks of the River Derwent, and what the comings and goings must have looked like to a child living on the grounds. It was a warm, nostalgic conversation; they each had memories of picnicking with family in gardens across the fence from Government House or attending functions in the Gothic Revival-style building that had housed the Crown's representative for more than one hundred and fifty years.

Allira refilled their glasses; she had already cleared the table. Any tension from earlier in the evening had dissipated, and Justin's lithe frame was draped across his chair, one elbow on the table. His stomach was satisfied, and a full glass of wine was in his hand. The clock on the wall showed 9.35 pm and Allira sensed that the time was ripe. Time to make her move before he drained the ruby liquid down his throat and called it a night.

'*Folk* is such a credit to you, Justin. Our city is so much better for it,' Allira began, keeping her voice even, understated. 'Obviously I love working on the magazine, but I wonder sometimes if you know how special it is?'

Justin's cool blue eyes flickered. He gulped his wine but didn't speak.

Allira continued. 'You don't hear the feedback firsthand like I do. I try to pass it on, but you should be really proud. Tasmanians love this publication. That's why it's going so well.'

Justin nodded awkwardly and turned his face to the city lights winking in the distance. Allira saw his jaw clench and he rubbed his chin.

Hamish squeezed Allira's knee under the table.

'It's okay,' she said. 'I know what's happening.' Her stomach was like a washing machine, but instead of shrivelling, her body was energised.

Justin's head snapped back to face her. 'And what's happening, Allira?' he said, his voice a steely coil.

'I know that we're behind on all our bills. I know Katy Driver hasn't been paid.' Justin's eyes were icicles. 'And you're not around much. I get the feeling you're losing interest. Tell me I'm wrong.' Allira's gaze was unrelenting; she was in too deep to backtrack now, so she held fast, just as Rae said she should. *'He'll try to make you feel small, but you're going to have to dig your heels in, girl!'*

Justin sneered. His hands were clasped beneath his chin as he held her gaze. 'I see what's happening here.'

'I don't know that you do. We'd like to make an offer on the magazine. We'd like to buy it, Justin. We'll take it as is, the outstanding debt, everything. You can walk away with cash in hand, and no one will know any different.'

Justin's aquiline nose reddened and his nostrils flared but his eyes remained icebergs. 'You think you could be editor, do you?' His voice was low and measured.

'You know I could.' Allira lifted her chin. 'I already fill in for you – gladly,' she added. She willed herself to breathe evenly, to keep her shoulders square and maintain unflinching eye contact. Her right hand twitched, the one that would ordinarily lift to her face to run a finger along that constellation of beauty spots. Her *tell*. Justin knew the gesture well.

He watched her now, reading her like he had read so many people before. Stoically reaching for her off switch, a way to shut her down. His aristocratic face was smoothed once more, even as he seethed beneath the surface, then he stood abruptly, the chair clattering behind him to the floor. He ignored the noise as his hosts scrambled to stand with him, their faces registering surprise. 'Well, it's been a lovely evening but I must be going.'

'Justin, please, can we just talk it through?' Allira retrieved a cardboard document wallet from the kitchen bench and thrust it into his hands. 'We want to help. Please. At least have a look at this. It's our offer.'

'This was your idea, wasn't it?' he sniped, pointing the cardboard folder at Hamish, jabbing its corner at his chest.

'No.' Hamish pressed his lips into a fine line and wrapped an arm around Allira's waist. 'You underestimate my wife. This was all her idea. To save the magazine, the jobs of your staff, and your arse, man. That folder in your hand means you can walk out of the mag's top job with your head high. People will still respect you. *We* will still respect you.'

Allira didn't trust herself to speak, but Hamish's words buttressed her resolve. He knew her so well.

Justin marched to the door, his expensive shoes tapping sharply on the tiles. 'You're not having my magazine.' He walked out, folder tucked under his arm, and slammed the door behind him.

Hamish and Allira were rooted to the spot, music still floating around them as they listened to Justin's car rev and drive away. A dog barked somewhere and a breeze sent leaves chattering across the concrete outside the door.

'That went well.' Hamish finally broke the silence.

Allira shoved him playfully. 'About as well as expected.' She sank to the floor right there in the hallway, draining her wine glass and kicking off her heels. She rubbed her neck, leaning against the wall, feeling the tension falling from her like chains. A maddening mix of disappointment and exhilaration swarmed in her chest, and she wasn't sure if she wanted to laugh or cry. 'It's weird, I actually feel relief, Hame.'

He sat down on the floor next to her and took her hand.

'It's all out in the open with him now and he can do what he likes with it.' She rubbed the tension from her face, not caring if her make-up smeared. 'At least he took the folder with him. I just hope some small part of him is interested in our offer.'

Hamish kissed her neck, his sandy hair tickling her face. 'Some small part of me is interested in you,' he said, slipping the strap of her dress down her shoulder and continuing his kisses.

'I hope your pick-up lines were better than that back in the day,' she said as she wriggled out of his reach and got up. She began heading to the kitchen, wanting to start cleaning up, then stopped. Stepped back into his arms. 'Thank you for what you said about me.' She stroked Hamish's face, pulling him towards her, guiding him down the hall. 'Perhaps you underestimated me tonight too,' she said suggestively, kissing him on the mouth. She flicked lights out as they went, leading him to the bedroom.

Later, Allira lay in the dark, wide awake, staring at the ceiling. Hamish rolled over, wrapping an arm around her. 'Don't stew on it, babe. Things will work out, you'll see.'

'I wasn't thinking about work, actually,' she said softly. 'It's Nora. I just want to know more about her.'

'That's why you're the journalist,' Hamish murmured.

'Not like that. I mean, why didn't she marry, have kids? Why did she change her name? Why is there no one in the world concerned with her welfare?'

'There's you.'

'She doesn't even know who I am, Hame. She confused me with an ex-boyfriend's sister called Sabine the other day.'

'At least she's letting you in, opening up to you.'

'I guess so. I just wish I could help her.'

Chapter 19

Autumn 1953

Sleep seemed a distant mirage. She was too hot, then too cold. The night was too quiet, the dark too black. Evelyn pushed back her blanket and unplaited her hair, which was pulling at her scalp, letting it fall like a stain across her white cotton nightdress. She walked to the window, seeking the moon, but saw light from Daddy's workshop. And she knew she would find him there.

He couldn't have heard her bare feet on the concrete floor, but he turned. Like he was waiting for her. A single lamp threw a white circle of light on the bench in front of him, feathering to amber, apricot, caramel. Dripping warmth. The whittling tool was still in his hand, the honeyed timber already taking form. Eye, beak, wing. Another wren. She imagined it sitting with the first, on the shelf beside her bed. Two birds from his hands.

'But I have nothing to give you,' Evelyn whispered.

Michał set the bird aside and stood before her, beholding her, his dusty fingers twining in her hair. The musky smell of him and the soapy smell of her. Their mouths were full and urgent, kissing to satiate the gaping hunger that had opened in them, two bodies moving like the crocus flower preparing to give up its precious spice. Opening, opening. His hand slipped beneath her collar, clammy, clutching at the fullness. She pressed his stomach, hip, the crevice that carved downwards. Sweat mingled.

Michał stepped back abruptly, and Evelyn saw him dragging his eyes away from her body shaping the single layer of cotton. She was a gushing stream in a desert. Sweet water she longed for him to taste. His fingers curled into fists and he sucked his cheeks, taking another step backwards. The floor was like burning sand and Evelyn imagined that his tongue was too parched to speak.

Her eyes followed him, mute with knowing. She felt it too. She stooped to retrieve something from the workshop floor: a thick curl of blond timber. So familiar. The medium of her father, and now her – what? What was he? She stepped towards him, reached for his hand.

'I will only thirst for you, I set myself apart for you,' she said, sliding the ring of timber past his knuckle. A breeze rustled in the orchard outside the little workshop window and when she turned, she saw the netting billow, luminescent with moon-shine, and all the trees with their arms aloft, their scarlet fruit plump for picking.

'My beloved,' Michał rasped, 'I am yours until death.' He followed her lead and looped a wooden thread around her finger. And as they kissed again, the thirsty ground was a bubbling spring, their feet splashing in the coolness. Michał's chest rumbled with barely contained laughter, leaping like a deer. It gurgled in her too. Set free. Redeemed.

They fell naked into the pool of their longing. The sweetness dripped. They drank. Rhythm. Breath. Immersion. They were one.

Peter's pa died in a tractor accident on the first Monday of winter. On Tuesday, the little Chudleigh schoolyard was abuzz with gossip, students exchanging tidbits of information, trying to piece together the full puzzle of how it had happened. Evelyn sat a few paces from the huddle of senior students leaning against the weatherboard schoolhouse or sprawled on the grass nearby. She unwrapped corned beef sandwiches and watched the upper primary kids hooting as they leapt and dashed in a vigorous game of dodgeball. The tang of mustard filled her mouth as a flock of black cockatoos flew overhead. Soon, the sombre discussion would turn to her. They would remember that she was the undertaker's daughter and come asking questions, pretending that the information would gain her entry into their exclusive friendship groups.

'What do you know about Peter's pa?' The question was pitched eventually by Eugene, whose parents ran the butcher shop. Evelyn knew every gruesome detail. Possibly enough to make even the butcher boy's toes curl. If it had been just the two of them, Evelyn might've thought about sharing. Surely he would understand what it was like to look at a body with the life drained out. But one of the first things Daddy had taught her as she was growing up was the importance of discretion. To be a trustworthy custodian of information. The solemnity of that lesson wasn't lost on her, even all those years ago.

'I know he was a solid wicketkeeper, and I could see his field of sunflowers all the way up Mother Cummings in summer,' she replied, loudly enough for the whole bunch of schoolyard detectives to overhear.

'Sod off!' one of the kids called, then belched. Eugene just nodded soberly and sauntered away.

Evelyn would really prefer not to have known about Peter's pa. The image of his bloodied body laid out in the hay shed under a grease-stained wool blanket was something that could not be unseen. It had been a rollover. A rusty old Massey Ferguson had careened and toppled when the gentle-mannered war hero and cricket fanatic had wrenched the steering wheel too hard. The slope, an obstinate rock under the front wheel, and the farmer's overzealous manoeuvre had proved fatal.

It wasn't the sight of his chest caved inwards or his disfigured face that had shaken Evelyn up, it was the stench. Daddy had handed her a cloth and a tub of warm water and asked her to clean the blood from his face. She nodded mutely and waited for him to walk away, across the farmyard to the house where he would speak with the family about the merits of a closed coffin in such circumstances. The smell of blood and urine was potent. They weren't uncommon odours in this occupation, but that day, it was like someone had turned up her smell gauge as far as the needle would go, and it was melting her usually cast-iron stomach. Evelyn mopped at his face, breathing through her mouth, or not breathing at all. After a few minutes, she scrambled out of the shed and around the back where she vomited onto the dirt, hoping to expunge the reek from her system.

'I'm sorry you had to do that, Nor. I should've done it myself,' Daddy said on the way home as she gulped air through the window. The metallic blood smell still lingered, mingling with Daddy's aftershave. It was as though he'd spilt the whole bottle over himself, the spicy scent was so thick.

'I'm usually fine,' she said with a swallow. 'Must've been that I know Peter from school.'

But that wasn't the reason, though she was happy for Daddy to think it.

Mrs Pike was ringing the bell for class to resume, her high-pitched voice urging students not to dilly-dally. Evelyn brushed crumbs from her school dress and collected her lunch bag. Poor Peter. He deserved every kindness, not horrendous tales about the way his pa's life had ended. To have survived the war and returned home only to lose a battle with an old tractor seemed very unfair.

Evelyn passed Peter's best mate Jono in the corridor. His eyes were red. 'Please give my sympathies to Peter,' Evelyn said, touching Jono on the shoulder. He was a few years younger than her and a whole head shorter. His petite frame wasn't helped by the fact that his mother refused to buy him clothes that fit, and he was forced to wear hand-me-downs from his seventeen-year-old brother, who was built like a bull.

Jono's bottom lip quivered. 'Should I go see 'im, then? I don't know what to do. Never lost so much as a pet rabbit in my life.'

Evelyn smiled sadly. She'd noticed this before, the fear of what to say and what to do, as though people became different, untouchable, when they lost a loved one. 'Go visit. Peter will want you there. You're his best mate in the whole world!'

Relief flooded Jono's face and his shoulders dropped. 'I will,' he said with a grim smile at Evelyn before running off to class.

After school, Evelyn took the long way home, through Mole Creek to Honeycomb Cave. Mother would still be at a church meeting so she wouldn't be missed for some time yet. She lay in the grass, her forget-me-not blue dress hiked above her knees to allow the delicious sunshine to warm her skin. Through eyelashes half closed she saw light leaping, fracturing. A chill breeze blew, a harbinger of winter. But autumn had been a slow, gentle arch out of Tasmania's warmest months, and Evelyn had been lulled into thinking the summery days might carry on forever. She always felt warm lately, especially when pressed against the earth, cheek to dirt.

She hummed, an evolving tune of all her curious observations: leaves turning, the smell of fresh-cut hay, the perplexing things her school friends said and did. She lifted a leg in the air, pointed her toes and watched her muscles pull taut. She flexed and pointed, again watching the lengthening of her muscles from thigh to knee to calf and ankle, then dropped her leg back onto the flattened grass.

School had become so complicated. These legs that were fun to sprint on, to dance and jump and kneel upon at bedtime to pray were suddenly something else – too long and too stick-like, too shapeless, and too blanched of colour. Suddenly the boys looked at her chest instead of her face, and the girls noticed their furtive glances, whispering behind their hands and pitching narrowed eyes and wounded expressions at Evelyn. And perhaps the most perplexing thing of all was that she didn't give a damn. Not any more. She barely even acknowledged their insults, their sniping. Just smiled dimly and walked away to find quiet and space for her thoughts to wrap around Michał. She only cared what he thought about her ghost-skin, her freckles, her carrot top. If only he were here.

The yearning plunged and climbed. When the girls organised a trip to Mole Creek for ice cream or a swim at Union Bridge without her, she rode her bike out to the caves to burn off the rejection, standing in their ancient gaping mouths and yelling her lonely questions into their bellies. The answers echoed back in icy draughts that pimpled her arms and pushed her stumbling back into the sunlight.

The black scared her. She had never ventured inside, not even when David, preying on his little sister's fear, had scrambled within and minutes later wailed that he'd broken his leg. Seven-year-old Evelyn had pedalled her bike faster than ever before to fetch Daddy, who'd arrived at full throttle in the Buick to find David lounging nearby reading a book, infuriatingly nonchalant and clearly unscathed.

'Evelyn's daydreaming again,' he'd declared dismissively.

Daddy's face had been a study of disappointment, and Evelyn's eyes had stung with hot tears. David was grounded for a week, but she had felt the discipline like it was her own. Why hadn't she just ventured inside to check on her impetuous brother?

Evelyn lifted her face to the sun and smiled at the warmth filling every pore of her face, running like a spark along each strand of her tangled mane of hair. This. This wonderful simplicity was all she desired. A head full of imaginings, daisies nodding beside her, the sun spilt like apple juice down her dress.

The throb of living she found when staring into the inordinately round eyes of a Jersey cow (was there any creature so gentle?), or riding Daphne with her arms flung skyward, her dress flapping against bare thighs. Plunging into the pools beneath Lobster Falls, the water biting her skin, prickling and aching before the shroud of numbness allowed her to dive and float on her back like a starfish, wearing just her bra and school bloomers. If only he was here to do it all with her. When would he return?

She straightened her dress and let her hands fall onto her flattened stomach. There was a changing in her body; she'd known for a while now. Every scent was heightened; every food that touched her tongue had a hundredfold zest. The stench of Peter's pa and the way she had responded, even though she had encountered countless cadavers, though not many so mutilated. Evelyn again counted the days back to when Michał left. Nearly six weeks. Her breasts were sore, swollen too. No wonder the boys at school gaped. And she hadn't bled. Not since he'd gone. The breeze swirled around Evelyn's imprint in the swaying grass and she shivered. What a strange thing it was to behold a life-force sculpting her body from within. She didn't know how she should behave, but there was electricity in her veins. The feeling that caught in her throat was the same as how she felt before setting off on a new adventure, exploring a new landscape.

But the black throats of the caves still greedily swallowed her conflicted sobs. What would she do?

Mother would be livid. She already objected to everything Evelyn embodied, railing against her 'idle frivolity'. Her happiness hinged upon seeing Evelyn married off to a respectable young man with a steady income, the sort who could provide for a family. What 'respectable young man' would want her now, though? Evelyn didn't mind that so much, but Mother would be quick to canvass a life of drudgery as a spinster.

Daddy would sit mutely, nursing the shock of his daughter's pregnancy with few or no words. Where did people find words for such a thing? He would be angry, of course, but the anger would be aimed squarely at himself. The stupidity of letting his daughter roam the countryside with a stranger – a German at that.

Evelyn lifted the wood shaving from beneath the bodice of her dress, tied around her neck with a length of fishing line. It wouldn't last long like this, but she wanted to keep it close. It was too loose on her finger, and she'd been afraid it might fly out of her pocket. The curl of wood used to pledge commitment was so fragile that a light wind would blow it away, and a stomp of a work boot would grind it to sawdust. Was that the reality of what happened with Michał? A meaningless heart's flutter? But the letter he had already sent her was warm, if brief and sounding as though his mama had been looking over his shoulder as he wrote. It would be so easy for him to forget her, to cut her out of his future. Yet he had written to her swiftly, first a postcard from Melbourne and then the letter, with its subtle assurances. He wouldn't be back anytime soon, but his heart was hers. She was happy to wait. Or was she, given the circumstances? How would she tell him that her body was slowly distending with a new life of their creating? The night in the workshop remained untouched. Not a single word had been exchanged about what happened under the watch of the moon and Mother Cummings. It remained an uncommon prism, a rainbow that reached full circle.

Daddy had once pointed to a circular rainbow in the sky, gathering her into his arm. 'That's called a glory,' he'd said as she gaped at all the colours. That was how she stepped around that one night with Michał. Like a holy visitation.

But that night of holding one another, of whispered covenants and moonlit skin had made a vessel of her.

Chapter 20

Summer 2019

It was Allira's turn to sit in the ancient fraying armchair, the only option in Nora's room. Once bright and bold, the volume had been turned down over time, but it curved comfortably around her body, hugging her shoulders and hips, tilting her backwards so her head rested against its back. She could sleep like this. But not today. The dream still scraped against her eyelids if she let them close for too long. She wouldn't stay. Just a few minutes to check in.

Nora was fast asleep on the bed, lying on her side above the coverlet, baby doll cradled in the void between her folded knees and chest. Her breath was ragged. The urge to share the dream with Nora had been strong enough to carry Allira here on a Sunday morning when Hamish was off surfing with his mates. When she'd described the dream to him over breakfast he said it would be worth seeing a counsellor about it and his eyes crumpled at the edges with worry. She agreed, knowing even as she did that she wouldn't. So it seemed like a compromise to come here and tell Nora. *Yes, tell an eighty-one-year-old woman with dementia instead of a counsellor. That makes perfect sense, Allira.*

She let the slant of the old chair catch her head and closed her eyes. The dream was still there, still scratching. She knew she must travel its path again if she were to be free, and her stomach clenched with the acid feelings it stirred. The toxic exchange with Justin just a few nights earlier was eating at her, his seething words still fresh in her mind. Allira grit her teeth, hesitated, then plunged forward. Maybe it didn't matter that Nora was asleep.

'Nora, I had a dream last night. I've had it before but this time it was slightly different.' She opened one eye to see if Nora had stirred, but the old woman's woolly hair was still splayed across her pillow, her breathing dragging her through sleep.

'I was holding a little girl's hand and we walked barefoot down my front lawn. It was one of those balmy days when the breeze was warm, stirring the trees to whisper. Only these trees were whispering the name of the little girl. Not a name I can recall, just syllables of sound that I knew belonged to her. A sweet, joyful sound. We followed the slope of the yard down to a tree shaped like a chalice, with great big leaves and plump figs.' Allira articulated the recurring dream sequence slowly, pausing every so often to make sure she had the details right. The girl with Hamish's features. The fruit. The white glowing dresses.

Allira took a deep breath and checked on Nora's still form once more. This was silly. What was she doing? She imagined someone walking in and her having to explain why she was talking to a sleeping woman with dementia. Yet, even as the thought formed in her head, she could hear Rae's voice from long ago when she was new to Allira's school, egging her on. 'Who cares what other people think? If it feels right, do it!' Rae had been hanging upside down from monkeybars, baring pink thighs and bottle-green bloomers to the playground.

'I will then,' Allira said, hoisting herself up to join Rae, looking at the world from upside down. And she had invited the new girl to her twelfth birthday party – the girl who rarely wore school uniform and was, frankly, rather abrupt and struggled to make friends as a result. Rae had become one of her closest friends and she came to appreciate her no-nonsense manner.

Allira squeezed her eyes shut and continued, recalling the terror she'd felt when the snake appeared. The familiar horror of this repeating nightmare.

'I wanted to wake up before the scales closed around my neck, but my body wasn't letting me. I was standing there in front of the fig tree and it felt like too long. I looked up and a beautiful wren with feathers the colour of a gas flame was flitting above my head, darting and weaving. I turned and realised it was distracting the python, diving towards its face and retreating again. Its wings were a blur, they were moving so fast. Such a tiny thing, it wouldn't have been half a mouthful for this snake. But it was too quick for him. I jumped to my feet and ran. That's when I woke up.'

Allira's hands were shaking, her skin clammy. Why was she so affected by this? It was just a dream.

'I have a bird.'

Allira sat bolt upright in Nora's tapestry chair. The old woman was now sitting on the edge of the bed, the baby resting in the crook of her arm. Her finger jabbed the air, directing Allira's eyes to the little shelf mounted above her bedside table, which held a brown gift box tied with twine, a framed pressed buttercup, and a carved wooden bird.

'You're awake! Ah – how much of what I said did you hear?'

'Over there, dear, on the shelf.' Nora's finger continued stabbing at the wall.

Allira crossed the room and lifted the golden bird from its place. She had noticed it before, but never stopped to look at it closely, thinking it was just a trinket, a mass-produced pretty thing that had caught the old woman's eye once. As she turned it over in her hands, though, she realised that it had been hand-carved by someone with a keen eye for detail. And the bird was a wren, just like the one in her dream, its wings lifted like it was about to take flight. It had a determined look about it; despite the soft, honeyed timber it was rendered from and its sweet musky scent, there was a hardness about it, a steely resilience.

'Michał made him for me. When he stayed in Daddy's work-shop. It's made from . . . oh, what's the name of the stuff . . . you know what I mean, don't you?' Her voice was a frail thread of hope.

Allira sat beside her on the bed. Nora had placed the doll on her pillow and was knotting and unknotting her hands, swaying. Allira handed the bird to her. 'Do you mean wood?' she asked gently.

'Of course it's wood, silly!' Nora snapped. 'No. No. No. Ohh,' she moaned, 'I've got glass in my head . . . it's . . . it's the timber that Daddy ordered from the west, the colour of lemon curd, bits of it floated around the workshop like dandelion seeds.'

Nora touched her nose to the bird's head and inhaled deeply. She stared blankly at the wall, hands moving across the bird's features as if reading it with her fingers. She turned back to Allira, her eyes stark with confusion.

'Huon pine?' Allira tried again. She could see that it sparked something in Nora, and she rubbed her arm, willing her to remember.

'Yes, dear, that's it. How did you know?' Nora lifted the bird to her nose again. 'Ohhh,' she said, 'what a painful smell.' Her eyes were on the wall, reflecting the vacant plane, irises white-washed, her face expressionless.

They sat there for some time, Allira happy to simply wait. Just when she checked her watch and shifted to say goodbye, Nora spoke.

'There was one wee bird for me, and one for you,' she said, turning to the doll marooned on her pillow, stroking its cheek.

'Where is the other bird?'

Nora ignored the question, scooping the doll into her arms and rocking it gently, humming.

'Perhaps it flew into my dream,' Allira said as she stood to leave, looping her handbag over her shoulder.

'What a funny thing to say!' Nora said.

Allira looked down at the crumpled body of a woman nearly three times her age. 'It is funny, isn't it?' She smiled and squatted down in front of her, marvelling at how Nora's often abrasive comments didn't injure her like they used to. She felt lighter than when she'd arrived, despite the confusing exchange. What a strange coincidence to have found the bird of her dream on a shelf in Nora's room. Perhaps she should actually see a psychiatrist, not just a counsellor.

She took Nora's hand and stroked it firmly, running her hand from wrist to fingertips, along her palm and the sun-spotted back of her hand. She had read that physical touch was a special kind of gift to those living in aged care facilities, especially those without family. It reduced agitation and anxiety. Ever since, she had taken time to greet and farewell Nora with an embrace. She wrapped her arms around Nora's shoulders and squeezed.

'You're a very good mother,' Nora responded with watery eyes, leaving Allira to puzzle over what kind of mother the old woman knew her to be.

Chapter 21

Winter 1953

Evelyn pulled stitch after stitch through the puckered cotton with its muted blue stripes. The motion was so familiar, she barely looked at her fingers as they poked and pulled, poked and pulled, creating the lining for the coffin Peter's pa would be laid into. The repetition was calming, and she thought back to a day when she was twelve. It had been a grim, overcast day, the Tiers shouldering storm clouds as she'd pedalled home from school early with blood congealing on the knuckles of her right hand. A shaking Evelyn had to explain that she'd been expelled for the rest of the week because she'd punched Clancy in the nose. Maybe even broken it.

'He stole my journal from my bag and was reading it to everyone at lunchtime,' she seethed, indignant, as Mother's colour rose and Daddy rubbed his moustache, barely concealing the laughter in his eyes. And there was the time she'd had to own up to picking every last bloom from Mother's rose garden to lay across old Mrs Felton's coffin, who had not a soul in the world to attend her funeral but always sung a cheery 'Hullooo!'

and handed peppermints to Evelyn from her picket fence in Chudleigh.

She knotted the cotton and discreetly tucked the ends out of sight before re-threading the needle. Her fingernails were ragged from nervous biting, and her mouth tugged downwards at the corners. None of the scrapes of the past would come close to the news she must deliver soon. Before they guessed. Should she wait until she was further along? Or choose a day when both were in high spirits? Perhaps it would be best to just tell Daddy, and let him break the news to Mother in his own gentle way. She had opened her mouth so many times to upend the truth to him. But he would step out of the workshop for a smoke just as she garnered courage, or start hammering noisily with nail against hardwood, or she would prick her thumb and became distracted with making sure the blood didn't spoil the fabric.

At dinner, her knife dragged heavily through meatloaf, her fork clumsily stabbing at broccoli florets and potatoes. Mother was jabbering away about a letter she'd received from David that day announcing his engagement to the daughter of a merchant banker in Melbourne. It only made Evelyn think about Michał. She tried to smile in all the right places, to look spritely. She wanted to know why David hadn't sent a telegram with the news. And since when did he live in Melbourne? But she hadn't the energy to ask, and Mother was already talking about honeymoons and grandchildren.

'I'll call him after dinner to give him our congratulations,' Mother said between tiny mouthfuls of meatloaf.

Daddy smiled. Evelyn knew it pleased him to see his wife happy, and her parents had made no secret of their view that it would do David well to have some responsibility in his life. Hopefully children would come early in their marriage.

'I'm pregnant.'

The words leapt out of Evelyn's mouth before she realised she had chosen this moment, with news of David's engagement still clotting the air. Silence. Mother's arms hovered, her elbows like chicken wings frozen at right angles, her hands gripping her fork and knife above her plate. She stared at Evelyn. Daddy dropped his hands to his lap, his shoulders slumped. The clock ticked noisily. The wireless was a fuzz of white noise from the kitchen.

This was not how it had happened with Clancy's blood nose or the roses for Mrs Felton. The rage had been immediate then, Mother's demeanour flicking from cold to hot in a heartbeat.

Finally, Mother's knife and fork clattered to the plate and her lips curled. 'Oh no, you don't.' Her eyes were empty buttonholes. 'I won't have you dragging our family name through the sewers.'

'Who did this to you, Nor?' Daddy asked.

'Isn't it obvious?' Mother snarled. 'It was that German rat you welcomed into our home.'

Daddy raked his silvery hair with a work-roughened hand. Evelyn said nothing. *It's okay, it's okay,* she soothed herself. *This is the worst of it. It will get better from here.*

'I'll tell you this, Evelyn Nora Grayson'—Mother picked up her fork and jabbed the air in front of her daughter's face—'you will not undo David's good fortune and you will not unravel this family's honour. You weren't torn out of my womb to dismantle us!' Her voice shook and her throat was corded above the neckline of her housedress. 'You worthless little—'

'Thelm—'

'No, Stanley.' Her nostrils flared, her voice a sledgehammer. 'We've worked hard to get where we are today, and this thankless child with her head in the clouds will trample us into the mud in one fell swoop.' Mother swept an arm, collecting her dinner plate and propelling it like a missile into the wall behind her where it shattered. The sound was like an explosion. Meatloaf, vegetables and shards of handpainted Royal Doulton mashed into a grotesque sculpture on the carpet. She stood abruptly and hurled the matching bread and butter plate at the other wall. 'How dare you!' she screamed. 'Have you no shame?'

She planted her palms on the floral tablecloth, leaning so close that Evelyn could feel the heat of her breath on her cheek. Her voice dropped to a scorching rasp. 'You reckless, selfish creature. You're no child of mine.' She hovered in the splintering silence before calmly sitting back down, lacing her fingers where her plate should have been and coaxing her features back to their usual posts. Her skin was blotchy; the only crack in her statuesque composure. She watched coldly as Evelyn's face crumpled.

Daddy said nothing.

'You must be two months gone,' Mother said, her voice a seam of lava. 'That gives us enough time to take care of things.'

'What do you mean?' Evelyn sat upright, her eyes wide.

'I mean that we will dispose of this pregnancy before it sabotages everything,' Mother said, a vein on her temple pulsing.

Evelyn gasped. The room spun, and her arms wrapped reflexively around her stomach as the wallpaper swarmed like ants and she felt the blood draining from her face. She looked to Daddy with pleading eyes, but he was scrutinising the table-cloth. *Please say something!* But he only looked sideways to Mother.

Dink, dink, dink.

A persistent tapping came from somewhere behind Evelyn and she turned to see a wren drumming his beak against the glass, challenging the brilliant blue reflection of himself to a duel. Or maybe he was attracted to the brilliant last rays of daylight. Daddy looked up and Mother snapped her head towards the sound, arching a brow. They all watched the pretty creature hovering, his wings a blur as he stabbed his beak at the window. His call was a high-pitched trill, a sonorous alarm.

Evelyn could have wept. The musky aroma of Huon pine was in her nostrils and she imagined running her hands across the delicate knife-marks of the two wrens sitting on the shelf in her bedroom. The wrens Michał had given her on days so foreign, so altered, it was like she recalled them through smoked glass.

Dink, dink, dink. The little wren hovered and tapped, his wings a furious blur of activity. He retreated for half a second only to return, beating against the glass at Evelyn's eyeline like he was communicating an urgent message in Morse code.

Evelyn turned slowly back to her parents and the wren abandoned his reflection. She had expected them to shoo the creature away, or to at least comment on the nuisance. But they did neither. 'No,' Evelyn said firmly. 'No, Mother, I won't do that. I will do whatever you ask of me to keep my baby a secret, but I will not do that.' She rose from her place at the table and walked from the room slowly, deliberately. What was the look on Mother's face as she left – relief? Her stiff posture softened ever so slightly, the terse lips slackening. Evelyn walked upstairs to her bedroom and stood at the window, chin cradled in her palms, her eyes tracing the outline of Mother Cummings with the deliberate contemplation one takes to walk a labyrinth. She heard her parents switching off lights and clicking the door closed to their bedroom. They'd been talking about her. Planning. Making decisions about the course of her future. And the future of Michał's child growing within her.

Egg sandwiches, jelly slice, savoury toast, pigs in a blanket. The little hall at the back of the Caveside Anglican Church was positively heaving with the 'bring a plate' interpretations of the congregation's womenfolk. Once a month the churchgoers congregated for lunch, lining up at the urn for tea the colour of the tannin rivers in the highlands. An enormous pineapple upside-down cake was captivating a group of children who tugged at their mothers' skirts for a slice. Evelyn watched as mother after mother ignored their child's pleas, the women absorbed in trading details of the recent coronation. It was the talk of every homemaker even now, more than two months after the Motherland crowned its new queen.

Evelyn winked at one of the children, beckoning him to the table. She sliced the cake and handed each child a piece on a paper napkin. Their faces were alight as they scampered to the other end of the hall and scooted under a table to feast together.

'Thelma, what's this about Evelyn moving away?' The conversation turned to home.

Evelyn braced herself for her mother's response. 'My sister is in need of a helper for a little while, down south in Huonville, and we thought the experience would do her well.' Thelma had clearly rehearsed the line and it came without hesitation. 'Philippa has ten children, you know, and her husband has been poorly with the gout, all while trying to run his busy medical practice. Evelyn will help about the house and free Philippa up.'

'What a sweet thing to give up her schooling for her family,' Agnes Lawrence said, her blue pillbox hat bobbing softly as she spoke. The Lawrences were new to the area and Evelyn knew her mother wanted to make a good impression.

Mother cleared her throat. 'She will continue her education from home, of course.'

The gaggle of women smiled and nodded. 'When does she leave?' asked Bronwyn Hardy, the baker's wife, her face pulled like she'd eaten sour cherries.

'Saturday.'

The collective gasp and exclamation of 'So soon?' was a mirror of Evelyn's own internal monologue. *Why Saturday?* Her head raced. She would have to say a strange goodbye to her class on Friday and then disappear. She would take Daphne for a ride every afternoon this week, she decided. Up into the foothills, those places heavy with knowing. She would say goodbye to the dirt, the gums with their pale grey trunks, the wrens. Her foot wouldn't fall there for at least six months. Half a year. She could barely comprehend what that meant.

Evelyn's arms hung beside her in the circus tent of a dress that Mother had insisted she wear. Not that she was showing yet – not in the slightest. At three and a half months, the slight rounding of her abdomen would be dismissed as the result of a hearty breakfast. The hideous dress ballooned to below her knees and a thick woollen coat cloaked her shoulders and pro-tected against any suspicious glances that might dart towards her décolletage, which even Evelyn conceded was much fuller than normal.

She was not going to her aunt and uncle's. That would have been a dream, but Mother wouldn't risk her being seen there with a swollen belly. After Evelyn's shocking admission at the dinner table six weeks ago, Mother had concocted a plan. It was all finalised over breakfast the next morning. Who would've thought so much could change in a girl's life between mealtimes.

'Everyone will be told you have gone to help Philippa and Trevor with their ridiculously large rabble of children,' Mother said. Evelyn wouldn't have been surprised to see her referring to notes like she was delivering a regiment its orders. 'I will call them today and give them the news so they know to mention you from time to time, and especially if they bump into our set. We will actually travel down south to visit them on the weekend you begin your confinement. I will take photographs of you with the children doing various things to back up the story over the six months that you're hidden.'

'Hidden? Confinement?' Evelyn said.

'I'm getting to that,' Mother snapped, looking down her nose at her daughter, who was still wearing pyjamas and a dressing gown. 'On the drive home, you will hide out of sight so

that anyone who sees us on the road will only recall two occu-
pants in our motor vehicle.'

'Really, Mother? Is this necessary?' Evelyn looked at Daddy,
who was avoiding eye contact, shovelling scrambled eggs into
his mouth.

'You forfeited all rights when you refused my first sugges-
tion, remember?' Mother's voice dropped to a gravelly rumble.
'After that, you will spend your confinement in the workshop.
Meals will be brought to you. There will be a slop bucket for
your business, and after nightfall you will be permitted half an
hour outside, but only on our say-so. And only in the orchard,
as it can't be seen from the driveway. If we have guests or know
the neighbouring farms to be working nights, you will need to
stay indoors.'

Evelyn clenched her jaw at the smug expression on her
mother's face. How she would love to do what she had done to
Clancy's. 'Why in blazes do I have to be in the workshop?'

'We have people coming and going from the house all day
long, and I won't be on tenterhooks because my daughter
doesn't know how to keep her legs shut.'

'But I could just stay upstairs in my bedroom.'

'And leave me having to explain the creak of floorboards
overhead to the ladies at the Croquet Association meetings?
I think not! Besides, you'll be earning your keep by helping your
father with the coffins.'

The association had never met at the Graysons'. But Evelyn
knew The Plan was not only about protecting the family name.
It was Mother's carefully curated vengeance for disrupting her
social equilibrium. 'Certainly, Mother. You know what's best.

May I have a heater, please?' Evelyn replied in a sing-song voice.

Mother narrowed her eyes and cocked her head. 'I will see what I can find.'

'There's one already in there, poss, in the cupboard under the workbench.'

Mother glared at Daddy, her mouth pinched, before she continued, punching out details like a drill sergeant. 'Once a week you will come to the house to bathe. We will ring a bell thrice from the kitchen window if there is an emergency requiring your particular discretion. You will assume responsibility for all mending and darning, and any other household tasks required. As I've already said, you will continue to help your father with the coffins. You are not permitted any visitors. Absolutely no one must know that you are here. No correspondence may be sent out from you, but you will be required to write postcards and letters from time to time, giving the impression you are having a lovely stay with your Aunt Philippa. I will send them to her in an envelope and she will send them back so that the dating and stamps are plausible.'

Mother paused to relish Evelyn's sharp intake of breath. *Half an hour outdoors each day. No rides on Daphne. No crawling onto the rooftop to behold the thickening night. No marvelling at the glistening dew-spray on morning meanders through the paddocks. No letters. No writing to Michał!*

'Do you understand, Evelyn?'

'Yes, Mother,' she replied in the humblest voice she could muster while resolving that she would find a way to continue correspondence with Michał. A brown cardboard box tied with string held his postcard from Melbourne and the fragile wood shaving ring, hidden in the back of her wardrobe beneath rows of shoes. The postcard said he had purchased passage on the *Castel Felice*, a steamship, and thanked Daddy and Mother for their hospitality – a short, cheery line of gratitude on the back of a photograph of Flinders Street Station. It had been fixed to the fridge for a week or so but wasn't missed when Evelyn carried it to her room.

'Philippa has a pile of books for you on the finer details of pregnancy and all the gestational markers. You are to read these, Evelyn. They are your doctor. We cannot risk you seeing a medical practitioner, so you must arm yourself with knowledge of your own volition. I am not your nurse. I have no intention of caring for you like some kind of invalid. You are to be the manager of your own condition, understood? I will be on hand to help with the delivery, and that is all.'

Evelyn blinked. 'I won't have a doctor here for the delivery? Not even Uncle Trevor?'

'Absolutely not. He is much too busy and too far away to bother with this. You got yourself into this mess and you can get yourself out of it too.' Mother snapped her notebook shut and removed her glasses. 'Women have been successfully giving birth since Eve – it's not a new phenomenon. Any questions?'

'Yes.' Evelyn's voice was brittle, a pale blue eggshell. She felt small in the voluminous folds of her dressing gown, like a child waiting to hear how she would be disciplined. 'What will happen to my baby?'

Mother stood to leave, the notebook under one arm against her waspish waist. 'Let's take this one step at a time. No point getting ahead of ourselves,' she said slowly. Her murky hazel eyes travelled to Evelyn's pelvis. 'Your hips are as narrow as a ten-year-old boy's,' she muttered. 'If this baby does survive, I shall find a solution. Never fear, darling, I am most capable at these matters.'

Perhaps it was genuinely meant to reassure her, but her mother's words were like a slap in the face and Evelyn felt the sting even now as she sat in the church hall chewing on an egg sandwich. Perhaps Mother was right; her body was too young and underdeveloped to carry a baby, much less to endure labour and deliver a healthy child.

Labour. The word was loaded. It had the whiff of farm-hands crouched over potato fields. The May sisters had said their ma screamed and hollered all night long when their little brother was born, but Georgie's ma went to the hospital one afternoon and a week later came back all skinny and with a bubby in a basket on the back seat. All of pregnancy was a peculiar chimera. It seemed that women who were *expecting* or *in the family way* went from normal to hobbling around in floaty dresses with peter pan collars. Then something happened behind closed doors and, wham-bam, she was suddenly carting a mewling newborn around with her. In the animal world, it seemed so much less complicated. As a little girl she'd watched the bulls and rams mounting the female of their kind. Evelyn wasn't silly. She'd noticed the subsequent rounding of bellies and then the strange smears of red in the grass around the same time as fresh lambs and calves staggered on new legs. One spring, she saw that a ewe had separated herself from the flock in the paddocks across the road and was pawing the ground, lying down and getting up again. Within an hour she had pushed her lamb into the world and it was feeding at her engorged teats. It all seemed so simple and natural. No momentous event, just a short journey that took some work, and then carrying on with eating grass, with life. Surely it could be simple for her too. She certainly wasn't afraid of hard work.

'Heard you're goin' away,' Tommy interrupted Evelyn's reverie. His shirt was buttoned wrong, a shoelace undone. He dipped his chin, hands in pockets.

'Yes,' she said, sighing. 'Mother thought it would be good for me. You know how it is.'

Tommy grinned. He did. His own mother ran a tight ship. 'You'll be missed,' he said slowly and leaned in closer, 'I didn't say a word about . . . y'know.'

Evelyn smiled. She wanted to hug him for his sweetness. 'You're a good friend,' she said instead, and Tommy blushed to the tips of his ears.

Chapter 22

Summer 2019

What would the dancers think? Allira often wondered how the previous inhabitants of the *Folk* magazine headquarters would respond to the partitioned grey desks, the ergonomic chairs rolling scratch over scratch into the sprung timber floors and the droll conversation about the correct use of parentheses and whether contractions were overused. At first she thought it a lyrical continuation of the space's story, from one artform to another: dance to literature. What was writing if not a kind of dance, a choreography with words brought to life by the creator, taking the audience on a journey? These days, the emphasis on art and expression in her writing sadly fell between the gaps of the wizened floorboards under her feet. The flow, the spark, the beauty, the muse – all those words that described a creative person's drive – had been somehow thwarted, dimmed.

Allira hovered at the doorway to the expansive office space, the morning light glaring through the glass. The *Folk* wall was in upheaval. Most of the clipboards meant to delineate each page of the next issue were in a pile on the floor, the remainder hanging like errant blackbirds on a wire. Justin had his back to her as he stood at the desk of the part-time advertising rep, his hands flailing aggressively. Allira sighed. It was her first day back at work since Justin had walked out of their dinner party. She hadn't heard a peep about the offer.

The lift pinged behind her and the doors rattled open. 'One word, Al,' Rae said as she walked up to Allira, hanging an arm across her shoulders and leaning a bright, smiling face into her ear. 'Mohair,' she whispered. 'Pure, luxurious mohair.' She turned Allira around to face her, showing off a deep purple jumper. 'Got it at an op shop for five dollars, can you believe it?' She did a turn before plonking her handbag on the floor and peeling the jumper off. 'Ironically, Tassie's weather isn't cold enough at the moment for me to wear it for more than ten minutes,' she muttered.

A bemused Allira waited for Rae to put herself together again, then watched her crimson lips form the question she was expecting: 'Have you heard from him?'

Allira grimaced and jerked her head sideways in Justin's direction.

'Lunch, then?' Rae asked. They agreed to meet at noon to talk in detail about all the things that could not be said within the four walls of the converted dance studio.

As Allira made her way to her desk, she imagined that the clack-clack-clack of fingers on keyboards was a metronome beat for dancers to climb in the windows and rush through the door, leaping and spinning among the office furniture, inviting energy and unity through their elongated arms, legs, necks. She had gone to one of the dance troupe's performances once, the group who had used this space to practise, choreograph and hone the expression of their bodies. It was called *Eunoia*. The programme had explained the dual meaning of the unfamiliar word and Allira had ripped it out and stuck it in her journal with all the other words she had collected over the years, like 'lethologica', 'zephyr' and 'mellifluous'. 'A beautiful and healthy mind. Goodwill between a speaker and his or her audience, receptivity,' the programme explained.

There were five dancers, male and female, lithe and lean. They were dressed in skin-coloured leotards and tights, barefoot. The music lifted them at first in a hectic sequence that tested the extremes of flexibility, strength and stamina. Heads flicking through maddening pirouettes, legs pushed beyond flexibility to contortion, muscles quivering under exertion and strain. One by one they faltered. Allira could feel the tension in the room as the audience tried to make sense of what was happening, what to do with the failure. There was a strained murmuring and then the intimate theatre room went black. Silence. Shuffling in chairs. No music.

Then, slowly, the lights came up and the dancers were in the aisles on the tiered steps, each holding a length of cord. They chose willing participants from the audience, one each, and led them onto the stage. The volunteers were self-conscious, pulling at their clothes, smoothing their hair, waving at friends back in the audience. Then the music started. Like water trickling, the sound of a woman's unaccompanied voice melded with the dancers as they moved gently around their partners, joined by the length of cord. Their movements were fluid, restrained, yet masterful. The restriction of dancing in the realm of an unaccomplished partner gave their movements sympathy, and it wasn't long before the audience members were participating, leaning as they did, countering their weight, lifting an arm or kneeling so they could dance at floor level. They watched each other, their bodies speaking without sound, just the round warmth of the female vocalist filling the black room. When the music stopped, the dancers hugged their partners and encouraged them back to their seats. There was no applause; it seemed irreverent. The expression on the stage hadn't been performance so much as engagement, an exchange of goodwill between creator and observer. Eunoia. Allira walked away wishing she had been chosen.

Now, Allira flicked through her calendar – just one interview today. She would spend the rest of her time tidying up the article she had completed on Friday. Allira liked to give her stories a couple of days to rest before she launched into the final edit; the distance gave her clarity to identify her own mistakes. She looked up as Justin marched to her desk, his long arms swinging in a designer pinstripe blazer.

'Let's talk,' he said gruffly. 'My office.'

'Coming,' she sang, as if it were the most natural summons in the world. But she felt the storm of his mood, black as licorice, as she followed Justin into his office, closing the door behind her.

He barely waited for her to sit down. 'The answer is still no. I looked at your offer and I cannot accept.' His eyes were bloodshot, his arms folded across his chest. 'If you have career aspirations beyond what I can offer you here, you should start looking elsewhere.'

Allira's eyes widened, her mouth was dry. Was he trying to get rid of her?

'However,' he continued, 'if you feel you can continue in your current capacity, I won't stand in your way.' He cleared his throat and the stench of alcohol reached Allira's nostrils.

'I . . . I'm sorry, Justin. I never meant to offend you.'

'Why would I be offended by you sneaking behind my back and digging up dirt on me to suit your own purposes?' His acerbic voice was tight with barely contained anger. 'Count yourself fortunate I'm not showing you the door.'

Allira's face dropped. She felt sick. 'I only hoped we could help. How are you going to continue?'

'That is none of your business,' he said, his face red, fists clenched.

Allira stepped backwards, her hand flinching to the row of beauty spots marking her cheekbone. 'You misunderstand my motives, Justin. But I am sorry. I'm so sorry.'

Justin took a deep breath, his face resuming its olive tone. 'Let's not speak of it again.' He turned to face the window where a flock of sparrows swarmed the sky.

Allira went to leave, but he spoke again.

'I've moved your story from the front page of the next issue. It doesn't work. I'm writing a replacement.' He turned glacial eyes on his best writer's face, seeming to take pleasure in the clenching of her jaw.

'You know what's best. I'll tell Dale,' Allira replied. The magazine's only sub-editor would have already laid the story out, ready for print. He wouldn't be impressed.

'He already knows.'

Allira lifted her chin and walked back to her desk, her pencil skirt and fitted shirt squeezing her like that hideous snake visiting her dreams. *What have I done?* She felt breathless, like she was about to stumble in front of an audience that didn't understand the stamina, flexibility and strength demanded of her. The maddening turns, the screaming muscles. She put her earphones in, focusing on the blank screen of her computer and allowing the music to soothe her. Without thinking, she opened a new document and started typing. Stream of consciousness, like she used to do as a teenager, letting the words flow out of her unbridled, not stopping to correct typos or labour over punctuation. Sentences stretched long, unstopping, and jagged red lines underscored more and more words, but she kept typing. It was about Nora.

A nurse had flung open Nora's mint green door with its rudimentary name slot as Allira had approached in the corridor last night.

'I don't have time for this,' she'd muttered before spotting Allira. The staff recognised her instantly as Nora's friend now. 'Oh hi, Allira. I've just spent a good hour trying to get her to put some clothes on so she can come down for dinner.' The stout nurse talked loud and fast. 'Maybe she'll listen to you.'

Allira had peered in, unsure what she would find. Sure enough, Nora was in nude-coloured underwear, humming as she dance-shuffled with her eyes closed, the imaginary music moving her. Tears pricked Allira's eyes. It felt wrong to be watching her, so vulnerable. But Allira didn't want to leave.

'Hello, Nora,' she said to announce her presence, and waited to see what her response would be today.

Nora's eyes opened slowly and suspicion permeated her features. 'Are you going to tell me to get dressed, too?'

Allira gave Nora her customary hug despite the harsh ring of her tone. 'It's nearly dinner time,' she said.

'Oh poppycock! That gruel is inedible, and you know it.' Nora's eyes were bright and clear. 'I just want to dance. What's the harm in dancing?' Her eyelids slid shut and she swayed her hips like she was tracing voluptuous figure-eights.

Allira gulped. She tried to dismiss the idea forming in her mind, but it was persistent. Obnoxiously tempting. She went to the door and closed it firmly before opening a music app on her phone and hitting play on a retro-inspired dance mix. She arrowed the volume up as far as it would go. 'Well, let's do it properly then,' she said, watching Nora's face come alive. Allira undid her fly, stepped out of her jeans, lifted her t-shirt over her head, removed her socks and stood before Nora, her dancing friend.

'Imagine what your mother would say,' Nora said, giggling behind a hand, and closing her eyes again, swaying to this new rhythm. Allira did the same, shutting off her brain to the cacophony outside this energised moment. She caught Nora's hand and they started taking cues from one another, moving up and down, sidestepping and swinging with gentle synchronicity.

'You did what?' Hamish had asked later. 'You got your kit off with your old lady friend?' And he'd laughed out loud.

Allira laughed too because she could hardly believe she'd done it. 'I don't regret it,' she said when the laughter subsided, 'It's like we were on an even plane. I entered into her world rather than expecting her to make sense of mine, you know? It was really . . . it was profound.'

Allira gathered up the memory of that visit, and all the subconscious musings that followed, and continued delivering them through her fingers to her keyboard in a furious stream. She ignored her phone vibrating on the desk beside her, didn't notice Justin striding past her or the pitter-patter of rain as it began to drive against the tin roof.

We are in a womb of your creating. Sing-song. Sway.
Lace and nude. Slack skin and stretch marks. Moving,
slow-turning. Gulping music into thirsty bodies.
Self-conscious? Yes. For a blink. Then it all falls away as
I see you properly, see your naked acceptance of time and
space. But do you know what they are, the where and the
when? In your way, you do. Who am I to correct your
mind's wanderlust? This journey has its purpose – I see
your eyes flutter shut, inviting peace like a balm smoothed
across your skin. You glow. Sing-song. Sway. Lace and
nude. Panties up to your belly button, buttocks jiggling
as you move. We move. I have to hush my nerves, tell
them to play dead. And I take your hand, guiding you to
turn, to wiggle this way and that, the music throbbing as
we cackle in abandonment. Your eyes are crinkly. Hands
fluttering. The walls give nothing away, deadpan faces on a
bodacious happenstance. La-la-la! You sing with eyes shut.
Broad smile, infecting me. We dance faster. Harder. Arms
lifted, shaking chests, rolling shoulders.
When the music stops we paddle in the silence, we hug.
Skin on skin. There are no words. It seems irreverent. I just
walk away. Pull on my jeans as you go back to clucking

over your doll. I'm thinking. Bubbling. Chewing. Lacing shoes. Suddenly I know that I've been given a second chance. I've been chosen from the audience to stand nervously before others and eventually respond to the dancer with her sinuous movement. Moves that perplex me, but entice me just the same. The invitation and the response. Back and forth and up and down. Turning me inside out. You are my eunoia.

Chapter 23

Spring 1953

Dear little Evelyn Nora,

*My darling niece! I call you little, though you are now
a woman, a woman entering motherhood. I know the
circumstances aren't of our choosing, but seek out the beauty,
sweet niece, as I know you will. We haven't spent much time
together through your childhood, not nearly so much as
I would like, thanks to this husband of mine with his heart
harnessed to his medical practice and all his patients. But
I know you to be a charming person who engages with the
world wholeheartedly. Don't let that go. Embrace it all
the more as your body changes to accommodate the little
one growing within you. Remember his or her innocence
and vulnerability and potential. Allow yourself to dream of
who they will be. It is a mother's special privilege to give
herself to her child, and that does not have to begin with
birth. It begins with the mere idea of a new child.*

*I hope these old books will help you prepare and
make sense of all the strange adjustments and stages you*

will face. Don't be afraid of them. God made us the more robust sex (don't tell Uncle Trevor I said such a thing, or your father!) with good reason. You are more than capable of pregnancy, labour and motherhood. You are young, yes. But that gives you more energy, more propensity for healing, more flexibility and strength. Harness them all, my lovely one. Fear only ties us in knots. I will pray peace on you, whatever you face.

You know I ramble on, and I am trying to keep this brief, but I didn't have the chance when you were here to whisper in your ear the words I wanted you to hold. This way, of course, you have them to read over and over.

I see the way my dear sister looks at you, the way she speaks to you. I gather you receive it as a harsh rebuke of your condition, and understandably so. Permit me to show you another way to consider it. Fear is a fickle thing. Sometimes it renders us a trembling, incapacitated mess. Other times it puts the fight in us and we lash out, even at the ones we love the most. Your mother loves you, Evelyn, more than you might know. Her own hurts prevent such expression. And I'll say no more on the topic, but to say show her mercy, the mercy you wish to have extended in your own direction.

I bless you, Nora, I bless your body, I bless your baby and I bless your future.

With all the love the world can hold,
Aunty Philippa

The letter was tucked within the cover of one of the books she gave Evelyn, wrapped discreetly in brown paper and nestled with her valise in the boot of the Buick. Evelyn sighed. How she wished her 'confinement', as Mother had taken to calling it, could indeed be endured within the rambling family home of her aunt and uncle, with all their rambunctiously delightful children. She knew why it couldn't. But Aunty Philippa's mother hen warmth was as redolent as the perfumed writing paper on her lap, and how she yearned for it. To be part of a family with so many members that what one daughter said and did and wore wasn't under constant scrutiny.

Evelyn folded the letter and tucked it back into the book. She'd read it every morning since they returned from the weekend at Huonville, with her crouched uncomfortably in the footwell of the back seat. It was the only letter she had. There'd been nothing from Michał since she asked Daddy to secretly mail the letter revealing her pregnancy. *You are to be a father!* she had boldly written, hoping that he would be thrilled with his new title. What she hadn't written was that she was convinced it was a boy, a sense she couldn't explain. She'd waited and waited, and a chime of doubt had wormed its way into her head. What if he was angered or embarrassed by the letter? What if this news was more than he could handle with a sick mother and a sister to care for? *That's probably it.* Or did he get it at all? Mother's pinched face declaring, 'No correspondence!' flashed in her mind. But Daddy would have delivered it. She trusted him.

Evelyn leaned back against her bed, wrapping a woollen blanket tighter around her shoulders. The days were thawing.

Spring was blooming, but the workshop had been an uncomfortable bedroom. She rubbed the orb of her growing stomach. More than six months along now, and she was visibly carrying. 'You're not very big for your gestation,' Mother had said the last time she brought her a meal. Evelyn tried not to linger on the harsh observations that Mother doled out, like spoonfuls of bitter medicine. That was why Aunty Philippa's letter had become a sacred part of her daily routine. That, and watching sunrise and sunset, taking walks through the orchard at dusk and sometimes sneaking out in the night to lie in the dewy grass. Her legs were restless for the ground, her whole body hungry for the brush of leaves and grasses, the smell of gum trees and cow dung, the sound of bees. She wanted to discover it all afresh for her baby, to be his tour guide to a world that kept giving.

Evelyn closed her eyes and imagined wrapping her baby tightly against her chest, the way some tribal women did, perhaps even those who'd once walked this land. Mrs Pike's eyes had been sad when she told the class of the Pallittorre people, who called this land beneath the Tiers their home when it was still bogs and bushland, before disease and conflict with first settlers decimated their population. *I will tell him that too*. She wanted him to know all the stories embedded in the land. Evelyn imagined the weight of his little body against hers, his skin against hers rather than within her. And in her mind, she rode the five-kilometre stretch between home and school, speaking to him all the way, explaining the sights to him as they went. The *maa-maa* of gangly new lambs before they found their mother's teat and tugged aggressively for milk. The daffodils lining the road's verge, sheep's wool caught in barbed wire making a line of white bunting. She would slow at the township, checking for smoke plumes from each inhabited cottage. No smoke in winter guaranteed a neighbour's knock on the door by midday with offers of kindling and chicken broth. She would stop at the pond near Big Tom's place to hear the chorus of frogs chirping their cheery anthem into the new day. Perhaps they would be there as Big Tom was out on his verandah, clanging a saucepan with a metal spoon and singing, 'Oh sheep-oh, oh lamb-oh, come 'n' get yer milk-oh!' Half-a-dozen long-tailed lambs would come scampering onto the deck for their daily warmed milk from the soft-hearted man, who reminded Evelyn of Tweedledum or Tweedledee. He would nod at her, but his words were for the lambs, never for human sorts. The girls at school used to say he lived off possum meat and spent all his money on milk and feed for his growing flock of orphaned sheep.

Evelyn would pull the wrap down a little so her child could feel the bracing air. The outdoors made her feel alive. She didn't even mind the sting of cold mountain air on her lungs, expanding them, scraping them clean. She just pedalled harder until the warmth came. Look, a plover, a kookaburra, a magpie; she would point out the birds and their calls, their dominions. The anxious *ke-ke-ke* of plovers protecting their young, and the lone kookaburra always sitting at the end of a rusty plough, his alien progeny.

Evelyn opened her eyes. She could barely believe she was carrying a real baby, let alone imagine holding him in her arms, caring for him, lifting him to her breast to suckle like the calves she saw in the paddocks every spring. She reached for another of the books from Aunty Philippa. It was a textbook, a week-by-week account of pregnancy with line drawings of female anatomy, as if detailing a new specimen of jellyfish. In fact, it looked like something Uncle Trevor might have studied when training in the medical profession. When Evelyn had first picked up the book, months ago now, she wondered what her aunt had been thinking by including such a brutal rundown of maternity. A paragraph in, Evelyn had been ready to stoke a fire with it. She'd rifled through the pages, intending a quick, non-committal perusal when a note dropped into her lap: *Week six: your baby is the size of a peppercorn.*

The writing was in her aunt's bold, looping hand with fine flourishes. Beneath it was a miniature watercolour painting of a pile of peppercorns. Evelyn skipped ahead to the next chapter and the next. Each section contained a note with the same format: a comparison of her baby's size with a fruit or vegetable and a hand-painted illustration below. They were colourful and whimsical. Evelyn imagined her aunt seated at the kitchen table, children running around her, interrupting her to ask for food or where their gumboots were or could they do some painting too? And she would reply happily, stopping to hug away tears or listen to a grievance, before picking up her paintbrush again to finish all of the little pregnancy cards. Every week, Evelyn pulled a new card from the book. There was joy in her heart, for the love her aunt had gone to the trouble of expressing, and the wonder that her baby had grown from a cherry to a fig to a lime in size.

Today, the card she pulled out revealed a swede, the colours blending from deepest purple to a custard yellow. *Week 28.*

She spread her hands across her stomach, her chest light, and dipped her chin as far as she could manage. 'You hear that in there? You're the size of a big swede!' The baby responded with a firm boot beneath her ribs and Evelyn giggled with giddy delight, wiggling her toes and hugging her stomach. 'We're going to be okay, aren't we?' she whispered to her navel. 'At least we have each other.'

Chapter 24

Summer 2019

Allira strapped Nora into the passenger seat of her car. Mercy Place had a deep clean of its rooms scheduled today and Sally had suggested taking Nora for a drive.

'It could be swapping one stressful situation for another, but Nora hasn't seen much of the outside world since she was admitted,' Sally had said, her brows knitting together. 'Apart from her Houdini performance, of course.'

The timing couldn't have been more perfect. Hamish was working the weekend and Allira was keen to put as much distance between herself and her work situation as she could. Geographical distance – even better. Rae offered to catch up for lunch, but Allira knew that her bouncy bestie would want to dissect the week's happenings, word by juicy word, and she was all talked out.

'How does that feel?' Allira asked Nora, checking that the seatbelt was positioned comfortably across her chest.

'Very good, thank you, dear.' Nora's doll was dressed in a short-sleeved romper and sunhat, tied with a bow under its chin. Nora smiled widely at the expansive sky through the windscreen. 'It's going to be a marvellous day,' she said. 'Now, where are we going?'

Allira squatted beside her, the open car door resting against her shoulder. Her hair fell in a glossy sheet down her back, and she wore a light cotton dress. It wasn't her style at all, something Hamish had bought her, but she wanted to feel feminine and free today. She took Nora's hand and squeezed it warmly. 'We're going home.'

They drove with the windows down and music blaring, the same 1950s dance mix that had them jiggling in their knickers the other night. Allira kicked off her sneakers to drive barefoot, her attention flicking between the black highway west of Launceston and Nora's face in her periphery. She was as placid as the baby doll in her arms. The wind lifted and shook her mass of grey curls, but her face remained serene, eyelids resting closed every so often, but eager to take in all the landmarks on the way.

They stopped at a roadside supermarket in Deloraine to gather supplies for a picnic lunch of sandwiches and apple juice. Allira was on her way to the counter when she noticed Nora slipping a Turkish Delight under her doll's wrap. Nobody else was watching. Nora walked to a bench to sit down and wait, rocking the doll gently as if nothing had happened.

'My . . . my grandmother has very bad dementia and she has developed a habit of taking chocolate bars when we're at shops,' Allira explained to the checkout assistant as she scanned the sandwiches. 'Can I please pay for the Turkish Delight I saw her slip into her doll's blanket rather than upset her by taking it from her?'

The middle-aged woman smiled kindly. 'My aunt has dementia and developed all these habits that are completely out of character. It's hard to see, isn't it?'

Allira nodded mutely.

'Of course, honey, I'll just look up the code.'

In the car, Nora pulled out the Turkish Delight and fiddled with the wrapping, closing her eyes as she sank her teeth into the first mouthful.

'Where did you get that?' Allira asked.

'At the shop, while you were buying your things,' Nora replied. 'You should try one – it's heavenly.' Her lips were coated with chocolate.

Allira manoeuvred the car around the top Deloraine round-about, accelerating onto the road with signs pointing to Mole Creek, Chudleigh, Dairy Plains and Caveside. The car zipped past the big, rusted yellow teapot made from a grain silo, the old site of the Bendigo Pottery factory. They pressed onwards into ever-greening countryside. Nora sat forward in her seat, clutching her doll to her chest and Allira turned down the music. She wanted to be alert to this hallowed place in Nora's history. They passed a football oval with sheep grazing, and the turn-off to Montana Falls, a hazelnut grove, ploughed paddocks and lakes like sky-mirrors. Copses of bush merged into flat green pastures dotted with Friesian cattle, their noses to the grass. Farmhouses were set back from the road which hurtled past like an arrow.

'Lobster Falls,' Nora murmured, straining to see out Allira's window, 'and Chudleigh straight . . .' Nora's voice dropped to a whisper as the mountains opened up before her, a cerulean embrace. 'The Tiers . . .'

'Are you okay, Nora?' Allira asked it three times before Nora turned her way. *Is this too much for her?* She second-guessed her decision for the umpteenth time that day. The landscape must have been swollen with history; how could she possibly know what painful memories were patched into the streets and streams and laneways? 'Would you like me to pull over for a bit?' she asked as she slowed through the township of Chudleigh, past the General Store with its expired petrol pump and lavender hedges. She went to take the road's natural bend to the right.

'That way, silly.' Nora stabbed a finger at the smaller road straight ahead, roughly clutching at Allira's elbow. She quickly corrected and turned the car onto the road that looked like nothing more than a side street, lined with weatherboard cottages and rundown chook sheds.

The wind buffeted through her window and Nora jabbed at the button to wind it down further. The road was empty, and Allira crawled along, forty kilometres on the speedo. Nora squeezed the doll tighter still against her chest and tilted her head towards the gaping window. The pure air was a tonic, it seemed, and Allira sensed her plunging deep into the past. The road zigged, then zagged, then zigged again before opening up, gently undulating.

Allira imagined Nora pedalling her bike on this very road, fiery hair wrestling with draughts, knotting, weaving; a net for insects and dandelion seeds. Her hands might have been flung skywards, fingers skimming the powderpuff clouds. This road that knew the soles of Nora's feet, the tread of her tyres. This part here, where she had probably pedalled with her bottom off the seat, putting all her weight behind her quads as they powered uphill. Then the coasting, the clunk-clunk of railway sleepers that made up the little bridge over Cubits Creek that would have been so slippery in winter. The flat, rambling stretches where she imagined Nora talking to bewildered new lambs and craning her neck at eagles. She saw Nora a thousand different ways. Dancing in that uncut straw, dancing with her Mr Darcy, sashaying patterns into the gold. Over there, leaning against the dairy wall, there she was, fluttering her hands at Heathcliff, beguiling him with her wit. By the duck pond there, look, look, pushing the rowboat out amongst the reeds to lay her head on Romeo's lap as he stroked her hair. But where was Nora's Michał?

Allira came to an intersection, slowed, waiting for Nora's directions. She was nearly at a standstill when she swung the wheel towards the old woman's rooted attention, turning left at the shed and past a line of pine trees.

'Are we close?' Allira tried to make conversation. 'We don't have to keep going, Nora. We can turn back, find somewhere to eat.' A little cream weatherboard church came into view. *I'll stop there*, Allira thought. It would be a nice spot for their picnic. She pulled into the churchyard, parking on the grass and pulling on the handbrake.

Nora had turned in on herself, rocking the doll as much as she was rocking herself. Her eyelids were heavy and she looked as if she might sleep.

'I'm just going for a little walk around. Would you like to come?' Allira received no reply, so she set out alone to walk the perimeter of the church with its steeply gabled roofline and minimalist landscaping; it looked as if it had been plonked in the middle of a paddock. She rounded the back corner of the modest building and the vista unfolded before her: Mother Cummings tall and imperial to her left, and the Great Western Tiers tumbling the remaining breadth of the scene. It reminded her of something – a painting she'd once seen: 'Spirit of the Plains' by Sydney Long. A lone woman or girl, clothed in nothing but her red-brown hair draped over one shoulder, pastel moonlight, and golden grass to her knees. The painted girl played a flute as she walked against a backdrop of silvery gums. A flock of brolgas brayed and flapped in thrall to the subdued enchantress, their awkward necks and beaks stretched forward and skyward and doubled back towards her where the moon silhouetted her face. Allira had stood in front of that painting at the Brisbane gallery for longer than all the others, even the visiting Monets. There was a thrilling tension about the red-haired, female pied piper stepping barefoot through a softened Australian landscape, a place she trusted her vulnerability to. Looking at Mother Cummings and the Tiers felt like déjà vu of seeing that painting of the girl with her brolgas – the girl she imagined Nora once was.

Allira kept wandering, past the adjoining hall and the cement brick toilet block addition. Calves across the fence eyed her with disinterest from their spot in the shade of a Blackwood tree, among rusted farm ploughs. There was a movement on the road and Allira's heart quickened. She jogged into the open. Nora wasn't in the car. She ran, seeing the old woman's stooped figure walking decisively along the middle of the lonely road. Allira picked up her pace, sprinting towards her, grateful that she'd chosen sneakers instead of thongs that morning, and praying that a car didn't come hurtling headlong around the corner up ahead. She reached Nora and linked arms with her, breathless. 'Where are you going?'

'Home, dear. You said you were taking me home, but you stopped a tad early.'

The older woman's face was determined and Allira walked with her for a few minutes. As they reached the top of a long gravel driveway lined with ancient oak trees, Allira caught Nora by the shoulders and stopped her from continuing straight down the private road.

'Nora, someone else lives there now.' A shudder of confusion ran across Nora's features and Allira took pity. 'This is where you lived, is it?' She smiled and brushed a curl of hair from Nora's eyes. 'Is this where your baby lived too?'

Nora's eyes dropped to the plastic face of her doll in its blue romper.

It wouldn't hurt, would it? Surely the new owners wouldn't mind us walking down the driveway to see the place, maybe a stroll through the garden? It might even be therapeutic. 'Come on then, let's take a quick look,' Allira said, linking her arm with Nora's once more and stepping towards the dappled driveway. Acorns crunched underfoot and Allira imagined Nora playing hide and seek among the hefty trunks of the oaks or collecting the nuts to draw faces on the slippery surfaces.

Nora suddenly stopped dead in her tracks. They had come to the end of the driveway, which opened onto a teardrop-shaped turning circle in front of a grand old Victorian-era homestead. Entry to the white weatherboard house was through a wrought-iron gate into a walled rose garden. Allira guessed that the front door was at the end of the path beyond her view.

'Where's Daddy's workshop?' Nora's voice tremored. 'The orchard . . .'

'What is it, Nora? What's the matter?' Allira wrapped an arm around her shoulders.

'They're gone. Where have they gone?' The arm holding her doll hung loose, threatening to spill it onto the gravel.

'Can I help you?' A head poked above the brick wall and Allira hurried over.

'Hello there, I'm so sorry for the intrusion.' She proffered a hand across the wall, glimpsing more of the stunning rose garden. 'I'm Allira, and this is my friend Nora. She lived here many, many years ago and we thought it might be helpful to revisit such a familiar place.'

The woman, who wore an apron and a terry towelling hat, shook Allira's hand, smiling a gap-toothed smile. 'I'm Heather, and you're very welcome.'

'What have you done with Daddy's workshop, and the orchard?' Nora glowered.

Heather looked at Allira and back to Nora. 'That's interesting you ask about the workshop.' She rested her elbows on the brick wall, a pair of bright pink gardening gloves nearby. 'My husband and I have had this place for about ten years now, and we heard from the previous owners – and a few of the locals confirmed the story – that there was indeed a workshop over there where our new garage is.' She pointed over their shoulders at the freshly painted metalwork, lattice, and corrugated iron roof. 'It burnt down in the bushfires of 1953 to '54 apparently and took out the orchard as well. It was a wonder the embers didn't reach the house and gobble that up too.' She paused, trying to catch Nora's eye. 'What did your daddy build in the workshop, love?'

Nora rocked her doll, soothing him, humming. She wouldn't look at Heather, her body angled away. 'We'd better go now; he needs his sleep. Come along, we'd better go,' she said, tugging at Allira's arm.

'Okay, Nora. You start walking and I'll catch up to you.' Allira smiled reassuringly and waited until she was out of earshot. 'Do you know anything else about that fire?' she asked Heather.

'They were a well-known family, him an undertaker and carpenter, very much involved in the community. But after the fire, they packed up and left. Some say there was a young one who died in the blaze, but I wouldn't know about that. These parts are riddled with gossip and wardrobe skeletons, you know.' She flashed her gappy teeth. 'Wait on . . . there's a scrapbook I found belonging to them and it had clippings about that fire. Would you like to see it?'

Allira glanced towards the drive, but Nora hadn't moved far. She was picking acorns from the driveway, polishing them on her sleeve and dropping them into her pockets like misshapen marbles. 'Yes, please.'

Heather hurried inside. The house was freshly painted, the pavers around the rose garden's central water feature newly laid, yet it had a sense of sympathy with the surrounding landscaping. Dormer windows protruded from the roof, and Allira wondered which one had been Nora's room. She would have chosen the one above the rose garden, surely, the one that saw the comings and goings and with the best view of the Tiers.

'Here it is, love.' Heather bustled along the pathway beyond the walled garden, waving a book over her head. Nora was still within eyeshot, polishing acorns, her pockets bulging. The scrapbook was covered in wrapping paper of white roses, leaves and golden wedding bands. The pages were curled and smeared with dirt and grease that obscured elegant, looping handwriting with a bold underline and date: *Thelma Grayson, 1952.*

'Forgive the condition. We only found it recently when we finally replaced the oven, one of those freestanding ones. We hadn't actually been using it. The kitchen's enormous – it already had a newer oven. I was rather attached to the old ceramic stove, even if it was just for looks. Anyway, this had slipped down the side, all but forgotten for six decades, I suppose! Makes for interesting reading.' Heather barely drew breath, her words coming out as one long stream. She stepped outside the gate into the turning circle, holding the scrapbook out to Allira. She hesitated. 'Do you really think your friend was part of this family?'

Allira was nodding before Heather finished the question. 'I do. I think what you're holding could bring closure to my friend.' She swallowed and licked her lips. 'If you would be so kind as to lend it to me, I will return it in the same condition and promptly.' Allira felt lightheaded from holding her breath and from the possibilities whirring through her head.

Heather nodded. 'Sure. You'll tell me all about it? Whatever you discover, you'll come back and tell me about it?'

'Of course, you will be first to know. I owe you that. Here, I'll leave you my business card.' Allira rummaged in her handbag and dropped her voice. 'But this is just between you and me, okay?' Allira knew Heather's sort. The whiff of intrigue and the promise of fodder for her next coffee date would get her over the line.

Sure enough, the woman released the scrapbook into Allira's open hands, her eyes shining. Allira thanked her and hurried to catch up with Nora, who heard her coming and swung around, juggling the doll with hands full of acorns.

'Daddy . . .' Nora's voice was a pale pink thread sewing together pretty fabric scraps of her past. 'He understood me. I . . . I thought he understood me.' She stopped. Her eyes had that faraway look of swimming someplace she could not return from, the memories slapping and surging. They coursed through her nose, her throat, her eyes, sucking and gurgling. She gasped, coughed. Eyes snapped open; green lifeboats. 'It had to burn,' she blurted, brooding. 'She made it a prison. It had to burn.' The acorns crackled and snapped in her hands, her arthritic fingers crushing them against her palm until they dropped into the mottled leaf litter.

Chapter 25

Spring 1953

Evelyn's cough was like the bark of an angry dog. The windows were steamy and Daddy's little heater with its two orange bars was pulled close to her bed, although its warmth eluded her. She had barely moved for a week, buried beneath countless blankets. The overturned fruit crate held a tall cut-glass jug with a mix of lemon juice, honey and apple cider vinegar under a muslin cover weighted with amber beads. Her body ached and she could not get comfortable. She was too hot, too cold, too cramped, too agitated. By day she dozed and by night she lay wide awake, her only comfort the fluttering kicks and squirms of the baby growing within her.

Daddy's workshop had become a peculiar clash of masculine and feminine. His tools hanging on the wall, the hefty work-bench, the curls of timber and sawdust carpeting the concrete floor, offcuts leaning against the wall – all of the familiar workshop activity contrasting with a clothes rack drying Evelyn's underwear, a trunk trimmed with floral wallpaper stuffed with her clothes, books and journals, and a screen of ruched curtain fabric behind the door giving her a place to dress and toilet. Daddy hadn't said a word, but the impingement on his space and the lack of privacy added to Evelyn's shame. He tried to do his work outdoors, the sanding and planing, the coats of shellac and the loud hammering. But sometimes a deadline encroached as the Tiers pressed inclement weather down onto the farmland, the air damp and heavy. On those days, Evelyn endured the scraping and sawing, and she opened the windows and door to expel the stench of chemicals that made her head spin.

The cough racked her chest again, tightening the muscles around her stomach. How must that feel from within, she wondered, for your whole womb-world to be clenched and shaken? Evelyn tried to bite the coughs back, to let them out gently. But there was no stopping their severity. 'I'm sorry,' she rasped. 'I'm so sorry.' She sipped some of the remedy that Mother delivered to her bedside yesterday. She hadn't visited for three whole days, and her face had shown alarm when she saw Evelyn crumpled beneath the covers.

'You've been wandering outside in the cold again,' she said.

'No, Mother. The nights are cold in the workshop. I can't get warm.' Her voice was listless, her lips pale, and she barely opened her eyes.

Mother had come back with a pile of blankets, a hot water bottle and the lemon drink.

Evelyn rolled over to find the Huon pine wrens, as she always did when her heart plunged heavily in her chest. From the very first day of her confinement, they had been propped on the window ledge above Daddy's workbench, where they wouldn't be knocked over and Mother would be less likely to take interest. She stayed away from 'the dirty side of Stanley's business', only taking charge of the paperwork. The moonlight was like a rain shower on the wrens' bodies and she could imagine their merry heads shaking droplets across their feathered backs, flirting with light and water. The bird on the left had her wings raised, her chest puffed and head jaunty as if she was about to take flight; she was the one Michał had given her when he'd said goodbye the first time. The wren on the right was tender, her head tilted towards the other, wings tucked away, feathers fluffed.

It would be romantic to consider them a rendering of two lovebirds: Michał and Evelyn, one proud and protective, the other demure and gentle. At first, that was how she positioned them, with the second bird tucked beneath the wingspan of the first. But in time she realised that the two Huon pine wrens were his interpretation of the girl he loved. Two sides of her. One with her wings spread, ready to launch into the limitless sky, the other nestled and nurtured, stilled in the knowing that her spirit would not be imprisoned. That Michał could intuit the essence of her as his rough hands curved around the carving tool and cut into the buttery Huon pine was what Evelyn saw when she gazed at the wrens on the windowsill.

Still, his letters didn't come. She couldn't shake the sense of him somehow caring and approving from afar, but her mind naturally slipped into bleak prophecies. *Perhaps his ship didn't make it. Maybe his family disapproves of me. Is he ashamed, or not ready to be a father?*

Daddy dutifully delivered her letters. At first, he had refused. Evelyn thought it was because he didn't want to go behind

Mother's back, but one day, as he hammered a dovetail joint into place, he'd snarled about the 'vermin' who slept with his daughter and then skipped the country.

'Daddy!' Evelyn had gasped.

He kept hammering.

'I love him!'

She was surprised by the strength of the words that tore from her throat. The hammering stopped and Daddy eyed her suspiciously.

'How do you know that, Nor?'

She didn't need to craft a response; it was already there, sitting on her tongue. 'I know because it was like we knew each other before we met, Daddy. He is gentle and funny and generous and kind. He spoke to me like he was on the edge of his seat, waiting for my every thought and word.' She stopped, checking herself. 'Michał is so different to me, Daddy, in a way that fits us together.'

Daddy's eyes were far away, swimming into the past. What was keeping him there? Evelyn wondered if he'd been carried away to the Hobart dance hall where he'd first spied an eighteen-year-old Thelma, glossy hair rippling down to her svelte waist. Did they talk into the night with a magnetism they couldn't explain? Did she beguile him in the same way that he grounded her? Were they consumed with one another, every waking moment spent in worship, nervously hoping the other felt the same? He had looked down at the dovetail joint he was working on, rubbing his thumb against the two pieces of timber that fit snugly together. He'd nodded sadly without looking up, and Evelyn truly thought he must have known what it was to be in love.

Another coughing fit left Evelyn gasping for breath, jolting her from the memory. Her forehead was slick with sweat and her ears rushed with the sound of her own heartbeat, or was it Daphne galloping circles in the paddock? She lay flat on her back, panting, and tried to concentrate on breathing, fingers stretched across her rounded stomach waiting for the familiar jab of an elbow or heel. The two wrens glowed in the moonlight, Mother Cummings a blackened cut-out behind them. She waited. An owl called across the orchard and the leaves rustled in reply. But there was no movement from Evelyn's distended stomach tonight. She waited all night for the flutter of life and finally fell into a torturous sleep as light crawled into a new day.

There was a scratching at the door. Evelyn stirred, rubbing her eyes. Her teeth were the velvet of days without brushing, and she could smell her armpits and other fetid odours. How many days had she lain here unwell? There were all kinds of brown-bottled remedies on the fruit crate at her bedside, and a hot water bottle lay on the floor next to a tray with an untouched crust of bread and a bowl of broth. She inhaled deeply and savoured the way her breath slipped easily down her windpipe, no longer reefing at her chest like fishhooks.

Scretch-scretch-scritch. The scraping again. *Yee-owl!* Evelyn manoeuvred herself from the bed, waiting for the fuzzy brain stars to dissipate before walking gingerly to the door on bare feet. It was Marmaduke, his white whiskers springing as he howled loudly at his mistress. The limp body of a field mouse sat beside him and before Evelyn had the chance to shoo him aside, the agile cat scooped the rodent into his mouth and carried it to her bedside. He dropped it on the tray beside the bread and broth.

Every muscle in Evelyn's body dragged downwards, the effort of the few steps to the door and back wearying her so that she wanted to plonk herself back on her bed. The grey offering was a lump of slick fur, pink roped tail and grisly neck. Marmaduke's ears pricked as he rubbed pompously against her legs. 'Silly old cat,' she cajoled, and her belly shook with laughter as she slumped down onto the bed, gathering Marmaduke into her arms, letting him nuzzle her face and neck. His back feet stood on her stomach, his front paws on her shoulder, then he suddenly pounced away, dancing backwards with his ginger hair standing on end.

Evelyn wiggled with a mix of awe and discomfort. She lifted her nightdress to watch the skin of her stomach shift of its own accord, distorted with the cramped acrobatics of her baby. The movement was slow and cumbersome, like the Great Western Tiers themselves had rolled over in bed to create a new landscape. The new position eased pressure on her ribs, but she suddenly felt the urge to wee. 'I knew you were okay,' she whispered, hugging her belly. 'I knew you were strong!'

Humming, Evelyn busied herself with the routine that had developed of her days. She toileted and washed her face and body with a sponge and pitcher behind the makeshift privy room. Later, Daddy would take the cloth-covered chamber pan and bring it back cleaned, the water in the pitcher refreshed. She pulled on a colourful dress, one she'd never seen until Mother came with an armload of clothes one Sunday afternoon, all of them carrying the stench of mothballs. 'You're bursting out of everything,' she'd harrumphed at her daughter. 'It's unsightly.' Evelyn washed each garment by hand in vinegar and fabric softener, hanging them to dry in the patch of sunlight by the orchard window. Most were too big by miles, but it became a creative challenge to pick up needle and thread and transform each garment into something that skimmed prettily across her new curves. It also provided a welcome reprieve from the monotony of seersucker cotton coffin linings and darning Daddy's black woolly socks.

'When I die, Daddy, please line my coffin with something merry,' she said one day as she threaded a needle.

Daddy abruptly stopped sanding at the workbench.

'Something like this.' She flounced the skirt of the dress spread across her lap. 'Then it will be like I'm just sleeping in a garden.' The fabric had a verdant green background lush with white, yellow and orange daisies. 'Can you imagine it?' Evelyn's face was bright as she pulled the needle up and down, stitching a new neckline in the grassy fabric.

'No, kitten, I can't, and I won't imagine it. You're to outlive me, you hear?' Daddy's elbow was propped on the pitted wooden bench and he swiped sawdust from his nose with the back of a hand.

Evelyn's laugh was like a wind chime but for once, Daddy's scratchy moustache and green-flecked eyes remained unmoved by her sparkly chatter.

'I mean it, girl, and what's more I don't care a jot what you line my coffin with. Dirt and ash will be just fine.'

Evelyn dropped the sewing to her lap and her eyes grew serious. It was raining outside, just a sprinkle, but the clouds shifted uneasily across the Tiers. Her voice sank to a whisper. 'But Daddy, what if—'

'No!'

'Mother said—'

'No, Nora.'

Her bottom lip quivered and Daddy knelt in front of her, his hands firmly gripping the tops of her arms.

'Women have been birthing babies since time immemorial. Young women. Jesus's mum was only fifteen. I've heard Reverend Green say it himself.'

Evelyn nodded mutely. She'd heard it before too.

'You're a bright flame, my Nor. You're going to breeze through this, and if that bub has any of your blood in its veins, it'll be a fighter too!'

Daddy hugged her then, tucked her under his chin and pressed her against his chest, Adam's apple working up and down his throat.

'Have any letters come for me from Michał?' Evelyn asked when Daddy pulled back and affectionately tousled her hair.

He stood up abruptly, turning away.

'Please tell me,' Evelyn's voice reached out.

'Don't ask me that, Nor.' He rubbed his moustache.

Evelyn sat upright, her eyes full of hope. 'He's written, hasn't he? I knew it, I knew it! How many letters has he written?'

Daddy glanced out the window and lowered his mouth to Evelyn's ear. 'Seems to me there's a foreign stamped letter in the mail every second week.'

'Why didn't you bring them to me?' Her voice hacked steeply. 'Why didn't you tell me? All this time?'

Daddy winced, didn't know where to look. 'I – well, it's your mother. She said the excitement would be bad in your condition. Said you might miscarry or have a stillborn.' His eyes were bright with worry. 'She told me to burn them.'

'You burnt them?' Evelyn spat. Her heart thumped in confusion, and she paced. *Michał is writing to me. He hasn't lost interest.* But the betrayal of her father's actions was like a bullet in the flesh of the very news she had yearned for.

He was shaking his head. 'No, I couldn't, Nor. I've kept them someplace safe.'

'Give them to me!' Evelyn stomped her foot before dissolving into sobs. 'How could you do this?'

Daddy guided her to the bed and sat her down beside him. 'It's for the good, bloss. I know you love him, but you're still so young. Like your ma said, let's focus on one thing at a time.'

'But I'm strong, Daddy. You know I am.' Evelyn jumped to her feet, her hands balled into fists at her sides. 'I guess you lied about sending my letters too?' She thought of all the tender words she had tucked into envelopes for Michał's eyes only.

Daddy looked at her sadly. She couldn't tell if the droop of his eyes was because of her anger or because he was realising that his daughter no longer needed him. 'Of course I've been sending your letters, Nora. Every single one of them. And I'll give you Michał's letters as soon as this baby makes its entrance.' He gently patted the roundness of her belly just as its occupant gave a hearty boot. He laughed and Evelyn grabbed his hand, holding it against the spot. There was another kick and a shifting movement against Daddy's palm, and they chuckled at the strength of it. 'You have my word, love,' he said, eyes locked with Evelyn's. 'I will keep those letters for you.'

Evelyn wanted to scream and punch at his chest, to shake him and name the unfairness of her position. Of his position. She despaired at the way he bent to Mother's every command. But relief made her generous and she let the anger slip away. Michał was writing to her, and regularly. And Daddy was here with her now, sharing in the delight of this baby's movements. She couldn't help but forgive his weakness.

Daddy's often-wordless presence in the workshop was a panacea for the warring of Evelyn's thoughts. His shuffling from saw and plane to hammer and chisel was all she needed to convert the dusty workshop from a solitary confinement cell to a place of gentle reverie, even though some days they barely exchanged a word. Evelyn had become more subdued. She tired easily. Her thoughts quickly turned inwards and she lost track of time. She imagined herself a painter as she looked out the window at the same view each day, seeking out the colours she would pick from her palette. She marvelled to find pink and yellow in the whitest fists of cloud, or a dimpling of magenta as the sun's yolk dipped.

Aunty Philippa's watercolour paintings were a tall pile now, tucked beneath the fruit crate. Today's card was silverbeet. *Week 37.* Evelyn tried to imagine the big leafy stalks curled within her stomach. He felt much fatter than silverbeet, but the length was no doubt right. The severe maternity book said that a baby at thirty-seven weeks gestation would measure about eighteen or nineteen inches. Evelyn fetched one of Daddy's rulers and placed her thumb at the right striations. 'Baby, you're so big,' she whispered. Just three weeks to go. Evelyn had written in her latest letter to Michał that she felt tight to bursting, and surely their baby would be born earlier.

> *I think he will be born this year, 1953, the year we met and loved, a year of more wonder than I ever thought possible. I want his numbers to be the same as our numbers, all tied together. And you see I'm still writing 'he'. I can't explain it, Michał. I just know our baby is a boy. And your name will be his. Although I fear what Mother will say and I don't know how I will stand up to her. Please come back soon. Please write . . .*

Her letters willed him into being. If she kept writing, he still existed. To stop would be to give up hope. Her pages of words re-created him, there at the workshop with Huon pine shavings hanging from his shirt, pedalling to keep up with Daphne's clopping hooves, lying on the grass in the shadow of Mother Cummings. Those Blue Willow eyes with prominent eyebrow verandas. She kept him alive by writing. Evelyn wondered if Michał had kept writing to her for the same reason.

A single string of tinsel flapped at the foot of Evelyn's bed. All those days eaten up . . . Tomorrow was Christmas. Daddy and Mother would go to church in the morning and then the Lawrences were coming for lunch. Their own family was overseas, and Mother was thinking of asking Agnes to join the croquet committee.

'I will explain that you were detained at my sister's for the Christmas season, but will join us again in the New Year,'

Mother had said with a scrupulous nod of her head. Evelyn was to remain in the workshop until the guests had gone and then she would join her parents for a supper of leftovers in the house, a rare excursion beyond the workshop.

'Can we have a picnic outside instead?' Evelyn asked. But that would have been too exposed, too risky, her mother said.

'We'll open the windows,' Mother said, and Evelyn looked at her shoes. 'You'll need to be back in your room by seven, as we're expecting a telephone call from David and Muriel.' As if they would somehow see her condition through the phone. Muriel. It wasn't quite as exotic a name as Sabine, but Evelyn wondered what talents her new sister-in-law would bring to the family. Perhaps she could sing too, or speak another language. Evelyn hoped she was adventurous, mischievous even, and she imagined them sharing conspiratorial glances during family dinners.

'Fortuitously'—Mother did love to use frilly words—'David and Muriel are unable to join us for Christmas due to a large gathering of her father's side of the family. I think it would be wise for David to attend ahead of their wedding, anyhow.'

Christmas would be much the same as every other day for Evelyn. She hoped that all her gifts would be for the baby. Booties and bonnets, rompers and singlets. The stocking on the hearth stuffed with soft toys and rattles. Imagine if there was a pram, one of those elegant contraptions with fine wheels and an arching handle, with a shade canopy stretched like a bat's wing, all in palest green. Or blue. White would even be okay, she supposed. Although then it might look more like a fancy casket on wheels. Daddy had a catalogue of glossy coffins from a mainland business that he flicked through from time to time 'for inspiration'. Evelyn thought they were all soulless. Daddy's timber coffins were the most honouring vessel of a family's mourning, the whorls in the honey or chocolate wood grain revealing rings of another life. Decades etched like a fingerprint and given likewise.

Perhaps she would read the nativity story while Daddy and Mother were at church. Yes, Mother would approve of that. And besides, Evelyn always enjoyed hearing the perplexing account of a God willingly sacrificing his son for a planet full of people who didn't even really care for him. There was a Bible in the stack of pregnancy books. Hopefully Christmas would be a fine day and she could sit at the orchard window with the sun warming her face. And she would read of the long journey, the star and the baby born to a fifteen-year-old girl hidden away in a dirty old shed.

Chapter 26

Summer 2019

'Hello? Rae?'

'Mmm?' Rae's voice was muffled.

'Have I caught you at a bad time?'

'Noo-aww . . . Ah've got a clay maahsk on . . . can't move mah moooth.'

'Raging social life you've got there!'

'Hey! Ah can hang uh, y'know.'

'Don't understand a word you're saying!' Allira laughed. 'Listen, I've found something, but I need your help. It's about Nora. Can you get us into the archive room at the *Tas Herald*? You're still chummy with Nathan there, right?'

'Uh-huh.'

'Meet me there in an hour?'

'Ets seven aclock on a Sat-ay!'

'Which means skeleton night staff. Can you be there?'

'Ah-kay, ah-kay.'

Allira hung up the phone and looked again at the scrapbook open in front of her. She couldn't get home quickly enough after Heather had handed her the yellowed book with its grease-smeared cover. She'd tried to ignore its tantalising presence on the back seat of the car as she spent the rest of the day exploring the bucolic Caveside area with Nora. A fire. A death. A prison. She itched to open its pages. They spread a picnic rug near Honeycomb Caves and tucked into chicken sandwiches, Nora mumbling disjointed things about books from Aunt Philippa and secret notes about vegetables and fruit as she intermittently stole glances at the Tiers, checking they hadn't disappeared, that their brooding blue presence wasn't a figment of her imagination.

Allira watched her with new eyes. It was like discovering that the familiar old painting on your wall was part of a triptych. It was a captivating wedge of landscape alone, yet in its proper place the vista opened threefold and multiplied its glory like a prism.

After ensuring Nora was safely back in her room at Mercy Place, Allira had pulled into her driveway at five o'clock on the dot, dumped her handbag and lunch leftovers on the kitchen bench, and sat down at the dining table, the scrapbook in front of her. She tucked her feet under her and rested her hands on the cover. She had an hour before Hamish would be home. He'd be exhausted; they would have dinner together and he'd be in bed an hour later. Tonight, she didn't mind.

Thelma Grayson, 1952. The name she'd read in the red almanac from the antique shop. Nora's mother. Thelma's own hand had clutched a pen and pressed those letters into the wrapping paper cover all those years ago. Allira took a deep breath, a prayer-breath that the mouldering pages would hold some kind of hope for the old woman at Mercy Place.

Glued to the inside cover was a family photograph in sepia. Stanley's wide, shaggy moustache and dancing eyes stared over the shoulder of his wife's rigid figure. She didn't look angry or indignant so much as smug, her chin tilted to display a small, forced smile. A tall young man – she guessed it was Nora's older brother – wore an easy, larrikin grin, the kind that made friends in a heartbeat. And there was Nora. Nearly as tall as her brother, and with uncanny resemblance, but thinner, paler. Her long neck was arched ever so slightly away from the group, her eyes not quite held by the lens. Her smile was a secretive, glowing thing, emanating from within.

Allira touched the stiff corners of the photograph. To behold this tangible proof of the Grayson family was surreal. She had been drawing shapeless stick figures in her mind for so long that seeing their true volume and impression was at once exhilarating and disappointing. It represented a little death of the stage play or novella her mind had been inadvertently writing. The end had begun.

Thelma was a meticulous keeper of records. The pages held neat clippings from magazines, church bulletins, association minutes, newspapers and gift cards that ran in rigid lines to minimise wasted space, with occasional notes adjacent: a date, comments on recipes ('required ten minutes additional baking time'), number of people in attendance ('twenty people' at the Croquet Association AGM), and even rainfall. Thelma's scrapbook recorded all the local deaths that involved the family's undertaking business, including the type of timber used for the coffin and the fee ('Jane Leonard: Tasmanian oak, brass fittings, £40'). There were floral embossed cards from David addressed to 'Dear, dear Mama' asking for varying amounts of money, post-stamped Hobart and, later, Melbourne. A two-page spread was devoted entirely to the queen's coronation on 2 June, 1953. Images of the crown jewels, the state coach, the velvet and ermine robes worn by the queen's peers and the Duke of Edinburgh in full uniform were cut neatly from an edition of the *Australian Women's Weekly*. Allira tried to slow her hands, tried not to skip too quickly to the end. Her eye was drawn to a handwritten recipe for Kołaczki, some sort of pastry, but not recorded in Thelma's elongated hand. The letters were small and rounded. The only hint Thelma had given was the date in the margin, February 1953.

Allira slowly turned the pages, past Caveside Anglican Church bulletins, Chudleigh school newsletters and another card from David, this time announcing his engagement. She yawned and rested her chin on her hands. She'd hoped there would be more than this. She flicked idly through the remaining blank pages. Thelma would have missed this book, she thought, as a slip of blue paper fluttered to the table. Another church bulletin, but it didn't look like the others. She turned it over. Sheffield Baptist Hall. About forty kilometres from Caveside. February 1954. Allira skimmed the front page, which listed the senior minister and elders and gave an update on scheduled maintenance and an invitation to a church picnic. She turned the page and immediately wanted to wrap a blanket around her goosebumped arms. There, in the centre, was a picture of the minister, his wife and three children aged from toddler to teens. But the blurry black-and-white image also showed that the wife, a chubby, matronly woman, was nursing a baby.

A fourth child. *Minister and wife adopt baby*, the headline proclaimed. 'We are thrilled to inform our church family that we have adopted the orphaned child left on the steps of the manse door after Christmastime. He will be dearly loved and we thank you for making him welcome in our congregation.'

Allira checked the dates again. The baby's adoption announcement was marked February 1954. What did it mean? And where did Nora fit into this?

Rae was waiting at the staff entrance when Allira arrived. She wore black, from her shoes right to the black felt hat propped on her head. Allira didn't think she'd ever seen Rae wear anything so colourless in her life. Even at her dad's funeral three years ago, she had worn an aqua and yellow Hawaiian shirt in an ode to her father's disgraceful dress sense.

Before Allira could speak, Rae's index finger was at her lips. 'Shhh! We have half an hour. Nathan gave me his security card. In and out. Let's go.' She pressed herself against the wall beside the staff door before peering in the window and swiping Nathan's card. They tiptoed downstairs to the archive room. It would be unlucky if anyone on night shift came down at this hour. Allira knew any stories requiring that level of research were usually shelved for a reporter to pick up the following day. Online search engines made many of these resources redundant for all but the few who knew the treasures that could be found in dusty tomes.

The room was cold and still. Rae flicked on the single light-bulb to reveal three rows of shelving, staggering beneath the weight of decades of newspapers. The corners were in shadow, the inky puddles threatening to spread to the shelves and seep into the brittle pages and their black and white secrets. Carpet squares muted any sound underfoot and when Allira called Rae over to the '50s volumes, her voice was dampened, one-dimensional.

The newspapers were archived in quarters, the three months' worth of daily newsprint bound into volumes and dated before finding their place down here in the bowels of the building. The newest were shiny black with a red title band bearing the masthead and date in gold letters. As the volumes crawled back in time, there was a period of sage green hardcover binding with leather spine and gold embossed writing. Back further and the leather was cracked, taped up, the faded lettering replaced with handwritten date cards, stuck haphazardly on the spines. Some were mere sticky notes.

Allira breathed in the smells that had become so nostalgic to her. The sharp stench of newsprint with its porous, smeary ink. The ink that rubbed off on her hands and streaked her face when she brushed hair from her eyes when she was on daily rounds. And the soak. She imagined all the pages in this room and how they had marinated. Cigarette smoke and ash. Coffee stains and newsroom gossip. Panic at sirens sounding down at the fire department, the emergency rounds journalist grabbing his notebook and running for the door. The solemnity of obituaries and staff cuts and fatalities first reported to the mash-up of professionals clacking at typewriters in the city's foremost newsroom. She hugged her arms, looking for 1953–1954.

'Found it!' Rae carried two hefty volumes to a lone table and chair parked beside the door, slapping them down and stepping back. 'I'll let you do the honours.'

Allira grinned, rubbing her hands together. The covers were weary, the spines fraying, with bright, white cards sticky-taped to the spines: *Oct–Dec 1953* and *Jan–Mar 1954*. She gingerly opened the first immense book, turning chunks of pages back to the window of time she was looking for. *What am I looking for? Why is it not enough to just spend time with Nora?* She sifted methodically through yellowed pages while her mind stumbled down labyrinthine halls of nebulous thought. *Surely I can find something to bring Nora peace in the dusk of her life.* Her eyes darted across headlines and grainy black-and-white photos, waiting for a face or a word to snag. *I have to know. There has to be something I can give her.*

Allira always capitulated to neat endings and predictable res-olutions. She never had more than one book on the go. It irked her to stop a movie before the end. A little thunderstorm brewed inside her when an author or screenwriter didn't deliver a sat-isfying ending. She'd once stayed with a boyfriend for way too long because he was stable, dependable and her parents liked him. It was Rae who had talked her out of him.

Allira kept flicking, slower now, scouring every column. There were some editions missing from early January. The pages whispered through her fingers as hope ebbed, and she was nearly into February 1954 when she clapped a hand to her mouth as if it was a wound.

Nora looked up at her from the page. There was no mistaking her defiant countenance. *Missing person. Evelyn Nora Grayson, aged 16. Last seen on the Bass Highway near Deloraine one week prior. Unknown which direction she was travelling. Call Tasmania Police if you have any information on her whereabouts.*

'Rae . . . are you seeing this?'

'It's her, isn't it?'

Allira nodded her head without looking up from the photograph of a young, freckle-nosed Nora, her mouth set in a conspiratorial half-smile. 'Where were you going, Nora?'

Chapter 27

Summer 1953

'What colour are your dreams?' Evelyn could remember asking Mother the question as a child. She closed her eyes and the familiar hot tint seeped in, like a drop of pigment in a bowl of water. It started off a deep burgundy, the colour of tree sap, swirled, spreading and merging, illuminating to a stain like Flanders poppies and tomato juice. Her dreams were always red, like closing her eyes meant immersing herself in her own veins, to swim their canals and discover their mysteries. She thought it was the same for everyone, that all dreams were painted with a brush dipped in the colour of an eyelid's underside.

'Good grief you talk nonsense!' Mother had said when she shared one of her red dreams at breakfast. It was a ripper, full of fantastical creatures with wings and horns and hooked claws, all of them red as Mr Herbert's ruddy nose.

'Aren't your dreams red too, Mother?' she asked.

Mother's only response was a stroppy *harrumph* as she cleared the table.

Daddy smiled into his Vegemite toast. 'None of my dreams are so spritely coloured, kitten. Must be a gift,' he said. That made her feel good, like God had given her a special lens. She didn't talk about it again, but always asked for red balloons at her birthday parties. She would peer through their translucent film, imagining the hazy red fuss of bodies had a peculiar meaning for her to grasp, a heavenly directive.

Evelyn leaned her head out the workshop window, trying to glimpse the sun's gleaming disk as it slid beneath the horizon. Her stomach pressed against the windowsill and her right hand absently sat atop the impressive dome. It would be similar for her baby, she thought, her belly skin like an eyelid casting everything into red obscurity. Like her dreams: a warm, safe anonymity that cradled who she was. Who he was.

Evelyn's stomach tightened, a sensation like her skin and muscles were shrinking around her womb. She hobbled to the pallet bed and lowered herself onto it stiffly. Braxton Hicks contractions, Aunty Philippa's books called them. She wanted to fling open the door and walk them off, walk around the horse paddock or up and down the drive beneath the arms of the oak trees. But there was a fancy-looking motor vehicle in the driveway. 'No lights. No noise. No outdoor wanderings.' Those had been the directives for the evening. No reading. No music. No fresh air. Just her vermilion thoughts, as fiery and dishevelled as her unruly hair that had grown to reach the small of her back.

She tried not to entertain the fear, tried to shut it out with activity, but on nights like tonight it was a deceivingly friendly suitor. *Michał doesn't care*, it whispered. *There are no letters. Your father said that to make you feel better.* It felt like truth. *Your baby isn't wanted. There's no place or plan for your baby.* The voice was a tantalising viper. *Mother hid you to save face – do you think she will allow a baby in her house?*

Evelyn gulped, knotting and unknotting her hands. It was true there had been no baby gifts at Christmas like she hoped there might be. No rattles or rompers. Just books, a summer dress and a bag of jelly babies. As she had helped Mother clean up the kitchen that afternoon four days ago, she had asked again what would happen to her baby. Mother had wiped her hands on her apron, slowly turning to face her.

'I told you I will take care of things.'

'But I want to know,' Evelyn implored. 'Why won't you tell me? This is my baby we're talking about.' Her hands were wrapped across her belly.

Mother nodded her head, sucking her cheeks thoughtfully. 'We will find a home for the child.'

'You're going to have my baby adopted?' Evelyn blanched. 'But I don't want that. I want to keep him. I love him!'

'Or her,' Mother quipped. 'Like you loved your Michał, who hasn't sent so much as a letter?'

Evelyn opened her mouth and closed it again. She couldn't let on that she knew about the letters or she might never see them.

'Darling.' Mother's tone shifted and she laced an arm around Evelyn's shoulders. 'You're too young to be a mother. That adventurous spirit of yours would be trampled if you kept this baby. Trust me, your world would only shrink. Another family will give your baby the care it needs and you will be free to follow your dreams.'

'But he is my dream now.'

Mother smiled sadly. 'You're just confused. This is the best decision, not only for you Evelyn, but for the child too. Do you know how to be a mother?'

Evelyn didn't reply. Of course she didn't know how to be a mother, but she could learn. How did any young woman become a mother if not by learning as she went? But a worm of doubt burrowed into Evelyn's thoughts that day, and in the darkness of night when she couldn't sleep she returned to wondering if Mother was right, if someone more experienced would do a better job of raising her baby.

The memory of that conversation still hurt and Evelyn massaged her temples and hummed. *Help help help help*, her spirit screeched. She pressed her palms to her eyes and the hot colour bloomed against her eyelids. *Please help.*

She went to sleep in the red terror, but not for long. Soon a droplet of pure, silken peace commanded its retreat. In her mind's eye was the ripple and the swift withdrawal, the red receding, ebbing, ebbing. And rushing in, the water, colourless and quenching, splashing. She exhaled. Fell back against the bed, curved within the covers as the waves lapped, gentle strokes of comfort. Her dreaming was formless, empty but for the sensation of one hovering above her, broad and loving. She was not in the water, nor on it. She *was* the water, flowing, flowing. Going where the hovering one willed. Winding in green pastures, settling in still pools of sky-tint. The searching and knowing were inextricably linked between the hovering and the water, formless and then formed. A cavernous grief opened up, yawning, bottomless. But the water flowed in, bringing light and the presence, always hovering.

At midnight Evelyn woke and water gushed from her.

Chapter 28

Autumn 2019

The bar heaved with people taking shelter from the teeming rain at the end of another work week. The storm had brewed all day and finally, at clock-off time, a finger of lightning soundlessly split the sky before the clouds opened on suited office workers fleeing beneath flimsy umbrellas from one stuffy building to another. The sodden creatures lined the bar, knocking back ales as the sky lowered.

It had been months since Allira had joined the *Folk* magazine staff for after-work drinks at the White Hart. The untidy din was never her choice for social gatherings. Allira craned her neck to see above the crowd and spotted the crew at a table in a far corner. Katy had handed in her resignation last week and this was her farewell. Allira didn't need to ask her to know that Justin's constant scrutiny, and the feeling that she needed to prove her value to the magazine, had finally got to her. Maybe she still hadn't been paid, too. It was a huge loss for *Folk*, although Allira was certain Justin wouldn't agree. 'Photographers are a dime a dozen,' he'd say. But Katy's eye for portraiture had become one of the defining elements of the publication, and Allira wasn't sure she'd be so easily replaced.

She joined them, giving Katy a long hug that said more than anything she could holler over the crowded bar's din. They ordered bar snacks and talked about the way mountain-biking was taking off in Tassie, the effects of global warming and whether the government should bite the bullet and change the date of Australia Day. The bar emptied as people headed home to families or moved through to the bistro for dinner. Justin drained another glass of red wine. Allira was surprised he'd even bothered to come. She checked her phone – eight o'clock already, and a message from Hame: *I'll come join you, be there soon.* That was from twenty minutes ago. She would have pre-ferred to call it a night, but he would be here any minute.

Sure enough, he arrived a moment later. 'Hey folks, thought I'd come crash your party, and bid you farewell in your new career path, Katy.' Hamish kissed Allira on the cheek before pulling a chair up beside her. He was well liked in the office, never missing an opportunity to mingle with the people his wife spent her weekdays with. He nodded at Justin, who was taking a mouthful of a fresh glass of wine.

'Sorry, chap, but it might be a case of too little too late. I'm ready to call a cab,' Justin said coolly, his words slurring.

A dozen or so staff were still at the bar, most of them clearly expecting to make a night of it. 'C'mon boss, you said you'd show us the ropes,' a young subeditor quipped.

Katy joined in, 'Yeah, I can't have my people thinking my send-off ended before the streetlights turned on.' The truth was, while the boss was here, the tab was still open, but Justin's ego met the challenge.

'Okay, okay, let's kick on for a bit longer. Hamish, how about you get us the next round?'

Hamish didn't miss a beat. 'Sure thing,' he said, jumping to his feet.

Allira joined him at the bar. 'He's toying with you, Hame.'

'I know. But we can't keep avoiding him. If you're going to stay on, he's going to have to get over it at some point.' He ordered a few jugs of beer and two bottles of wine. 'The way I figure, we can dazzle him with kindness or get ourselves all bent out of shape with bitterness.'

'Hamish, you're so darn good, it disgusts me.'

'How good?' He held a jug of beer in each hand and pretended to take a slurp.

Allira rolled her eyes and they returned to the table, a waitress following with the wine and fresh glasses.

'The pool table's free,' Rae said, dragging her eyes away from her phone. *She must be seeing someone*, Allira thought. It wasn't like her to be subdued in a social setting. That, or she was as furious with Justin as Allira was and couldn't even bear to look at him across the table.

'Good idea. Let's grab it before someone else does.' Justin thumped his wineglass onto the table, sending the red liquid into a sloshing whirlpool.

The billiards room was a dogleg space behind the bar that hadn't made the cut in the last reno. The lurid green felt tabletop was stained, and the cues leaning against the sides had seen better days. Allira stood by the window with Rae and Katy as Hamish, Justin and two of the now-depleted *Folk* entourage began a game of doubles. The sharp clack of ball against ball punctuated their discussion on what Katy would do next.

'I'm just doing the freelance thing,' she said. 'It's fun working for a magazine but my lifestyle is always better when I'm my own boss.' She smiled diplomatically. Burning bridges was never wise in a little place like Launceston. Rae and Allira both knew there was more at play, but they didn't push. Rain continued to pummel the window. The road was slick with it, tail lights bouncing red haze into a blank night. Allira's thoughts kept sliding to home, where she could swap her skirt and heels for trackies and Uggs. Nora was on her mind again too.

She'd gone for a quick visit before work that morning, carrying a fistful of yellow daisies hurriedly picked from the garden. Nora hadn't even stirred when she knocked and entered with a cheery 'Hello!' She was sitting in that gaudy upholstered chair, which looked like a gaping mouth about to swallow her emaciated body. Eyes glassy, hair dishevelled, doll in one arm. It had been like the first time they met: that forlorn, unseeing expression. The most the old woman could manage was a wan smile. A flag of defeat, like her spirit was surrendering to the corrosive confinement of her condition. Allira had been left trying to make conversation with a husk.

Allira found Sally in her office, her arms resting on either side of a tiny laptop. 'Did you sedate her?'

'Allira . . .' Sally stood slowly, leaning heavily on the desk. 'Nora's gone downhill. Don't tell me you're only just noticing.' She squinted at Allira with the posy of flowers still in her hand,

and sighed. 'It's normal. Dementia is degenerative. You might still find she snaps out of it from time to time, but the last stage of dementia's a beast.' She moved to where Allira was standing in the doorframe and placed a heavy hand on her shoulder. 'Whatever you do, don't go Googling it. Everyone likes putting these sorts of things in boxes. What's happening to Nora is different to what's happening to Janet further down the hall. Different to what happened to my dad, too.' She smiled sadly.

Allira swiped hair from her face and rubbed her cheekbone with the heel of her hand.

'Be kind to yourself.' Sally patted her shoulder before opting for a brief hug instead and then brusquely pointed her out the office door.

Now Allira bit her lip to stop the tears and downed the rest of her drink. Rae was watching her and gave her a questioning look. Allira shrugged. 'I'm done. Have the boys finished yet?' She threw the focus back to the pool table, going to join Hamish who had just been utterly smashed by Justin.

'Good game, man!' Hamish slapped him on the back goodnaturedly and shook his hand. Glancing at Allira, he must have read her face because he continued. 'Looks like we're making tracks, thanks for tonight.' Allira was tugging him towards the door.

'Not so quickly.' Justin stood in their way, flashing wine-stained teeth. 'It's just getting fun. Let's increase the stakes.' His laugh was menacing. He stepped back too quickly and Hamish had to grab his elbow to stop him falling.

'I think the lady's pretty keen for some shut-eye, thanks, Justin.' Hamish wrapped an arm around Allira.

'You don't even want to hear the wager?' Justin's bloodshot eyes were trained on Allira. 'The winner takes the mag, holus-bolus.'

The couple froze.

'I'm deadly serious,' Justin said, his arms held out, palms open. 'One game and it could be yours.'

'I don't think that's wise, Justin.' Allira broke eye contact. 'You've had too much to drink to make such a massive wager.'

Hamish squeezed her waist, stopping her from marching out of the bar. 'So you're saying if I win this game of eight ball, Allira and I will be the new owners of *Folk* magazine?' Hamish asked slowly, deliberately.

Justin crossed his arms and nodded.

'And what if you win?'

Justin licked his lips. 'Your lovely wife becomes my PA for a year.'

Allira glared at him. 'Come on, Hame, let's get home.'

'A year, hey?'

'Hamish! I'm not some kind of bartering chip.'

'You're right, babe, which is why I think *you* should play.'

Allira's eyes snapped to Hamish's. His face was soft, urging her to take courage. Since they'd lost their baby, focusing on the silky swish of the cue between her fingers and the subsequent *clack-clack* of balls had become a way to dwell together in the pain without the complexity of words. Hamish squeezed her hand. She knew. He was asking her to try.

'Me?' she spluttered. 'I haven't played in forever!' She watched Justin's response carefully. Did he know? Had Rae boasted of her friend's hidden prowess? Surely he knew. Journalists made it their business to know.

'I think that's a smashing idea! Good man, Hamish – you know you'd never live it down if you lost that game.'

'But how do we know you're serious? How do we know that you're not going to go back on your word?' Allira said.

'I'm deadly serious!' Justin was indignant. 'Wait.' He grabbed a beer coaster and pulled a pen from his shirt pocket. 'We need a witness,' he muttered, looking around the room before latching on a barman clearing a table. Justin called the unsuspecting man over and quickly explained the plan. 'Will you witness?'

The barman's eyes were wide. 'You sure about this, dude? I mean, I'm no financial advisor, but that's a sweet gamble!' Colour rose from the twenty-something's neck, flushing his freckled face right to the roots of his white-blond buzz cut as Justin stared at him. 'All right, all right,' he said. 'Tell me where to sign.'

Justin leaned against the pool table as he read aloud what he was writing in a left-leaning scrawl on the small square of cardboard. 'The winner of this eight-ball game is the owner of *Folk* magazine. There. Now I'll sign here . . . You sign there, Allira, and the witness signature can go beneath.'

They shuffled the coaster between them. Three signatures on the back of a Boags beer coaster that was suddenly the most meaningful item in the room. Justin slapped his hand on it, pushing it to the rim of the pool table behind one of the middle pockets. The bartender was pouring drinks again, gesturing towards the billiards room, his face animated. Hamish squeezed Allira's hand and she went to choose the straightest cue in a pile of duds.

What on earth am I doing? She wanted to run. The bar was full again, the thrum of conversation underscored with bass notes from a three-piece outfit playing in the other room. Couples and small huddles of friends skirted the room, nursing their drinks and waiting for the game to begin. Katy looked incredulous. Rae winked. She had faith in her friend even if Allira's hands were shaking.

Allira approached the table where Justin had racked the balls and positioned the cue ball on the head string.

'You can break, m'lady,' he said and bowed with a full glass of wine raised haphazardly in the air.

Allira nodded stiffly and then removed her heels one by one and placed them neatly under the table. A ripple of laughter moved around the room, followed by scattered applause. For a moment she thought it was directed at the band in the next room, who had just finished a set. But the strumming and singing continued, and she realised the small crowd was invested in the game she was about to begin. Whispers in a Lonnie pub had pulled people to the billiards room to see if *Folk* magazine's top journalist could beat the boss at a game of eight ball that would sit her in the editor's seat. It was better entertainment than the skinny teenager crooning her angst into the mic for a crowd who, for the most part, was taking more delight in her gyrating hips than her voice.

Allira positioned the white cue ball slightly right of centre along the head string. She didn't hesitate, didn't wait for the nerves to freeze her wrists or skew her eye. She relied on muscle memory to drive the cue into the little white ball, easily splitting the triangular formation to send the colourful balls bouncing off the cushions. It was a firm, decisive shot and it sunk the thirteen; a striped ball. Allira quickly lined up her second shot. She would try to sink two this time. A strong stroke to graze the ten into the side pocket and continue onwards to nudge the nine in the far corner pocket. She fired again and watched it take the route she planned, chalking her cue as her second and third balls dropped into their pockets. The room had gone quiet and Allira looked around. All faces showed surprise; even Hamish feigned shock, his eyes popping like a cartoon.

'Beginner's luck?' she asked with a shrug, and the spell was broken.

Rae yelled, 'Go, girl!' and another woman echoed it on the other side of the room.

Justin blanched as the room erupted with raucous hoots of support. There was no clear shot this time, so she aimed for a cushion, sending the innocuous white ball ricocheting into one of her balls so it rolled directly towards a corner pocket. It teetered at the edge before settling against the green felt. 'Not enough grunt,' Allira muttered.

'My turn?' Justin sauntered to the table, sitting his empty glass on the lip. Allira had surreptitiously watched the previous games, and he wasn't a bad shot. The problem was, she hadn't been counting how many glasses of red he'd downed tonight. By her guess, it was more than the number of balls he needed to pocket. Justin sunk an easy shot and then wasted his follow-up by hitting the cue ball with such splintering force that the ball he was aiming for bounced back out of the pocket again.

She was up. The room closed in. More people had spread themselves around the walls and the bar staff were in a line, ignoring customers and polishing glassware as they kept track of the game. Allira blocked out the noise and activity around her and counted her heartbeat, willing it to slow down. *One, two, three, four.* This was not a game like those in the garage with Hamish, where the silence was a balm and the fierce focus the game demanded was a welcome relief. *Five, six, seven, eight.* Those games were delightfully inconsequential. Now, she cared more than she'd like to admit. For starters, there was no way she wanted to work a whole year as Justin's PA. Not a chance.

The next shot would need all her concentration. She calculated the angles, carefully positioning her cue. The audience was confused, watching her aim at an empty cushion. She tensed her biceps and rammed the cue ball with all of her might. It hit the cushion and rebounded sharply into the opposite green felt bumper, clacking loudly against the twelve. She held her breath. The twelve shot towards the pocket, colliding with the fifteen to sink it squarely. The twelve followed; two balls in one pocket.

The growing crowd roared, the buzz cut barman clapped his hands above his head and people had their phones out, filming. Allira allowed a faint smile before retreating to her place of focus. *Three balls to win the role of editor.* She tapped an easy line-up into a corner pocket. *Two.* One of Justin's solid balls was in her way, so she deftly tapped a shot that felled her last striped ball.

Justin laughed loudly and shouted, 'Bravo, bravo! She's quite the *player*.' He snarled the last word and stepped towards her but lost his balance, stumbling to his knees as wine sloshed onto the floor. Hamish helped him up and Allira walked over to them.

'Justin,' Allira whispered, 'we can stop this now. It's not fair to continue. Let's get you home.' His eyes were bloodshot, his skin pallid. A splatter of wine stained the cuff of his pinstriped shirt, unbuttoned at the collar. He pulled himself up to full height, shaking off Hamish's grip.

'Don't you dare!' He clenched his jaw and the deep dimples that usually lent a handsome punctuation to his face were like black pits. He handed Allira her cue from where it was propped against the table. 'Play,' he demanded.

Hamish and Allira exchanged a glance before she resumed. This was a bad idea. *Why did I let him convince me to go along with it?* A heavyset man with a shaved head was pumping his fists, starting an anthem with his blonde girlfriend in her skinny jeans and buckled boots. 'Go, go, go, go!' The whole room chanted. Her head spun. How was this ever going to end well?

It was Justin who finally raised his arms and stilled the ruckus. 'A bit of quiet for the lady,' he said, flashing that convivial smile as he half-bowed, 'as she whoops my ass!' The crowd laughed. They liked him again.

Allira flicked her hair over her shoulder and leaned down above the cue. Her eyes darted from white ball to black, estimating the distance, angle and speed she needed to gain a winning shot. *Do I even want to win this?* She exhaled. To fake a loss would be just as delicate a situation to navigate. Justin would know. Better to give it all she had. She thought of *Folk*, of all the incredible people she had interviewed and their powerful stories. She thought of Hamish and the baby they'd briefly held. She thought of Nora, the way they had cradled each other's pain beneath the apple trees that night. Allira steadied the bridge her left hand formed for the cue. She gripped the butt of the cue and tapped the white ball. It bumped against the cushion, avoiding one of Justin's balls, before chipping against the target. The eight ball crawled at an excruciating pace towards the middle pocket. The room was on mute, eyes tracing the green pathway of the black ball. Several bystanders were filming on their smart-phones, this suspended moment that would change everything. Their mouths were moving but Allira didn't hear them. Her eyes were like a magnet to the pocket beside the beer coaster and its three rushed signatures.

The winning ball hit the buffer, swayed, and dropped into the pocket.

Chapter 29

Summer 1953

Evelyn lay crumpled beside her bed, the hessian mat beneath her glistening with pink dampness. Blood galloped noisily through her veins, thundering like a cavalry charge and throbbing in her ears. Then it stopped. She looked out the window where a near-full moon illuminated the yard, the orchard, even the silhouette of Mother Cummings Peak up there on the ridge. She saw Daphne's palomino flank flash past. Her head swirled. It was the pounding of hooves, not her blood. Blood was on the floor, but paler, watered-down. Daphne was out there galloping frantically around her paddock in the middle of the night. Funny little horse. Not like her at all.

'Nora!' Daddy was beside her, his voice rubbed raw with worry. 'Oh darlin'!' He wrapped a brawny arm around her shoulder and kissed her on the forehead.

'I'm scared, Daddy.' Evelyn clutched her stomach's tight orb. It protruded from the synthetic flounces of one of Mother's old nightdresses. Her hair was still in braids.

'I'm here now. It's going to be okay. Pull all your bravest

bones together, Nor. This'll be hard, but you'll get through it. And I'll be right here the whole time.'

Daddy helped her onto the pallet bed and Evelyn wished she could believe him.

'Will you just, Stanley?'

Evelyn looked up to see Mother standing over them, mosquitoes and moths winging an agitated halo around her under the single, swinging lightbulb. She seemed to be gnawing on the mayhem of the scene, the shadows carving the angles of her cheekbones and shoulders sharper than usual. Her eyes roved across Daddy's workshop. Planes and chisels sat on the broad workbench, the shadow board revealing an outline of where they should have been stowed. A pile of sawdust was swept against the wall: pale blond Huon pine. Its sweet, musky scent would forever fragrance the memory that was unfolding before them.

'This is no place for a man. Now, go get me some towels and a basin of boiling water.'

Evelyn nearly snorted at the irony of it. Daddy's workshop, where he did the work of a man, a carpenter, would be the birthplace of her baby. She willed him to speak: *This is no place for a woman, and certainly no place for* my *daughter to give birth!* Yearned for him to whisk her away, to take control. Instead, Daddy slipped work-roughened fingers beneath Evelyn's chin and levered her face so that she couldn't help but look up into his sad eyes.

'Courage,' he whispered.

Evelyn nodded, an almost imperceptible movement, before he squeezed her hand and left the room, closing the door with a soft click behind him.

A bead of sweat dripped from Evelyn's forehead onto her inner thigh and mingled with her own blood. She curved into herself, chin to chest, panting like a lamb in drought. The pains came quicker and harder. They needled her spine to unfold, her mouth roaring to the ceiling. The sound cracked against the countryside stillness like a limb peeling from a tree.

'Hush, hush.' Mother's eyes darted to the door, the windows.

'The neighbours are bloody well miles away, Mother!' Evelyn grit her teeth, letting out another howl that finished in a long, defeated sob. Mother was kneeling at her side and sat back on her heels, glowering.

A fist pounded the workshop door. 'I'm calling the doc, Thelma. She needs some proper help.'

'Daddy . . .' Evelyn whimpered.

'Lord Almighty. I delivered my own sister, Stanley. This is completely normal.'

Evelyn could hear the heavy footfall of his Blundstones as he continued pacing outside his workshop. She screamed the sawdust into eddies and, in between, his pacing was a metronome of comfort.

A Bakelite clock radio, propped beside a family photo of the four of them, the happy Caveside family, showed 2.35 am as Evelyn's mouth finally hung slack after another harrowing contraction.

'I can see its head,' Mother reported. 'This blighter is in a hurry; another few pushes and we'll be done here.'

And she was right. Two more pushes and Mother was holding the slimy body of a tiny baby boy. The baby boy Evelyn had dreamed of and whispered to through the drum-tight skin of her stomach. Her chest surged with love like she'd never known. As fatigued as she was, she was euphoric with wonder. Mother hastily cut the cord and wrapped him in a pale-yellow towel, rubbing at his chest until the faintest mew escaped his lips. His feet kicked in slow motion and his head rolled to one side. Evelyn shifted onto an elbow so she could see Mother walking her baby to the window, where she stopped and stared down the orchard's line of apple trees, the outline of Mother Cummings pressing down on a horizon that would soon labour a new day.

'I'm sorry things aren't better,' the older woman rasped so quietly, it could have been a moth wing against the window. The boy squirmed and squeaked in her arms, his umbilical cord a mess of blood and sinew against the luminescence of new skin.

'Let me hold him.' Evelyn was lying where she gave birth, splayed on the pallet bed, her stained nightdress crumpled around her knees. 'Please, Mother. I want to feed him.'

At the window, Thelma swayed one way and then the other as if trying to decide which way to go. An apron was tied severely at her snap-thin waist and the light cast fingers of shadow like deep ravines down her dressing gown. She was silent for the longest time and then she turned, shielding the newborn from her daughter's view.

'I'm sorry, Evelyn. He's very sickly,' she said, not without tenderness. 'Tuck yourself into that bed and get some sleep. You'll be needing it. I'll be back with him soon.'

'Please,' Evelyn breathed.

But she had already gone.

Bewildered, Evelyn slumped back in her bed, listening to a murmured exchange between her parents outside the door and then the crunch of footsteps on gravel as they walked back to the house. *Where's Daddy? Why didn't he come in?* She wanted to muster the strength to march out there and hold her son close, to nurse him as she had dreamed she would, kissing his petal skin, his forehead, his toes. *If he's sick, let me nurse him.* She opened her mouth to scream, but nothing came out, only the sensation of nails raking her throat. Exhaustion quickly claimed her to a deep, incapacitating sleep.

Evelyn woke to the sound of a spade driving into stubborn soil, rocks screeching as the tool cut deeper and deeper into the ground. She winced as she swung her legs over the side of the pallet bed, her feet landing on the concrete floor. The hessian mat was gone.

Evelyn pushed tangled hair from her eyes. Everything was tender. From her buttocks and the soft place between her legs to her fingers, her jaw and her breasts. Her memory was dark fog but for one intense spotlight of clarity: gangly legs, turned-in toes and a mouth opening and closing like a little fish as he was held aloft after that last staggering heave. *My son, I have a son.* The spade stopped its hacking and Evelyn stumbled to the window.

Daddy. In the waning evening light she could see that he'd dug a deep hole in the place where one of the apple trees died a few months ago. She clung to the windowsill, her knees weak beneath her, and watched as he gently lifted a bundle of lemon-yellow towel and lowered it almost ceremoniously into the hole. Evelyn looked up to the kitchen window. Mother watched in her bleached apron, arms folded, her mouth a rigid line beneath unblinking eyes. Then Daddy was shovelling dirt back into that deep, deep hole. Partway through he stopped and lifted a sapling from the ground beside him, pointed its bare roots into the earth, and continued shovelling until he had finished, pounding the earth flat around the base of this new tree. He paused for a moment before walking slowly back to the kitchen, eyes on his boots, spade under one arm.

Evelyn was a stone wall. Her fingers were granite, her face was sandstone. She could not move, could not comprehend what she was seeing. Everything within her raced outside screaming into the stained evening air, her arms and fingers throbbing with the desire to wrench fistfuls of dirt away from that foreign tree's roots and press her baby boy to her chest. Yet she was rendered motionless, her mouth an open grave. *He was sickly. He died.* The words were a rope of grief winding ever tighter. Finally, as the Great Western Tiers swallowed the last light of the day, she gulped air into her starved lungs. Gasped. Her knees gave way and she sobbed into a sleep that was far bleaker than the last.

Chapter 30

Autumn 2019

Hamish launched at Allira with a chest-crushing bear hug before she even had a chance to lay down her cue. The billiards room at the White Hart went from tense silence to uproarious energy in a heartbeat. From Hamish's embrace, Allira quickly scanned the room. The crowd converged on her, clinking her glass in celebration or angling for a selfie with the new boss of *Folk* magazine. Justin was alone, gathering his jacket, finishing his wine.

'Get Justin into our car, Hame. We have to make this right,' Allira whispered into his ear. 'I'll meet you there.'

Hamish kissed her long and hard on the mouth, 'Love you, babe,' he said before moving away to do her bidding.

Rae and Katy squeezed through the crowd to hug and hop up and down around Allira's befuddled face. Katy was particularly perplexed. 'What— Where did you learn— I don't even know what to say,' she stammered.

'I want you to stay at *Folk*,' Allira said. 'Don't say anything now, but please at least give me the chance to win you back.'

Katy gave a short, astonished laugh. 'Right you are, boss lady,' she said with a salute. 'I think I'm going to enjoy this!'

Rae opened her mouth to speak but Allira got in first. 'I have to go. I'll call you,' she said with an apologetic shrug. She set off towards the door, ducking and weaving against bodies pressing towards her. They slapped her on the back as she passed, and she acquiesced to a few photos with strangers. She felt suffocated, like she needed air. The usual gentle buzz after winning a game against Hamish was replaced with an exhilarating but groundless sensation, like her heart was floating up through her throat. She felt nauseous.

'You're welcome back anytime,' the barman called out to her retreating figure. Allira laughed self-consciously and made a beeline for the door.

Rain pecked at her face. The sleek road bounced reflections of red and orange taillights like hectic fireflies. It was nearly 10.30 by the time Allira dashed to Hamish's beat-up Land Rover idling at the kerb, climbed in and slammed the door against the stinging rain. She looked in the back seat where Justin was slumped, the seatbelt slung beneath his chin.

'Out to it,' Hamish said.

'We have to get him sober.'

'I dunno, Allira. We might need to press pause on whatever plan is percolating in that pretty head of yours . . . I mean, look at him.'

'Let's take him to his place and give him a coffee, see what happens,' Allira pleaded. 'Wait, I don't even know where he lives.' She dropped her forehead into her hands. 'This is not going well.'

'Um, do you need me to remind you that you just smashed your boss at a game of eight ball and are now officially the owner and editor of this little town's pre-eminent magazine?' The windscreen wipers screeched across the glass.

'Am I, Hamish?' Allira's voice was thin, 'Or did I just participate in a humiliating charade? That's what it feels like right now.'

'A contract's a contract, Al, even if it is on the back of a beer coaster.'

'But where is it?'

'Give me some credit, Al.' Hamish waved the grimy coaster above her head before handing it to her. 'I also happened to prise Justin's address from him right before he told me he *lubbed* me and passed out on the back seat of my car. It's something like *sven furrrr-bean away*, which I've never heard of.' His eyes twinkled and Allira playfully punched his arm.

'Take us to seven Verbeena Way, you clown.'

The brick veneer house was sandwiched between renovated terraces. A dim streetlight revealed a facade the colour of chicken liver pâté, a cracked cement path and patches of lawn that needed a mow two weeks ago. The woven wire fence sagged and the letterbox leaned.

Allira wondered if she'd translated the address wrong. She looked for Justin's car, a little red MG, but realised he had probably left it at work. 'I'm not sure—'

'I'm good from here.' Justin stirred from his alcohol-induced coma and groped at the door handle. Hamish and Allira leapt from the car and helped him out, even as he swatted at them like pesky flies. 'Leave me be,' he said, stumbling onto the footpath. 'You've had your fun, leave me to lick my wounds.'

'I want to talk to you. Please, let's just have a quick coffee together.' Allira shielded her face from the driving rain. Her shirt was plastered to her back and water squelched between her toes.

A spotlight in the porch flared and the door of the modest little house creaked open on a tall man in slacks and a crisp shirt, his waist pushing at the buttonholes. They dashed up the cracked path and Justin brushed past him, his shoes in his hands.

'Come in out of this weather,' the balding man said in a gravelly voice. 'I'm Justin's dad. You can call me Horrie.'

Justin's dad? Allira felt as if her brain was firing more neurons than her body could bear. She took Hamish's lead and shook the man's outstretched hand, trying to reconcile the tumble-down house with Justin's high taste.

'I'm not as steady on my feet these days,' Horrie said in answer to their perplexed expressions. 'It's a balance disorder, but you're not interested in my medical history.' He waved a dismissive hand and Allira noticed the merry sparkle of his green eyes. 'I'm fortunate that Justin moved in to help last year.'

Allira smiled warmly. 'We shouldn't keep you up, Mr . . . Horrie.'

'No, no. Please come in. I don't get many visitors.' He practically pushed them indoors, down a dim hall of threadbare carpet and into a cramped sitting room. Justin was already sprawled on a tattered chaise longue beneath a window, the drapes pulled almost shut, and an oversized leather armchair took up most of the remaining space. There were no pictures, but every centimetre of wall space was filled with banjos, mandolins and ukuleles,

264

suspended from their necks on a line of hooks. The honeyed timber threw a warm glow across the draughty room, as though the light emanated from their bellies and not the floor lamp with its peach lace shade.

Horrie pointed at his son. 'Coffee, Aspro and Berocca for you, and how about you two?' He looked at Allira and Hamish.

'Coffee, please,' Hamish and Allira replied in unison, their eyes still on the instruments. Horrie chuckled as he moved into the adjoining kitchen and Justin lethargically made room on the chaise.

'Dad's a woodworker, a luthier to be precise. Mostly makes instruments like those on the wall: guitars and the odd violin too.'

Allira could hear Horrie humming as he clattered mugs onto the benchtop and a kettle onto the gas stove. 'He made all of these?'

Justin nodded. 'Why are you here? I mean, thanks for the lift, but let's not pretend to be friends. You got what you wanted. Perhaps you can leave me be now.'

The house groaned as a gust of wind jettisoned rain against the window, rattling the glass violently. Justin tugged the heavy brocade curtains closed behind him.

'Tonight wasn't fair, Justin. I don't want this,' Allira said. 'I absolutely want to step up as editor of the mag, but not this way. Our offer still stands. We'll buy it from you, with all the terms we already discussed.'

'What's this, a pity party then?' Justin sneered. The clattering in the kitchen stopped.

'Call it what you like. I won't be taking over the magazine based on a drunken game of eight ball.' Allira had raised her voice, tears stinging her eyes as she held her ground within the spot-light of Justin's icy composure. Hamish was at her side, his warm hand at the small of her back.

'Sounds fair to me.' Horrie's sandpaper voice accompanied the jangle of crockery balancing on a tray, which he placed on the card table beside Justin. 'Something's gotta change, son.' He pushed the lid of the French press slowly, the aroma of coffee placating them all.

Justin bowed his head as Horrie poured coffee into tiny orange espresso cups, and Allira's frustration puddled on the floor like the run-off from an umbrella.

Hamish broke the silence. 'Justin tells us you made all these. The handiwork is exceptional.' He had an eye for well-crafted furniture. Many a time Allira had feigned interest as he gaped at a dovetail joint or a parquetry tabletop.

He had clearly found Horrie's pet topic and, without any further prompting, the gentleman with the shiny head was sharing how he taught himself the art of woodwork when his family couldn't afford to buy him a guitar. He'd made the instru-ment out of offcuts scrounged from neighbours' sheds.

'There was a carpenter, a top bloke, and he'd drop by every so often with a load of his seconds and scraps. You wouldn't believe some of the timbers he gave me, just a squirt of a lad in his pre-teens. Huon, Sassafras, Blackwood, King Billy. The sort of timber that's well hard to come by these days, certainly without a wallet full of cash.'

Allira wondered why Justin hadn't written a story on his own dad for *Folk*, or at least put his name forward to be inter-viewed. Besides anything else, the room with its wallpapering of petite guitars would be a photographer's dream. She could already sense the texture of Horrie's story, the layers of grief, joy, triumph and mystery. Every family was layered like that, though some were easier to separate than others. The glue dissolved with gentle questioning and listening. Listening without interruption.

She sipped her coffee. Justin had withdrawn again, his eyes closed as he gulped his hot, tarry liquid. *Please say yes to our offer, Justin.* She wanted to shake him. *Can't you see that this would be good for all of us?* Her stomach fluttered with guilt. She'd noticed Justin had lost weight lately; lines feathered his sallow skin and his determined gait had lost its vigour. Who was she to decide what was good for this man, who was drowning some kind of pain with alcohol, barely keeping his business operational while living back with his father in his forties? She turned away, unable to look any more, but the rumble of Hamish and Horrie's conversation had stalled.

'Right, let's have this settled tonight then.' Horrie commanded the attention of the room with his booming voice.

Justin opened one eye, then the other.

'Allira, Hamish, I've seen your offer and I think it's downright reasonable.'

'Wait on, Pops. This's got nothing to do with you—'

'Seeing as we're housemates, son, and I've seen the state of your finances, I reckon it has everything to do with me.' A tenderness threaded through Horrie's posture and he lowered his voice. 'If you're going to make some good and proper changes, son, maybe unbridling yourself from the magazine would be a good place to start.'

Justin eyed his father. 'Thanks for your support, Dad,' he said wryly.

Horrie tapped the side of his coffee cup loudly with his spoon and Allira was reminded of the tinkling of crystal champagne flutes at a wedding before the best man's speech. The sudden hush. The nervous energy: would there be laughter, or would this moment be spoken of in years to come as poor taste, sour grapes, missed opportunity? Justin sighed and looked at his hands. Allira knew this wasn't the way he'd planned it. He hadn't planned to push everyone away and medicate his loneliness with the drink. In the early days of *Folk*, there was promise of a good working relationship. But she could see that Horrie's persistent tinkling for his 'speech' was like a death knell for Justin. Everything was tumbling down. She only hoped that one day he would have the strength to rebuild.

Justin looked around him. Everyone was silent. The roar of the rain only amplified the absence of human voices in that smarting moment.

'You'll publish my work from time to time?'

The room breathed again, the caramel woodgrain glowing more vibrantly. The sense of relief was palpable, but a shadow prowled around Justin like a hungry cat. He rose from the chaise and extended a hand, his eyes roaming everywhere except to Allira.

'Yes! I mean, of course!' Allira stammered. They shook hands and Allira threw her arms around Justin's neck, kissing him on the cheek. 'Are you sure?'

He nodded and smiled sadly, enough that dimples carved the corners of his mouth, a flash of the youthful charisma that had won him interviews with so many great minds and movers, once upon a time.

'Well, this is cause for celebration!' Horrie chuckled heartily. He thumped Justin and Allira on their backs before pushing between them to a squat little cupboard with leadlight doors. He unlocked it with a key from his pocket and retrieved an expensive-looking bottle. Hamish squeezed Allira in a breathtaking bear hug for the second time that night as Horrie poured port into their empty espresso cups.

'To health, happiness and new beginnings,' Horrie said with his bright cup in the air like a wedge of Valencia orange.

'Health, happiness and new beginnings,' they repeated before drinking.

Allira allowed the port to touch her lips only, licking the sweet syrup that tasted of sultanas and allspice. 'Wow, I can't believe this is happening!' She felt wide awake. 'Thank you, Justin, I won't let you down, you won't regret this,' she babbled, her cheeks shining from joyful tears.

'You've only got yourself to let down now,' he said drily.

Horrie chuckled again. 'I'm going to leave you young ones to celebrate. All this excitement has got me feeling rather exhausted.' He rammed the cork into the port bottle and sat it back in the little cabinet by the mantelpiece. As he went to shut the orange-and-green leadlight door, something caught Allira's eye. Small, smooth, the colour of honeycomb.

'Stop!' Her heart galloped, 'Horrie, can I have a look in there?'

He stepped back, the key in his hand. 'There's nothing much in there, love, just a few tipples I like to pour as a nightcap.'

Allira reached past him. She lifted the carving into the light and brushed dust from its back, her fingers tracing the patination of feathers, a tilted head, folded wings. It was carved into utter contentment. Masterfully carved. Just like the little bird on Nora's shelf. 'Wherever did you get this, Horrie?' she breathed, the bird cupped in her hand. The musky perfume of Huon pine muddled the air.

Horrie lifted the wooden figure like it was injured and gently set it down on the mantle. 'Deserves to be seen more, it does.' The bald orb of his head nodded. 'When I was a newborn baby left in a basket on the doorsteps of the Sheffield Baptist Church manse, this little fellow was tucked among my blankets.' He rubbed a handkerchief across the wren's head and chest. 'It's all I have of my birth mother.'

Chapter 31

Summer 1953

All was quiet in the workshop. It had been at least a quarter of an hour since the baby's first sound. There was a cough, a shuffling, muffled voices and another low, long groan, but then, silence. Stan paced at the door, hands jammed into armpits. He wanted to be in there, at his daughter's side, but Thelma said it was unseemly. His ticker raced worse than when Nora herself was born. An owl called, its wings whooshing through the inky air. Stan flinched before sitting down on a hefty round of wood, massaging his neck. *Blow it, I'm just going in there*, he was thinking as the door swung open and Thelma slid through, quickly latching it again behind her.

'He's a sickly child,' she said. Light from the kerosene lamp at Stan's feet strained, insipid, and he made out the shadowy features of the child, wrapped in a towel in Thelma's arms.

'A boy then!' Stan was on his feet again, marvelling at the bundle, a silly smile on his face. 'Hello, lad. Aren't you a tiny blighter?' he said, rubbing an index finger against the baby's cheek, sandpaper on silk. The child wriggled, squeaked, opened his eyes briefly and Stan wondered if he'd truly inherited his mother's riverine eyes, or if it was just wishful thinking, the light being so dim. 'How's Nora?' he asked, finally cutting the spider-web mesmer between his own chest and the wee scrap of life in his wife's hands.

Thelma turned away from the eyes that were indeed a mirror of their daughter's. 'She will be fine,' she said, her voice lowered. 'We need to take him away quickly now.' Thelma took a deep, harrowing breath. 'It's for the best.' She stepped away from the door, drawing Stan with her. He roped an arm around her birdlike shoulders, leaning towards his grandson.

'Shouldn't we wait a bit, let her say goodbye?'

Thelma shook her head. 'It will only make the parting more difficult. She is a determined girl. No, I have no doubt in my mind that Evelyn will thank us for this one day.'

'I don't know, Thelm. Look at him . . .'

Thelma's jaw clenched and she swallowed hard. 'She agreed with me, Stanley, that this child would only get in the way of her dreams. Her dreams with that German boy, no doubt.'

Stan's head snapped. Heat pricked beneath his salt-and-pepper moustache, and he pulled himself to full height.

'Now, now, Stanley,' Thelma said firmly. 'Calm down. You know the plan. Let's get moving so we can quickly put all of this messy business behind us.' The baby whimpered and they continued to the house, where Thelma would mix some formula and send Stan off on a hasty drive before dawn rinsed the shadows from the countryside.

*

Stan thought all mothers bonded naturally with their babies. There were scientific ways to describe it: chemical reactions, pheromones, oxytocin and whatnot. Not to be sentimental, but he always thought it had more to do with spiritual connection. Deep and mysterious, but there all the same. Like the bioluminescent algae flaming in the waves at the secluded beach on the East Coast during their honeymoon. The bright blue wonder had met them as they walked beneath the sickle moon, and they tore off their clothes to see the phosphorescence light up their wet skin. A rote explanation lay on the desk of a scientist somewhere, a clashing of molecules or some such thing, but the miracle was in the wonder. Piercing blue, two lovers, an otherworldly moment and utter abandon.

With David, Thelma took to motherhood like a duck to water. She was in her element, all the rhythms of washing, feeding, sleeping and cooking organised to within a minute and tracked in a blue-lined notebook that was her constant companion. Not only that, but Stan would come across his wife leaning over the edge of the sleeping child's cot, watching David as he dreamed. Stan always thought it was the best sight a husband could behold, the tenderness between his wife and their baby. Then along came Nora. Poor Nora. It wasn't her fault her birth was traumatic, and her ma struggled to feed her, struggled to love her. Stan would carry his daughter to Thelma at feed times and she would allow the child to find her breast, lying listless in her bed.

Perhaps Nora would have struggled to bond with her baby too. Perhaps it really was for the best. Still, the thought sat uncomfortably, like a burr in his sock.

Stan stole a glance to the back seat of the Buick where a wooden crate lined with blankets cradled his grandson. He was fast asleep. Thelma had fed him formula with an eye dropper and the tiny amount was obviously enough to satisfy him for now. Headlights flashed over farmland, lumpy mounds of sheep and dairy cows, the occasional darting wallaby. He pressed the accelerator harder. Sunrise was around 5.30; he must make the delivery before it was light, before people woke up and moved around. Before he lost his nerve.

Thelma shouldn't have done that, put sleeping draught in Nora's water. She reckoned it'd ensure she didn't wake in hysterics over the trauma of the labour. What was it she said? *'Quick labour, long recovery.'* He couldn't say what had given him the idea, but before driving off he'd crept into the workshop and fetched one of Nora's Huon wrens, the one with the peaceful look to it. It glowed in his hand and the musky perfume tickled at his nose. Nora didn't so much as stir, her face pale as the people he boxed up for a living. He held his hand in front of her mouth, only leaving when he felt the warm waft of her breath on his skin. It didn't feel right, what they were doing. He wanted to hear it from his daughter's lips – a single word of consent would do – but Thelma wouldn't be turned.

Stan slowed the car as he entered the township of Sheffield, dark and still but for a line of streetlights, their glow barely visible through the heavy fog. Fog or smoke from somewhere, or a murky mix of the two. He turned down a side street and pulled into the shadows of a Norfolk Island pine, cutting the engine. The manse was three doors down, the church next to it. He didn't want to risk being heard or seen. The baby was still asleep as Stan lifted the crate and walked the distance to the door. It was quick, and Stan realised too late that this was goodbye, a grandfather to his grandson. He knew he couldn't linger on the steps there in the garden of foxgloves and lavender, growing more colourful by the minute as the sun rose, so he dipped his stubbled chin to the boy and whispered, 'I'll find a way to know you, kid, you just see.'

Thump. Thump. Thump. Stan rapped at the door with clenched fist and slipped into the shadows beyond the house, crouching, catching his breath. A minute passed. Two. Should he go and knock again? Were they away? Then the door opened and a woman of short stature, soft with curves, a long plait trailing her back, stood framed in light. Her hands flew to her cheeks. A man quickly joined her and together they turned blinded eyes into the nightscape, trying to catch a glimpse of their donor. That was all Stan waited for. He made his retreat and the click of the manse door pulling shut registered like the slap of a back cover closing on a book. The end.

His Adam's apple rubbed up and down his throat on the way home as he drove through a countryside coming awake. Greening, yellowing, reddening. As the Buick roared along the hedgerows of Caveside, Stan barely noticed the decadent sunrise, bright as a Mai Tai. Smoke particles in the atmosphere refracted and multiplied the light until it appeared like the Sahara sky in a dust storm. Stan's thoughts were on the other unsavoury tasks ahead of him: the bloodied towels, the placenta, the hessian mat. Thelma said he must burn or bury them. He would bury them of course. A bonfire in this heat, with plumes even now curling from the ridge, would be sheer lunacy. There was the dead apple tree that he'd pulled out last season. He would bury the items there in the orchard, and plant the new sapling while he was at it. Quietly, of course, so Nora wouldn't see and add to her distress.

Wind swirled and pummelled the car's dusty bodywork as Stan turned into Western Creek Road. *How will I look at her?* Those eyes, the green puddles that followed his every movement and implored explanations of every observation. Like, why do gangs of black cockatoos come screeching off the mountain some days and not others? And why doesn't Billy feel terrible after he tortures skinks by driving nails into their bellies? Or how do you know when you're an adult? His Nora was an adult long ago, capitulated on her apprenticeship to the family business. Death was a sharp sniff of smelling salts. The fuzzy falsehoods and smeary grey of things untended or unaccepted violently snapped into focus when life met its full stop. There was only now, the eye-stinging shock of mortality filling the lungs but threatening never to do so again.

He remembered green lilypad eyes reflecting the pallor of dead neighbours' faces and swimming around the phenomenon of rigor mortis. It was the same awe she held reverently in the mountain places she rode to, bouncing in Daphne's saddle with clutches of the pony's barley-coloured mane laced between her fingers. It was fearful, this awe at life. A holding in the balance. The fear and the wonder.

Stan pressed the brake and eased the car down the neck of the Grayson driveway. He frowned and rubbed absently at his moustache. The last time he'd seen his daughter winding those elements together like a helix wasn't so long ago. She'd been in the workshop, belly full of baby, whispering, 'We're going to be okay.'

As he approached, Thelma ran towards the car. Stan wound his window down, pulse racing, an image rising like scum at the edge of a soup pot, of Nora laid out on the pallet bed. Or was it a casket?

'Thank the good Lord you're here, Stanley.' Thelma was breathless. 'It's the Frankes,' she gasped. 'Bushfires . . . Their shed is gone. The house is too close. You'd best get over there and lend a hand bringing it under control.'

Stan looked in the direction of the Franke farmhouse, further along Western Creek Road, nestled where the land began to slope into the foothills of Mother Cummings. There was nothing to see but the eerie glow of the sun trying to crack open the sky.

Chapter 32

Autumn 2019

'There's no such thing as a coincidence,' Allira's mum used to say when the world dealt her a lucky hand. It was her oft-repeated sentiment that came to mind when Allira struggled with the baffling discovery that Horrie was Nora's son. That her boss, or ex-boss, was Nora's grandson. *How does that even happen?* In the end, she had rolled her eyes at Rae and said, 'Only in Tassie!' Only on this island state where families tended to dig roots down deep did a discovery of this magnitude – of lies, love and shame – result in such a timely reunion. It was a divine appointment.

Allira met Horrie and Justin on Sunday afternoon in the sparse reception at Mercy Place with its plastic peace lilies and the local radio station playing just above a whisper. Horrie hadn't wanted to delay, so here they were the day after Allira had linked the dusty Huon pine wren in his liquor cabinet with its pair in Nora's room.

Sally pulled Allira aside while Horrie and Justin finished signing in. 'I'm not sure how to say this without sounding condescending, but I'm so proud of you.'

Allira flushed.

'What you've done for this family . . .' Sally shook her head, leaving the sentence hanging.

Allira placed a hand on Sally's arm and smiled. That was enough. She knew.

Sally turned to Horrie, sidestepping pleasantries to pump his hand energetically. 'In all the years I've worked here, Horrie, I've not had such a pleasure as reuniting a mother and son after more than sixty-five years.' She was still grasping his hand as she continued. 'When Allira told me about you, I wouldn't believe her, but now you're here . . .' Sally blinked rapidly.

Horrie looked as dumbfounded as she was. He'd told Allira that he'd given up hope of finding his birth family long ago, had always felt torn about the whole messy business. His adoptive parents, the Reverend Taylor and his wife, had never been called such. They were Ma and Pa, nothing more, nothing less. When they told him the reason he shared so few of their physical traits on his thirteenth birthday, it had barely registered. They treated him no differently; he was loved, a valued member of the Taylor tribe. It was only when Horrie had a child of his own who asked the questions he'd never thought to ask that he'd had a half-hearted scout through the adoption records. All dead ends. So he left it at that. He wasn't meant to find out, it seemed, and he never was the sort to poke his nose where there was likely to be a bad smell.

And then along came Allira late one night to spill the whole fantastical story on his hearth beneath the mysterious wooden wren on the mantelpiece. The same wren now cupped in his hand.

'To think . . . My mother, a wee girl of fifteen.' Horrie had plonked his big frame down in a chair in disbelief when Allira had told him about Nora last night. 'And my dad, a German-Polish carpenter. A lover of timbers just like me.' He'd cried when Allira had explained that his mum thought he was dead all these years. Sixty-five years of grief. He'd openly sobbed in front of Justin and Hamish and Allira, the guttural sounds rattling his teeth until there was nothing left. 'Phew,' he had finally said, offering a quavering grin through the sheen of tears. 'I guess it really does count for something, knowing my mother wanted me, even after all these years.'

Horrie turned the golden wren around in his hand. 'I'm as baffled as you are, let me assure you,' Horrie said to Sally. She told them that his mother had gone downhill lately, preparing them for disappointment, though Allira had already told Justin and Horrie that the bad days were now far outnumbering the good. It seemed to her that Justin was keeping the whole matter at arm's length, aloof from the intensity of emotions that were no doubt coursing through his dad, whose whole world had been remade.

'I'm ready,' he said. How did a 65-year-old prepare to meet his own mother for the first time in memory? Allira wondered. He'd been robbed of the gradual awakening to who she was, the one whose very body enveloped and nourished him into being, the woman-child who'd said yes to him before she clapped eyes on his pink body. She who felt his movements within her, the rhythmic pulsing of his bouts of hiccups, his sleep cycles, his swift kicks of protest. He didn't know her. Yet, he knew her. Strangely, it was how Allira could describe her own relationship with Nora, the cruelty of dementia obstructing any common connection, yet also ushering them to a different plane of understanding. No one else had empathised with the pain of her own loss quite like Nora had.

Nora didn't stir when they entered in single file, Sally taking the lead, Justin loitering in the doorway. Allira looked at her as if seeing her for the first time, acutely aware of the impression Horrie would be receiving. She had lost weight. Her shoulders and elbows and knees all pointed inwards like a quiver of arrows in her greying tapestry chair against the wall. Her hair hung limp around her face and her eyes were the colour of a snail's silvery trail. Someone had dressed her in an ill-matching rust cardigan and petrol-coloured slacks, a cream silk scarf slung like a fishing net around her neck. The baby doll rested in the crook of her left elbow beneath a yellow bunny rug, and she swayed from side to side, a waning pendulum.

Allira took her hand and massaged it gently, smoothing the skin along each knobbly finger while trying to find her eyes. *Look at me, Nora.* She willed the depleted woman to emerge from her stupor. 'Hello, Nora. It's me, Allira,' she said softly, 'I've brought someone very special to visit you today.' The air conditioning whirred, and a volley of laughter drifted from a conversation down the corridor. 'I'm your friend, Evelyn,' Allira tried her other name, the one connected to her childhood. 'You're one of my dearest friends.'

Nora tilted her head and stared vacantly, her face like melted wax. Horrie cleared his throat and closed the space between them, his knees popping and grinding as he lowered himself to her eye level. He lifted her hand from Allira, squeezed it, before addressing the hollowed woman. His mother.

'My name is Horrie,' he said, his voice like bark peeling from a tree trunk. 'I've got a story to tell that I think will interest you.'

Nora looked at him, from his shiny scalp to his clean-shaven chin, his broad shoulders and faintly familiar green eyes. 'They put arsenic in our soup here,' she hissed at him. 'Watch your back, dear. That's my advice.'

Horrie's eyes creased. 'Cripes, you must have a cast-iron stomach,' he said good-naturedly.

She gave a curt, mirthless nod and continued her swaying.

'Nora, when I was a newborn, just a day-old little tacker, I was left on the doorstep of a minister's family in Sheffield.' He watched for any flicker of understanding in her face before continuing. 'They took me in and for many years I believed them to be my real ma and pa, but on my thirteenth birthday they told me I was adopted. They didn't know who my birth mother and father were. They didn't know anything except for the old crate I was nestled in, and the little wooden bird tucked into my blankets.' He lifted his free hand, uncurling fingers to reveal the Huon pine wren nestled within, the carving so intricate it detailed puffed chest feathers, tilted head, gleaming eyes. 'Do you remember this?'

Nora looked at the bird in his hand and then looked at the bird on her shelf. There was a spark, a whiff of something, Allira saw. The potent perfume of the timber rose, beckoning Nora's synapses to fire, to recognise and remember. And she breathed it in with the baby on her arm, a visceral moment teetering at the cusp. But she fell backwards, a gasping retreat into the dark spaces of her consciousness. The shadows lurking.

'There's no soap, I'm all out of soap.' Her face was puckered. 'Where does a woman get a good bar of lavender soap around here?'

Allira watched as Horrie blew out the breath he'd been holding. She knew he was grateful even to meet her, but like Allira, he longed to set her free, this woman and her doll. He took a measured breath and Allira imagined him mustering strength for one more try.

'Nora, we think you might be my mother.' His voice splintered, and he waited, the wren in his hand.

Nora twitched, pushing the doll to her lap. She knotted and unknotted her hands, tugged at the scarf around her neck and then returned to the knotting and unknotting of her sun-spotted hands above the doll's unblinking face.

Sally stepped forward. 'Nora, this man is your baby, your son, see? All grown up now, but he's lived a long and full life. You gave that to him.'

The bewildered old woman looked at her doll, at Sally, at Horrie. No one dared move.

She looked at the doorway. 'Who's that?' Nora half-rose from the tattered chair, her eyes on Justin. Horrie gently steadied her. 'You! Look at me!' Her voice was a dissonant note.

Justin flinched in the doorway and Allira beckoned him in. He straightened and took a step into the room so that light fell across his scruffy hair and tanned complexion. Nora's mouth dropped open and she shambled forward, the doll flung behind her into the chair.

'Michał!' Her pupils dilated as she staggered towards Justin, who had begun backing away at the same pace, like a magnetic field was keeping them separated.

'That's my son, Justin,' Horrie scrambled to explain. 'Your grandson.'

Justin slipped out of view into the nursing home corridor. Allira could see that the spectre of grief was too much, and she watched Justin lean against the wall. His brow was slick with sweat and he clutched his stomach. She wondered if he'd had a drink this morning.

Nora stared at the vacant doorway, the cream silk scarf waving gently with each laboured breath. She was a plinth, a sandstone pillar, eyes turned hard. They allowed her time to gather herself, Allira hoping she would find some speck of the past to make sense of the present. Nora rubbed her forefinger and thumb together, over and over, lifting them to within a handspan of her face. Like water over a stone, her skin had been smoothed by the passage of time, and she scrutinised the pads of her fingers as if making a profound discovery.

'I have no fingerprint,' she said, lifting her face to Horrie. 'You see?' She offered her hand so he could inspect the whorls of markings. 'Nothing.' Her listless voice barely rustled the silk at her throat.

Horrie opened his mouth, closed it. Allira could see he couldn't speak, so he simply grasped her hand, his thick, sun-spotted mitt encompassing her withering digits. He drew her grainy, cracked skin to his lips. She couldn't help thinking of the little girl from her dreams, her luminescent skin and dirty finger-nails wrapped in the secure clasp of her hand. Mother and child.

In the dream, as with Horrie and Nora, it was the child holding the parent.

'It's the soap, of course!' Nora pulled her hand away, 'Worse than sandpaper! What I wouldn't give for a bar of pavlova . . .' She paused, eyebrows slanting downwards. 'Who are you?'

'I'm Horrie. Just a friendly visitor.' His eyes were sad.

'Well, Horrie, I'd be obliged if you made it your business to procure a bar for me.'

'Of pavlova?' He cleared his throat and exchanged a knowing look with Sally and Allira, who weren't trying nearly so hard to contain their amusement.

'The soap, Horrie. I do love my pavlova soap . . . but it doesn't sound right. The words are wrong again, I keep losing my words.'

'You said you wanted lavender soap before,' Horrie said gently.

'That's it, yes. Lavender.'

Horrie guided Nora to the armchair, where she settled back to nursing and clucking over the plastic doll. Allira retreated to the doorway with Justin. She didn't understand. This was no exultant reunion. Her gallant hopes of wrenching a barbed lie from Nora's past dissolved before her. Deep, lacerating sorrow engulfed her as she saw the tenderness of Nora's touch against the doll's plastic cheek, how she wrapped it snugly in the yellow blanket and rocked it in the crook of her arm. Back and forth she rocked. Her son right there beside her. It was just the two of them, sitting close, yet so very far away.

'He's a very good baby,' Nora said.

Horrie lifted himself from where he'd been crouching beside her chair, his knees popping and groaning again. 'Goodbye,

Nora.' He lifted the Huon pine wren and placed it on the shelf beside its pair. They glowed together, their perfume doubled. 'Goodbye, Ma,' he whispered.

'Don't forget the pavlova, mister,' Nora said without looking up, and Horrie walked slowly to the door.

Allira stood at the window, a mug of coffee going cold in her hand. She watched the industrious bustle on the other side of the Tamar River. A crane lifted cargo onto the berthed ship, a forklift buzzing in the background. Lights flashed in the darkening night and Allira imagined the urgency of the workers trying to get the job done before nightfall. The ship's hull sank lower into the murky water as it accepted more and more freight.

Allira blinked. The weight of Horrie's disappointment had pressed upon her all afternoon. It was not the reunion she had imagined. For all Sally's warnings and her own observation of dementia's cruel spiral, she had still hoped to see Nora's face flush with delight when Horrie revealed his identity. Allira tipped her untouched coffee down the sink and slumped onto the couch, pulling out her phone. Rae had sent her a message earlier, something about the *Tas Herald* archives: '*Hey Al, Nathan tells me the Tas Herald has just finished digitising its archives and gave me his login. Want it?*'

Allira remembered the missing editions down in the stuffy archive room and punched a reply: '*Of course!*' When Rae sent through the details a few minutes later, Allira already had her laptop ready and quickly navigated to the online archive's search function. *1953–1954. Grayson.* Allira hit the blinking search button and held her breath.

A list of three articles loaded onto the screen. The first was the missing persons notice, Nora's young face in grainy black and white. Nothing new there. Allira's eyes latched to the headline of another article: *Highland Fires Claim Five Buildings*. Allira scanned the article. Three houses. A shed. And the workshop of Caveside undertaker and carpenter Stanley Grayson. She checked the date: 2 January, 1954. One of the missing editions. She read the article again. Fires had burnt out of control below Mother Cummings. A windstorm blew embers across the farmland, lighting bush and threatening infrastructure. The Mole Creek and Deloraine fire services could not save the homes of the Abbott, Franke and Lee families. Fire had threatened the Grayson family home, but volunteers managed to contain it to the separate workshop building and the adjoining orchard. No mention of a daughter.

Allira zoomed in on the photo. There were two men in the background of the smouldering Abbott house remains, their faces blackened, leaning on spades. The shorter of the two had a wide, bushy moustache. Could it be? She retrieved Thelma's scrapbook from her desk and flipped to the family photograph glued to the inside cover. There was no mistaking it. The man in the newspaper article was Stanley Grayson. Gosh, Allira thought, maybe he was there while his own workshop was burning down. Allira's arms prickled.

The third article in the list was a short follow-up report three days later with estimated damage costs. Allira printed

the two pages of new information and slipped them into
Thelma's scrapbook before closing her laptop and rubbing
her eyes. It wasn't going to help Nora Gray – Evelyn Grayson –
comprehend that Horrie Taylor was her son, but it was another
piece to the puzzle.

Chapter 33

Summer 1953

Evelyn woke to the sensation of being pinned to her mattress. Her body was lead. She groaned and lifted her head to see pale arms and legs lying freely at her sides. No pins splaying her like a science class specimen. No bulky weights piled upon her. Light seared through a gap in the blanket that had been hung as a curtain across the window. She wanted to go back . . . back to the soft place of sleep. Her eyelids squeezed against the glare, and she was floating. Succumbing to the call.

Was it minutes or days that passed? Evelyn's head danced. The light was as grey as laundry water and there was an acrid, cloying stench to it. She rolled onto her side. Muscles and ligaments in her abdomen spasmed painfully, but she moved lightly. Evelyn reached a hand to her stomach and the past day's events flickered like a malevolent film reel. Water and blood. Mother at the window. A feeble cry. Arms reaching. Yellow towel.

Evelyn clutched at the loose skin around her belly button. She had been emptied. There was red on her nightdress. The shaping of her body for nearly nine months was finished. *Where's my baby?* The dizziness was a mercy. Black.

'Evelyn. Evelyn.' Someone called to her from so far away, the sound barely tickled her ears. The three syllables of her name slowly marched nearer, like a choral trio, sing-song and elongated. *Air-vah-len. Air-vah-len.* Her eyes twitched. She murmured.

'Evelyn!' The sound was blunt, an axe against hardwood, and Evelyn's eyes flew open to find Mother hovering above her with a glass of water. Her flawless skin was a creamy loom for almond-shaped eyes and pursed crimson lips.

'You're so beautiful.' The words fell out of Evelyn's mouth unbidden, and she watched her mother's chest and ears pinken and her pointed chin fall ever so slightly. Her hand darted to her throat, rustling the flounces of a smart, grey house dress and disturbing dust into the air. The perfume of Huon pine swirled, and Evelyn looked to the windowsill above Daddy's work bench. One of the birds was missing. The wren poised for flight cut a lonely figure, silhouetted against farmland and the Great Western Tiers. It must've been bumped onto the floor. *I'll check it later.*

'Silly girl. It's been a big couple of days,' Mother cooed. 'But everything can get back to normal now, darling. Your room is ready inside. You can have a few days 'battling a cold' to allow for your chest to settle, and then you can get on with things.'

Evelyn looked down at her chest. Her breasts were like rocks, and the front of her nightdress bore peculiar water-marks. She hugged her knees and shook her head. *Back to normal. Get on with things.* She shuddered, and behind the red film of her eyelids she remembered. The hushed voices outside the workshop door. The spade hacking into the orchard earth. The yellow bundle. Mother's expressionless face at the kitchen window. She remembered her son lifted from her into the dawn light, his petal skin glowing, legs kicking. *Her son.*

She wanted to run, to hide. She wanted to dig her hands into the soil and scream at the mountains. Instead, she bent her neck and wept into her hands. 'What did you do?' she asked, tears and dribble strung between her lips.

'I said I'd take care of you, Evelyn. I kept my promise.' There was steel in Mother's voice. 'It's okay, Evelyn, it's okay.' She rubbed her daughter's back, her wedding rings cutting over each bony vertebra. 'This is normal. Your hormones are all over the place. Everything will settle down soon.'

The affection was foreign to Evelyn, and she invited it and flinched away simultaneously, the sobs subsiding. Mother's touch was firm and real. Like when she had once gashed her head at a playground and the bleeding wouldn't stop. Mother's firm, rhythmic strokes on her back as she held a bandage to her head had lulled her. And when she first fell off Daphne onto a rock and badly grazed her arm, Mother had been brusquely attentive, cleaning and dressing the wound, assuring her that there would be no scarring before shooing her out of the kitchen.

The pregnancy and her baby felt an enigma. Did it even happen? Did she have a son? Maybe she could just carry on like

Mother said and pick up where she left off, unchanged. Perhaps the wound would scab over, and time would rub it away so that one day she would only hold a nebulous memory of it.

'Where's Daddy?' Evelyn took the glass of water from Mother's hand and drank.

'Helping at the Franke farm.' Mother walked to the window and pulled aside the curtain. 'There are fires in the highlands, and this fickle wind is blowing embers and starting spot fires. The Frankes have already lost a shed and every man this side of the Mersey River is over there working to save the house.'

The Tiers shouldered an opalescent sky. Evelyn had never seen so many colours brooding over the mountain ranges, yet Mother Cummings was obscured in a smoky stranglehold.

Chapter 34

Autumn 2019

It had been three weeks since Allira last visited Nora. Evelyn. She wasn't sure what to call her any more. Horrie had sent her a text a few days back, a muddled message of autocorrected typos. 'You should go visit Nora,' he said, among other things, including an update on Justin's admission to a rehab facility. It all made her feel terrible. She'd neglected Nora, though she was still coming to terms with the reason why. *Has it really been three weeks?*

The handover at *Folk* had been mercifully swift. A day holed up in Justin's office rifling through manila folders crammed into Reflex boxes and a hodgepodge of documents on an old hard drive. The staff clocked off early that Friday, catering was ordered and the bar fridge filled – non-alcoholic bevvies only – for a low-key farewell of their editor, who they could all admit had been extraordinary at times, if a little faded and bruised. He performed well, but Allira could see it cost him and there was nothing she could do to cushion the fall. Any intervention on her behalf would just diminish him further.

For all her celebration of his achievements, the speech lauding his gumption in taking the magazine into a new era as an independent publication, the toast to his bright future, there was still a point where he had to clear his desk. When Allira saw him carrying the cardboard box containing a potted succulent, the framed photograph of him receiving his Walkley Award, errant pens, his old SLR and a laptop, she wanted to run after him and beg him to stay.

'Over to you, boss,' Justin said with a wink.

Allira opened her mouth to say something meaningful, but his faded blues flickered away. *Don't*, they seemed to say. So she said, 'Bye, Justin,' instead, a limp farewell that dropped hollow as a vacated chrysalis behind him.

She watched him step into the elevator, heard the ping as the doors closed, and then stood alone in the old dance studio, trying to divorce the conflicting tides within her: the part that wanted to push the desks against the walls and dance on the cloud of primal energy rising within, and the other part that wanted to lie prostrate with guilt and let her tears wash the grimy floorboards.

Since then, Allira had worked solidly to understand the magazine's operations, building a clear picture of how far Justin had let things slide. There were relationships to patch up with disgruntled suppliers and stakeholders, which meant long and costly lunches. By the end of the first week, her jaw had ached with the constant effort of curating her face to show optimism and capability. She met one-on-one with every staff member and listened to their concerns, ideas, and visions, writing copious notes after every interaction, jotting down their strengths and weaknesses. She quickly identified two employees who would need to lift their game or leave, and many others with untapped talent.

Each night she used her last skerrick of energy to sink into the couch, letting Hamish cook dinner or order takeout while she updated him on the day's findings at the mag. She wanted him to be part of every decision and even held secret hopes that he would one day cut back his hours with the ambulance service to give a couple of days to *Folk*.

'Suze is an absolute rocket. I can't believe I didn't notice it before,' she prattled between mouthfuls of satay chicken stir-fry. 'She's just been undervalued, stuck in admin when her skills are more suited to management.' For all the crippling hours and delicate management, Allira was energised in a way she had rarely experienced before. It took her back to college days, when her creative writing teacher had asked her to have a go at editing the college magazine.

It was Saturday today. She slept in until 10.30, had a brunch of scrambled eggs and coffee, and decided to visit Nora before Hamish finished his shift that afternoon. Everything was the same as her last visit: the assault of smells as she pushed through the security door into the sterile corridor; the semi-circle of residents in front of a midday sit-com; the milky view across the car park.

A nurse hurried by, doubling back when she saw Allira. 'You're here!' Her face lit up. 'Make sure you go see Sally before you leave,' she said, marching off without further explanation.

Opera music played somewhere, the sound carrying along the hall. The notes wavered, split open. Allira remembered

Gilbert, the giant of a man with the baritone voice. A voice only for singing. It started again, tingling her spine, encouraging each vertebra to stand up. Any errant thought extinguished, any sluggish muscle revived.

Nora was in bed, pillows surrounding her head like an Elizabethan collar. A walking frame sat on the right-hand side of the bed, a vase of bearded irises, deep royal purple, next to it. From Horrie, Allira guessed. Nora's eyes were closed but they flickered and jittered as if she was having a vivid dream.

Allira perched on a chair beside her, mourning how different she looked after just three weeks. Her skin was like a dumpling wrapper boiled too long. Translucent, blue and grey and pink and yellow. Veins mapped her temples and her hair had been cut shorter, the coarse grey crop a woolly halo. Allira took her hand as she had done so often, gently massaging her palm as the old woman's eyes opened.

'Dear one,' Nora said, closing her eyes again, 'I heard you singing. It reminded me of the song you performed at Michał's thirtieth.' Her voice drifted off and Allira kept massaging her hand. The mysterious Michał.

'That was a great party. Where was it held again?'

'Hmm?' Nora lifted her chin, mottled greens peering at Allira. Something was different, but she couldn't place it.

'Where's Michał now?'

Nora dropped her head back against the pillows and squeezed her eyes closed. It was the wrong question.

'Who brought your flowers, Nora?'

'I don't know,' she said, water seeping from the corner of an eye. 'Have you come to take me away?'

'No, Nora, I'm a good friend. Just come to see how you're doing.' The papery eyelids drifted shut again and Allira wondered why Horrie had insisted she come. It was just as she had dreaded, a confirmation of why she had been so reticent to visit these past three weeks. Nora's dementia was full blown, and now she would never truly realise that her son was alive, that she had a family. Allira felt like a failure. She sat quietly for a quarter turn of the clock before standing, tucking her tee into the waist of her leggings, and turning to leave. Halfway to the door she swung around, her handbag whacking against her thigh. Something was not right. The thought was persistent. She closed her eyes, took a deep breath and then opened them again, drinking in every detail of Nora's room like she was seeing it for the first time. Ancient tapestry chair, sunken, scarred. Two Huon wrens beside the cardboard box tied with string. Nora dozing, a cotton nightie buttoned to her chin. The walking frame. Slippers.

Where is the doll? Allira tiptoed to Nora's bed again, checking that it wasn't tucked under the covers. But the bassinet was gone too. No bunny rug slung at the end of the bed, no romper or bibs in the drawer of the bedside table. Nora didn't stir as Allira opened the doors of the built-in wardrobe. No nappies, bottles, rattles or teddies, no lines of tiny shoes or piles of baby clothes in palest blue. Just Nora's own clothes in three drab piles and on a handful of coat hangers.

Allira flew from the room, her head buzzing. What had they done with Nora's doll, her only comfort? As if reading her mind, Sally was already marching towards her, the nursing home corridor retreating around her. She smiled as she reached Allira, steadying her with a steely hand on her shoulder.

'It's okay,' she said, stooping to catch Allira's eye. 'It happened after that first visit with Horrie, the one we thought was a raging flop. We didn't think she'd registered a word, did we? Well, the next morning, the bassinet was piled high with Nora's doll menagerie and pushed up against the door. The nurse thought she'd barricaded herself in!'

Allira grinned at the picture of a nurse calling security to barge into the door of Nora's room.

'We took the doll to her, thinking it was just a lapse or something, but by jeepers, the look she gave me, Allira!' Sally's shoulders shook, her hair bouncing. 'She gave me daggers for offering her the doll, and said in her most uppity voice, "Am I a child to you?" before pitching it across the room. It's a wonder she didn't put a dent in the wall.'

'She hasn't asked for it again?'

'Nope. Not once. It's like it didn't exist.'

Allira nodded, warmth spreading across her chest as realisation dawned. Sally nodded too, lopsided smiles on their faces. Horrie. Of course she didn't need the doll. Allira threw her arms around Sally's neck, jumping from one foot to the other. Sally was laughing, her eyes leaking, as Allira raced back to Nora's room, throwing a harried 'Thank you!' over her shoulder.

The gnarled old chair seemed the right place to sit, and before she'd even settled into the lumpy seat, Allira was pulling a notebook from the bottom of her handbag. She began to write. It started as a letter to Nora, merging into memoir and then autobiography, everything she knew of the green-eyed, fire-haired girl given shape and expression through the ink of her pen, linking and rushing out like electricity zipping along powerlines.

Nora rolled over in her sleep. A nurse raised his voice in the corridor, speaking slow and loud into an old man's ear. Allira's phone vibrated in her bag. Clouds darkened the sky and it began to rain. She barely registered any of it. Her hand zig-zagged down the page, flicking to one new sheet after the next. There was no time, no measure. She was a jar pouring out, spilling all her knowing with a gratefulness that anointed her hand.

Finally, it was done. Allira dropped the pen and notebook to her feet, her arms circling her stomach. She was exhausted and sleep came swiftly, carrying her to a familiar dream.

In the dream, the little girl with the Blue Willow eyes tugged at her arm, pulling until Allira tipped off balance and was running barefoot down the front yard on mossy grass that cushioned each footfall, so that it felt as if she was gliding. The breeze whispered. White cotton dresses billowed. The air was warm as a puppy's tongue and everything curved. The trees arched their branches ahead of them, a leafy arbour, and they pattered through, the light and whispers falling like blossoms in their hair.

The little girl's name shook the branches. Allira knew all this. Everything was familiar and her heart began drumming faster. She didn't want to continue. She wanted the dream to stop. But there she was with the beautiful child. What was her name? It was in the trees, flitting among the branches, so spry that she couldn't interpret the resonance.

The tree shaped like a chalice was ahead of them now, leaves like dinner plates serving up fat, juicy figs. *Don't eat the figs*, Allira thought as her dream self plucked one from the branch,

splitting it with her thumbs and laughing as the juice splattered
their dresses. The girl's olive skin was a fresh roll of brown
paper, unfurled, ready. A face full of her mother, leaning against
her thigh in the mild garden whimsy. The trees whispered her
name again, shaking it from their leaves and her dream self
strained to hear as her wanting-to-wake self filled with dread.
She knew what came next.

In the zephyr came a word that was name and bird. *Wren*,
it said, and lit on a branch. The blue of his cap was so incan-
descent, Allira flinched away. Their dresses glowed with the
reflected light of the little bird, and the girl named Wren giggled,
playing with the radiance that rubbed off on her hands and
imprinted everything she touched. She ran from flower to leaf,
insect to rock, lighting them up.

Then the bird opened its beak and trilled a warning. It
could not be anything else, the notes were so brutal against the
buoyant milieu. And there it was, the snake rearing up behind
her, scales rippling like a muscle, head flexed for attack. Allira
gulped air, looking for an exit, but her dream self was calm. She
noticed the snake's metamorphosis. This was no python. The
snake of her earlier dreams had shrunk to the length of a belt,
skinny and dull. Wren hovered behind her, tugging at her dress
and the bird's siren continued.

Allira lifted her foot and stomped on the snake's head, her
bare heel easily crushing the danger into the grass, where it dissipated to dirt. Wren whooped and squealed, kicking the dirt
into the air where it floated like ash, like dusty grey moth wings.

Allira woke in Nora's chair feeling like her gut had been
turned inside out. The dream was still cradled in her thoughts,

but its potency was diminished. She stretched her neck and lifted the pen and notebook from where she'd dropped them at her feet. The room was dark and quiet but for the snuffle of Nora's breathing; she was still asleep. Moonlight cast a stripe of light down the wall beside her bed, illuminating the Huon wrens.

Allira sat cross-legged on the lounge room floor. Hamish was singing in the shower and she could clearly make out his off-key rendition of Coldplay's 'A Sky Full of Stars'. How she loved him. Her heart ached with it, and she couldn't comprehend loving anyone more.

Spread out in front of her was everything she had connected with Nora. A notebook filled with pages of scrawl, recording what she could remember after each lucid day when Nora had stepped back six decades and re-lived a scene or a moment. The red Almanac from 1953 with sticky notes marking the significant pages. Thelma's scrapbook with its floral wrapping paper cover, smeared with grease and dated in her looping hand. Printouts of the *Tasmanian Herald* articles.

There were still so many gaps, and Allira knew that some of the answers lay bundled in that brown cardboard box in Nora's bedroom beside the two Huon pine wrens. The investigative journalist in her had wanted to whisk it away for a day and stitch together more of the picture. But when Justin called and asked a few tentative questions about Nora, his grandmother, she suddenly knew what she must do.

Allira wiped dusty hands on her jeans and lifted a gift box from the couch, carefully wrapping the books in tissue paper and placing everything neatly within. Last, she tied the box closed with a ribbon and slipped a notecard beneath the satin bow. The message was brief, just a few solitary lines: *I know now why I was so hesitant to write Nora's story. It's not my story to tell. It's yours, Justin. Here's everything I know, everything I found and everything Nora shared with me.*

The only piece she hadn't included was the stream of consciousness that had spilt from her on her last visit with Nora. That was tucked into her journal, perhaps to revisit many years down the track when her daughter was old enough to understand.

Hamish walked into the room, still humming. He kissed Allira on the head and massaged her shoulders. 'Ready to make this delivery, you two?' He leaned down further still and kissed the subtle roundness of her pregnant stomach. Twelve weeks today.

'Sure am.'

Justin answered the door in trackies and a faded Metallica t-shirt. Allira gripped the gift box awkwardly in front of her. Hamish was waiting in the car.

'Hi,' she said.

Justin's eyes were clear, his complexion like a fresh bagel. 'Allira.'

'I've compiled everything I learned about Nora, your grandmother, and I want you to have it. I think you'll be interested. And if you ever want to write her story, I promise you I'll publish it.' She grinned at him hopefully. 'But I realised a while ago that it's your story to tell.' She paused, her eyes sincere. 'Or not to tell.'

Justin took the box from her grasp and smiled his thanks. 'I'm glad you dropped by, I wanted to give you an explanation. An apology.'

Allira shook her head. 'You don't need—'

'No, hear me out,' Justin stood full height, his hands across his chest and Allira remembered the posture from his angry, erratic days in the office. She circled an arm around her stomach. 'I was a brute to you. You deserved better, and I'm so glad that you are editor of *Folk* now. Please forgive me. You are a great leader.'

'Oh, I—'

'Through all this mess I've discovered something about myself. I'm a stuffer. I stuff pain down deep inside and it eventually explodes. I'm afraid you bore the brunt of that.'

Allira couldn't hide the bewilderment from her face. 'Are you okay now?'

'When Mum died, I . . .' He leaned a shoulder into the doorway and paused to choose his words. 'I couldn't forgive myself for not being there for her. She died of cancer, you know.'

Allira nodded silently.

'I feel like I've been given a second chance, with Dad and Nora.' He gulped.

'Me too,' Allira whispered. She couldn't shake the notion that this pregnancy, this new baby, existed in part thanks to Nora and her mysteriously well-timed wisdom. She thought of the night beneath the apple trees when Nora had revealed the silvery scar on her palm. *'I don't ever want to forget it,'* she had said. *'I'm happy for the way the knife cut me.'* A little message-gift of embracing the pain as part of her story. And then there

303

was the presence of the Huon wren in Nora's room, looking every bit as jaunty as the wren in Allira's dreams. And she would never forget Nora's decisive declaration that had reached through the padding of her grief: 'You're a very good mother.'

'It's like she knows you, even though her dementia says otherwise.'

Allira looked up at Justin. They were the very words she had been trying to find.

Chapter 35

Summer 1954

As soon as Daddy handed her the stack of letters, Evelyn knew she couldn't stay. It was like a key had been turning and turning for so long, and then it clicked, the latch retreating to reveal a sense of clarity as pure as mountain water.

'You should have these,' he said solemnly. 'It wasn't right they were kept from you.'

It was such a big stack, twenty-two in all, wearing her name in crouching, rounded letters: *Evelyn Grayson*. All of the envelopes bore monotone postage stamps of buildings or droll men's heads, with *Deutsche Post* in block capitals. All sent from Berlin.

Evelyn wordlessly took the pile of letters from Daddy's hands, tears spilling down her cheeks. When she looked up, his eyes were scrunched, face crumpled, a dirty finger pawing his brow. She felt sorry for him. The sorrow bloomed in her chest, knowing that it was he who would be trapped in the memory of what he had done, not her.

'It was wrong, Nor, so wrong of us.' He sucked in his cheeks and then exhaled loudly through the shaggy overhang of his moustache. 'I'm so sorry.'

Mother was already at church heading a catering response to the fires, ensuring those fighting the blazes were fed, as well as the families who had lost homes. She didn't think Evelyn should be there for fear her first public appearance would only 'complicate matters'. It was just Daddy and Evelyn. And a stack of twenty-two letters.

Evelyn nodded. Over and again, she nodded, fingering the crisp corners of the envelopes in her hands like neat little razors.

'I . . . I need to tell you something else Nor,' Daddy fumbled. 'That is, I've got to explain something to you.'

Evelyn nodded absently again. That was the right thing to do, wasn't it? His voice was muffled, reaching her ears as through a long tunnel. He seemed so far away. Was he drifting? Was he being carried away in the wind?

'You need to hear it, the whole truth. I've been a fool, Nor, and I want to make things right.'

Her brows knit together with confusion.

'It's okay, poss. Let's talk tomorrow, or some other time, when you've had the chance to settle.'

Settle? Evelyn didn't know what he meant. *I should ask*. But then Daddy was talking again, saying something about fire, the Abbott farm and 'under threat'. He hugged her with his usual rough warmth, and she returned it as best she could, then listened to him drive away, the rumble of the engine petering out. Every farmer whose own property wasn't in the fire's path was at the Abbotts' trying desperately to save the house, which bordered thick bushland at the foothills of Mother Cummings.

Everyone was out fighting fires and Evelyn was suddenly alone with her thoughts. Utterly alone.

Evelyn carried the letters upstairs to her newly reclaimed bedroom. Calmly, she took out her pocketknife, chose the oldest envelope from the pile and slit it from edge to edge. She pulled out the creamy paper encased within and smoothed it on her lap.

> *My dearest Nora,*
>
> *I do not know what you expect me to say, yet I will be honest. When I read that our child is growing within you, I was overjoyed! You will be a wonderful mother. I will soon return and we will make a home together. A family. Please do not worry. I am needed here for now, or I would have been on the first ship back to Australia. My mother is very unwell. I'm not certain she will overcome her illness, and I am bracing myself for the possibility that she will soon enter heaven's gates . . .*

Evelyn pressed the letter to her chest. Michał had known about their baby. He had been willing. Their child was wanted and loved. *She* was wanted and loved. All she desired in that moment was to rip open every envelope and devour Michał's words, to drink them like healing medicine. But there was no time. The clarity was back and there were decisions to make. The clock's big hand drew two circles around its face while Evelyn sat, mute, at the edge of the bed, her hands folded atop the letter on her lap. Her breathing was even, her shoulders straight. Finally, she stood, her chin high. Ready.

There was much to do in the short few hours left of the afternoon before her parents were likely to get home. She quickly gathered the letters, retrieved a brown cardboard box from the back of her wardrobe and placed them within, on top of the postcard Michał had penned from Melbourne and the fragile ring of Huon pine. She closed the lid and tied it with string. From her bedroom window, she could barely make out the fence lines of their own paddocks. The air was thick, a murky yellow-pink, and ash blew against the glass, leaving tiny white trails.

Working methodically, she then filled a discarded military-issue rucksack from David's old room with bare necessities. A change of clothes. Food. Her journal. The brown cardboard box with Aunt Philippa's watercolour cards. Money from Daddy's bedside table, more than she'd ever handled before. She divided it in four and placed the folded notes in different pockets and places of the bag.

Finally, Evelyn wrapped her remaining Huon wren carefully in a tea towel and nestled it between her clothes. She couldn't find the second, more subdued of the two wrens. It wasn't on the workshop bench or floor. There was a little round patch of dustless window ledge where the bird had lived for her confinement. Her heart squeezed to think it was lost. *Did Mother notice them and take one? But why just the one?*

She didn't have time for the luxury of grief or to search further. The sky had reddened. Looking at it was like swimming through the red haze of one of her mercurial dreams. If it wasn't for the crystal coolness of her resolve, the apocalyptic sky would have quickened her pulse to a gallop. She could hear Daphne's hooves beating the ground and wondered if she should let her out.

So many decisions, and the clock kept ticking while the sun, somewhere, languished like a biscuit dropped into tea.

She didn't leave a note. She composed it a million times on Mother's lavender-scented notepaper. *I'm sorry I can't stay*. No, she wasn't sorry. *I forgive you*. No, that would take time. *How dare you!* No, Daddy's folded and crushed features visited her thoughts and all she could think of was the burden of guilt he carried. She would just slip out of their lives. That would be best. They could choose her ending, the one that suited them, while she lived out the one she had been dreaming of.

Evelyn walked to the orchard, Marmaduke trotting along beside her. She had one more thing to do. Tree limbs quaked in the whip-wind, which grew more violent as she approached the exposed end of the property. The new sapling was flanked by the worrying trees, the black earth disturbed, leaves limp. It was the wrong time of year to plant a fruit tree. Daddy knew it too.

She dropped to her knees and Marmaduke rubbed against her arm, soliciting for a pat. He cried. She carefully positioned a clutch of buttercups, tied with string, at the base of the tree. She ached all over, ached to wail with Marmaduke, an offering of mourning to her son. But she was empty, soundless. She sat on her knees with her palms pressed against the loamy soil. He had no coffin of Tasmanian oak, sanded until smooth with brass fittings attached. No lining fabric stitched lovingly by his mother. No wake with homemade scones and pies, and the well-wishes of friends. Just this unmarked earthen grave. She pulled out a pocketknife and began etching a crude cross in the juvenile tree flesh, imagining dirt and roots circling her son's body the way her womb once had. The cross was thick, deep and crooked. If it didn't kill the sickly tree, it would certainly scar it for life.

Finally, Evelyn grabbed her rucksack and heaved it onto her back. She pulled Daddy's tweed cap low over her eyes, her hair coiled within its baggy fabric. Overalls, workboots and an old shirt would hopefully detract attention from her on the road and in the streets.

Her feet crunched on the gravel, and she turned for one last time towards the stately weatherboard house, keeper of her childhood. Embers rained from the apricot sky, blown from the south. *I should be running a hose to the gutters, filling buckets of water.* The thought glowed and died just as quickly as most of the flying embers faded. As she turned to leave, her eye was dragged to the workshop roof; a curl of smoke, a tongue of flame. It disappeared and then reared up, red and hungry. She dropped the rucksack to her feet, her stomach lurching. Daddy's workshop! All his tools. The slabs of irreplaceable Tasmanian timbers. *I could stop it if I drag the hose from the orchard now.* Then she remembered her son's perfect toes, his petal skin and the ache of longing that opened up in her. She gulped. Her eyes stung as she pulled the rucksack onto her back and turned towards the oaks that led her out. Acorns crackled under her feet, or was that the fire? The wise old trees shielded her from the glare of her decision as the flames doubled and tripled, gorging on the roof, spreading to the walls. Before long it would be dirt and ash. Just like Daddy had said. Dirt and ash.

Evelyn quickened her pace to a jog, took the route past Tommy's place and slipped into the shambly cottage's backyard, praying he was outside with his siblings, playing on the pounded dirt beneath the clothesline or feeding the chickens. The yard was deserted and she turned to leave, not wanting to risk rapping on the front door. She could get stuck talking and then never leave. The back door suddenly swung open with a loud whack and there was Tommy, struggling with a rubbish bin.

'Tommy!' she hissed, and again, 'Tommy!'

He looked up, saw her and the way she hung uncertainly around the house's corner and carried on his business as if he hadn't seen a thing. His ma was watching at the window. Tommy continued to the rabble of sheds and she scurried to meet him there.

She hugged him tight, and the bewildered boy returned the squeeze. She pulled back. 'Oh, Tommy. I wish I could stop and tell you everything. Perhaps you wouldn't believe it, though.'

'Gimme a try!' Tommy grinned good-naturedly. He'd changed. The lanky-legged teenager had broadened, his voice deepened.

Evelyn flushed. 'I'm leaving, Tommy. Nothing's going to stop me, you hear?'

He scratched his head, breathed out, whistling through his teeth. 'Y'always did make your own way.'

She smiled then, her chest tight, and hugged him again. 'I need you to do something for me. Embers landed on the workshop and it's on fire.' She took a breath. 'Go tell Daddy at the Abbotts', and rally as many people to get over there and stop it spreading to the house.' Evelyn nodded at him, then the back door screeched open and she ran for the road.

She kept moving forward along the farm roads, hitching rides where she could until Mother Cummings was barely a nipple on the horizon. As she put the familiar landscapes behind her, she imagined her name left behind too; letters lashed by the wind, snagging in trees and burning to ash before fluttering like hapless grey butterflies across the Great Western Tiers. She was Evelyn no longer. That girl was gone.

In Launceston, she went straight to the ticket office, her stride purposeful, bold. She had drawn a line between her old self and this new, emerging woman. Her skin tingled beneath her clothes. It seemed as if her life was about to begin, and she would leave all her strife in Evelyn's lap while bundling her dreams, her letters and her golden wren into the arms of Nora. Nora. The name she loved. Nora, who would slowly heal, stitching up the chasm left by her precious, sick son who'd died before she could show him how much she loved him. *If only I could have held him.*

'Name, please,' the ticket clerk barked from his window, crouched over reams of paperwork.

Her heart skipped a beat. It was time. Was she brave enough? Would she be able to say it? 'David Grayson,' she said without hesitation. Like her future depended upon it.

'Identification, lad.'

Nora thanked God that her brother had left his passport in his bedside table and her mother had refused to trust it to the postal service, saying he could collect it next time he visited. It would expire next year anyway. People always said they looked alike. Here would be the test of it. She pulled herself to full height while dropping her chin. She handed him the passport and held her breath. *Please believe me*, she willed the wiry little man behind the window. He was scrutinising her while chewing the end of his pen. He coughed, looked down again.

'Right you are, lad.'

Nora kept her eyes lowered for fear their triumphant sparkle would give her away. She mumbled a harried, 'Thank you,' before exchanging the correct change for her ticket and moving on.

It was getting late. She would find a room for the night, somewhere quiet. Her ship sailed tomorrow. Just a few hours to keep out of sight. She straightened her cap and walked on.

There it was: the *Taroona*. The same old steamship that had carried Michał away. Its great, forest-green hull was submerged in the high tide of the Tamar River, a cheery yellow striping its girth. Workers carried crates and boxes up and down the back gangway, and people formed a line in front of the passenger bridge, hugging loved ones, straightening hats, rummaging through handbags to wipe children's noses.

Nora watched the merry scene from a distance. Wind rustled the reeds, and the tide licked the muddy riverbank. A pelican soared overhead, its shadow smearing across her face. Everything seemed to be moving in slow motion. *Is this really happening? Am I brave enough?* And then they were unlooping the rope barrier and ushering passengers up the bridge and onto the ship.

'Welcome aboard, ma'am,' she heard the porter's spritely greeting as the line progressed forward. Nora looked at her feet, willing them to move, but they were rooted to the spot, like all the grief of the past nine months was pressing her into the grimy street's gutter where she stood. It all flashed before her. Mother's dinner plate splintered against the dining room wall. Mother Cummings reduced to a window's height and width for six long months. The mew of a baby boy. The dense fog post-birth. Daddy's face bunched in shame. She couldn't go back, but could she go forward?

The *Taroona*'s horn blasted into the sleepy Launceston air. Two joyous sounds, punctuated with clouds of steam belching from its funnel.

Nora started, lifted her eyes and took a deep breath. The sky was limitless blue. She moved. One foot, then the other. Gripped the railing. Produced her ticket. Nodded at the porter's welcome. And as she moved forward, almost immediately the agony of emotions in her chest began to subside. She was caught up in the press of passengers moving onwards, forwards. The ship's decking was ahead, the same sturdy boards that supported Michał's weight, carrying him like they would carry her. Her heart leapt. She was already closer to him than she had been this time yesterday. Hope pricked her arms, surged through her veins. This was what she'd always wanted: to embark on an adventure. All around her, people were doing the same. The young woman in blue who intermittently pulled a pencil from behind her ear and scribbled in a tiny notebook. The freckle-faced infant who had barely stopped staring at the suited gentleman holding his hand. The couple with linked arms leaning across the railing to wave at family below.

She was one of them now. A traveller. Girl-mother emerged. The line was moving again and Nora patted her bulging rucksack to feel the edges of the box containing Michał's letters. She couldn't wait to find a quiet place to read them, all his beautiful words sinking into her like the remedy she had pined for. The hotel last night had been too loud, too dingy to undertake such a sacred thing. The Huon wren was there too, like a clandestine friend who had witnessed the spectrum of her grief. Secret-keeper of the rending of her heart in three directions; from her home to her child to her love.

Water slapped against the ship's side and Nora looked down, down to the black water that reflected a bleary image, a painterly smear of colours that she knew to be herself. And the water shone up at her, like a dark mirror to her soul. She had the peculiar sensation of change, of a new thing being wrought from old things. Hovering over the waters. Mirrored there in her face, in the smoky glass of slapping tide and departure. It sent a thrill all the way through her, a cool, splashing charge of expectation. Like a kiss, it bade farewell and hello at once, with the warmth of one who knows. And she rose from the dark glass of the river and stepped forward.

Chapter 36

Winter 2019

Allira felt she had been standing at the waterline for so long, and today her tears ran unbidden, torrents of emotion washing her face. She blamed it on the pregnancy hormones, her five-month baby bump making itself known. She looked around the room and her heart swelled again with gratitude. Nora was asleep, her breathing coming in gasps and sighs. She didn't have long. Horrie was holding her hand, bowed over her bed. Justin was reading a novel in a chair against the wall, glancing at his father intermittently. And Sabine was humming as she knitted standing up, looking as if she would prefer to waltz the moss green scarf's pattern into place. Allira could barely believe the elegant, silver-haired woman was here.

The idea to invite Sabine had formed after Allira had visited Nora a month ago, another hour spent silently hoping that Nora would stir. Allira's eyes had been drawn to the cardboard box on the shelf, the one she had never felt she should touch. That day, however, the air had been charged with permission, and even the wintry sun had pointed a finger of invitation. Allira slipped the box from the shelf and gingerly returned to the chair, removing the twine and lifting the lid.

A bundle of yellowed envelopes took up most of the space. There must have been at least twenty, Allira thought, all bearing the name *Evelyn Grayson* in the same hand, sent from Berlin. They were dated 1953, and Allira knew they must be from Nora's Michał.

There were exquisite watercolour paintings of fruit with copperplate handwriting, and poems on flowered notepaper, written in a language that didn't look quite like German. Polish? There were three black-and-white photographs: the same Grayson family photo she'd found tucked in Thelma's scrapbook, a studio portrait of an attractive young woman in operatic dress and make-up, signed *Sabine Friedrich* across one corner, and a candid photo of a young couple in swimming costumes at the beach, squinting and laughing into the lens, the man's arm protectively circled around the woman's waist. Nora was unmistakable. This was her and Michał. Allira had lifted the photo to catch the light. They were laughing. Nora's face was alive, glowing. She was happy.

On the top of the pile was a letter different to the others, its crisp white envelope dated only last year. *Dear Nora,* it began.

I took a picnic to Michał's grave today and wished you
were with me to sing and dance in the ripples of his life.
I know you will have remembered in your own way.
He left us too early, Nora. There was still so much
discovery left on the soles of our feet. I wish that time
could have continued forever. I miss your letters, as you

probably miss mine. Forgive me, my dear friend, the past is painful and cruel. Although it holds pleasant pools to look into . . .

It had taken no convincing at all for Sabine to agree to visit, and here she was, as poised in her old age as Nora was crumpled. Sabine had fluttered around the room when she first arrived, making soft exclamations in her velvety accent, before finally landing at Nora's side, stroking her face and singing what Allira guessed was a Polish lullaby. Nora had smiled like an enchanted child. And Sabine had delivered missing pieces of the puzzle. Horrie, Justin and Allira were on the edge of their seats as she had told them of Michał and Nora's wonderful reunion, of how Michał had wept bitterly to hear of his son's supposed death, and how they had grieved together, leaning in and allowing it to shape them. How they had travelled extensively and lived expansively. The furniture shop that they ran together until Michał's sudden death in a motorbike accident. And then Nora's travels that had become listless wanderings and eventually brought her back to Tasmania, to where it all began.

'Always, we had the sense that a part of her was here,' Sabine said. Allira noticed that Justin was recording Sabine's revelations on his phone, held discreetly at his side. He saw Allira watching and nodded, a sparkle in his eye. She was already imagining the page layout, how she would feature that shining photo of Michał and Nora on the beach. She knew Justin would make a masterpiece of Nora's story, that it would be a tribute and a celebration. She also sensed that it would throw light into the dark rooms of his family's past.

'Her heart knew what her head did not,' Sabine had whispered into the thickening atmosphere.

So here they were, invited by Sally to gather because she didn't expect Nora to hold on for much longer. While Allira was saddened by the news, her step was light when she joined the others at Nora's bedside. It was just as she had hoped. Nora was enveloped by family, both blood and of her making, all of them knotted around her when it mattered most. They lingered companionably in her presence, and Allira wondered if Nora could hear them through her slumber: murmurs of conversation, pages rustling, the click of knitting needles, the pop of groaning knees. To anyone else, it might have seemed like a rudderless silence. But Allira felt the weight of it. *Be still*, the room whispered. *Be still and know*. Nora's breath barely lifted the sheets. The pause stretched long, and the stillness was holy.

Eventually Horrie stood, and Justin followed, Sabine folding her knitting into her handbag. 'Are you sure you're okay to do this?' Horrie asked Allira, tapping his own rotund belly while looking to hers. She was on duty tonight. They had drawn up a roster so that Nora would never find herself alone in her final hours.

'Of course, I will be absolutely fine.' Allira smiled.

'Okay then. Call me if anything changes.'

Justin suddenly twigged. 'You're pregnant?'

Allira laughed at his brazenness. Very few people commented on the obvious condition of her body, but when they did, she loved it. Being pregnant made her feel doubly alive and she had found that the best remedy for the doubt and fear had been to throw herself wholeheartedly into the joy of the journey. 'Sure am!'

'Congratulations.' Justin beamed.

The three filed from the room, Sabine kissing Allira lightly on the cheek. The door clicked shut and Allira's tears fell again. *This is ridiculous, I'm like a water fountain!* She hiccupped and laughed at the same time. But the tears felt good, like a salt-water baptism.

She scooted closer to Nora, sidling up beneath the shelf and those two Huon wrens, like little golden guards. Did they dip their heads conspiratorially? Did their feathers quiver?

Allira pulled her attention back to the bed. 'Thank you, Nora,' she said, her fingers splayed across the orb of her belly. And there were no words adequate to acknowledge the strange twining of their lives, so she stroked Nora's hand gently, as she had done so many times before, until the sun immersed itself in the horizon.

Acknowledgements

It was September 2018. Hubby and I were sitting around a campfire near Mareeba in North Queensland, kids tucked up in bed in the caravan nearby. We listened as an eccentric fellow traveller told us of her many hats. Police officer. Nurse. Nomad. Who knows how much fiction and chardonnay were holding her storytelling together, but we didn't mind: it made for compelling listening. She told us how she came across a woman with advanced dementia at a nursing home and took interest in her when others had written her off. The old woman had a doll, and she would often mutter chilling sentences. 'Daddy took my baby behind the shed . . .'

That campfire story was the genesis of this book and the character of Nora. So I'd like to begin by tipping my travel-worn Akubra to the campfire woman, whose name remains unknown, as I have no way of contacting her. Thank you for telling stories.

My creative practice is a spiritual one. I begin each writing session by surrendering the work to the Creator himself. He created me with this insatiable desire to write, and he provides the inspiration and the opportunities to explore that. There is no one I am more grateful to.

You may as well know that I have the best husband in the world. A few years back, we were at an in-conversation event with international bestselling author and friend Katherine Scholes. During question time, he waved his hand in the air and asked her, as I shrunk in my chair, 'How can a husband best support his wife to write a book?' The room erupted in laughter and he quickly became the most popular man in the room. 'Give her space,' Kath said, 'and always say nice things about her writing.' Phill van Ryn, you do all that, and so much more. This is for you, because it simply could not have happened without your support.

My deep gratitude to Karen Mace, Sue Brown, Lauren Thompson, Kay Thompson, Bianca Ebdon, Fiona De Kievit, Beverly Vos, Anita Denholm, Paul O'Rourke, Madeleine Wiedemann and Mary Machen for reading early drafts and giving invaluable feedback. To Becky Beeston, who read it chapter by chapter as it was written and believed in its success from day dot. To Sarah Kirton (you know why). To Madeline Dingemanse (Chapter 22 is for you). To my wonderful writers' group. My love and appreciation to my family, who always enthusiastically encourage my writing: Rod and Lynn Dowling, Jack and Alie van Ryn, and my little cheerleaders Roman and Adelaide. Thank you, Agnieszka Sikorska-Meikle, for your last-minute help with Polish details. To Andrew Dean for the generous insights into undertaking in the 1950s. Heartfelt thanks to Robyn Mundy for the first edit and all the encouragement and advice thereafter, to Fiona Smith, my tenacious agent, to the

ACKNOWLEDGEMENTS

Penguin Random House family, including Ali Watts, Amanda Martin, Hannah Ludbrook and Debbie McGowan, and to cover designer Nikki Townsend. What a blessing it is to be enveloped in the resources and kindness of this incredible team.

This book is made of nostalgia for the place I was born. The heart tugs every time I visit the landscape detailed here. I am grateful for Walch's Tasmanian Almanac (1953), and *Ticklebelly Tales and Other Stories from the People of the Hydro* by Heather Felton (2013) for their help in building characters and place, as well as some beautiful 1950s editions of the *Australian Women's Weekly* that I picked up from a garage sale.

Finally, I thank you, dear reader. Sincerely, it is a most wondrous thing to know that you have chosen to read this, my first novel. Shalom.

Book Club Notes

1. Allira and Nora have a connection that at times transcends the usual modes of communication. What did you observe about their relationship?

2. The wren is a recurring motif throughout the novel, both in Nora's and Allira's story threads. What does it symbolise?

3. If Thelma had allowed her daughter to make her own decisions about her pregnancy, how do you think things might have turned out differently?

4. How significant is the 1950s era and the rural setting to the events that unfold in this story? How are things different today?

5. In the novel we learn that 'Evelyn would have done anything to please her mother.' Why do you think Thelma is the way she is?

6. How do Thelma and Nora explore and express their spiritual beliefs in different ways?

7. 'Nora loosened her grip on Allira's hand and lifted her palm into the moonlight. There it was. A tiny, triangular scar, embedded like a sliver of precious metal. "Beautiful, isn't it?"' Nora treasures her wound because of the memories it holds. Do you have similar scars, emotional or physical, that are precious to you?

8. Allira said, 'It's a part of your story, Evelyn. You're not you without it.' How did these discussions help Allira address her own recent trauma?

9. Discuss the theme of loneliness, and explore the different ways it plays out in this story.

10. Do you think Allira did the right thing by accepting Justin's challenge to a game of eight ball with the magazine at stake?

11. Do you have a friendship with someone many decades younger or older than you? How is it different from your other friendships?

12. When Nora is first introduced to Allira, she is described as having 'no family'. Discuss the role of nursing homes in today's society. Do you have any experience of these yourself?

Discover a
new favourite